Air's Vision

Book 3
The Elementals Trilogy

Jillian Jacobs

Published by Green Moose Productions
Copyright 2016 by Jillian Jacobs

ISBN: 978-1-942313-08-3

DEDICATION

To: All those who cannot see.

ACKNOWLEDGMENTS

To: My beta-girls.
Also thanks to Linda Carroll-Bradd. Best editor ever.
Any mistakes are my own.

PROLOGUE

1645

"How did Pillar take the news?" Mother Nature arched her thin red-gold brow and met Nodin's gaze. She made an almost comical picture beside him with her spindly legs spread out in the grass and her upper body propped up on her bent elbows. Her gold-hued skin sparkled with shades of green and yellow. As usual, she wore a flowing dress that covered her ankles, no shoes, and her sunset-colored hair tumbled over her shoulders and landed on the ground.

"Honestly." Nodin plucked at the tall grass at his side. "She blames you."

Spring had arrived once more upon the Tennessee River. However, the tiny flowers budding along the banks, the fresh scent of newly sprung leaves, and the green blades of grass did nothing to brighten Nodin's spirits as he considered his tribe's future trials. Yet, wasn't spring a time of rebirth, of change?

Nerida, the Water Elemental, sat at his other side. She shook her head and, in her heavily Greek accent, said, "Pillar must see that you need to return to your people. Your continued visions of the death and disease coming to your Chickasaw tribe must not be ignored, and your Air Elemental gifts will serve them in their time of need."

"Pillar's problem is that in order for me to return to the tribe after fulfilling my Elemental duties for thirty years, I must marry one of the Elder's

1

daughters. I've agreed. Pillar and I have been traveling this globe since I converted into an Elemental, and for seven years before I transformed, she was part of my life. I do love her, but I have a duty to my people and my element."

"Do you have to marry this girl?" Nerida arched a dark brow.

"I will marry her, but I will not consummate the marriage. The union will be in name only."

"I am not sure you can separate the two so easily." Mother tucked her tongue in her cheek. "You are not being fair to the poor girl, nor are you being fair to Pillar. I assume Pillar was enraged at your decision?"

"She has always been selfish where I am concerned. I trusted and followed her, because I love her." Nodin rubbed the back of his neck, knocking his long braid to the side. "But she and I have different visions for our future. For the past few years, we've fought about our purpose as extraordinary beings. Plus, she becomes angry when I spend any time with Nerida and Flint, and even angrier when I spend time with you, Mother."

"I have never understood Pillar's animosity towards me." Mother sat up and folded her long legs. "I was not responsible for her transformation, and she has never turned to me for guidance."

"Pillar is threatened by what she believes are negative influences over my life." Nodin heaved a sigh then settled onto his back and closed his eyes. Though he didn't want to discuss this next portion, he needed a female perspective. "And...well...the other day I was walking along this very river with my future bride, and she kissed me. I did not ask for this nor encourage her, but the girl doesn't truly understand who I am. I believe she holds some romantic feelings for me. As if that isn't enough of an issue, Pillar witnessed the whole thing, and I have not seen her since."

"Does she believe you betrayed her?" Nerida asked.

"Yes, though if she truly loved me, she'd allow me to explain." Nodin straightened, cupping a hand over his brow to block the sunlight glinting off the river. "Perhaps this was for the best. I cannot continue to pick and choose my Elemental duties based on Pillar's whims. Plus, my people need me." He shook his head as he remembered their heated fights. "She is overcome with jealousy. She believes Mother Nature is the reason I've chosen to stay, and why I am marrying another."

Mother patted his hand. "I am here as a friend. Though you did not ask for this life, you were predestined, and thirty years ago when the arrows of another tribesman pierced your heart, I transformed you into who you are today. I understand why you've had a hard time adjusting, but I, too, have duties I must fulfill. I must look out for the earth and make hard choices. I will not apologize, because though you've resented me for many years, I believe you are a wonderful Air Elemental."

"I agree, I did not ask for this. I would have preferred to die a warrior's death, but I'm beyond that now." Nodin stared out across the water before meeting Mother's gaze. "You have influenced me, and I have finally released my anger at having this life thrust upon me. I'd like to continue as an Elemental, tribesman, and Pillar's lover, but she refuses to see reason."

"That's not really fair." Nerida brushed away a strand of dark hair from her sea-green eyes. "You've spent the past thirty years doing as Pillar wished, and now that you've asked her for something in return, she walks away? A relationship is about compromise. Forgive me for saying this, but I've never seen love for you in her eyes, I've only glimpsed her pride at having captured you, and I must say I'm glad to see you finally breaking free."

"Nerida, our relationship is not one-sided. I am hopeful we will overcome our differences...though I find those differences more and more troublesome. She is quite selfish and domineering. While I started out so, I am no longer her puppet."

"And that is what Pillar wants—a puppet." Nerida shifted onto her side and placed a hand upon his knee. "I see your relationship from an outside perspective and, of course, the fact I've been around since the first gladiator fought in the Colosseum means you should listen to this old maid." She chuckled. "I've learned a lot about human nature since 85 AD, and one thing that generally rings true—people, whether gifted or not, tend to look out for themselves first. Elementals, by the very nature of what we've become, no longer have that choice."

Nerida's olive skin showed not even one wrinkle. Her long black hair waved down her back and her eyes were the color of an ocean wave, almost turquoise. Though she preferred more flowing, silky fabrics, she was currently adorned in a buckskin dress she must have picked up from his tribe or another. She and Flint held the same opinion about clothes. The finer, the better.

As usual, gold earrings and a piercing in her nose adorned her classically Roman face. He'd asked how they stayed in place even after her transformations into all forms of water and her answer was always the same, "They are a part of me."

Would he last as long as Nerida? Did he want to? Of late, his mind had turned to questioning the whys of life. He tossed a rock into the river, watching rings spiral out from where it landed. His life was the same; duty lay at the center, and everything else rippled out from there.

Spring showers were early in coming, so the river's current flowed at a steady pace.

A peaceful quiet settled over them all. Nodin closed his eyes and soaked in the sun, wishing Flint were a part of this conversation. The Fire Elemental always had a straightforward answer.

Nerida shot to her feet, releasing a torrent of words in her native tongue as she pointed across the river.

There on the other side stood Pillar and Quint.

Nodin staggered to his feet, fighting for air as though he'd been gut punched. "Pillar, what are you doing?"

Their voices carried easily over the short distance.

Mother held Nerida's arm. The Water Elemental's history with this vile creature began centuries ago. He'd not yet battled Quint in his short time as an Elemental, but Flint and Nerida had many war stories. Nerida's last foray with Quint had almost destroyed her.

Nodin stood in front of Mother and Nerida. "Mother won't be able to hold her long. Get him out of here."

"I found a solution." Pillar smiled. "A way we can be happy once again."

Nerida continued her barrage of words in a rhythm like spell casting then she spat on the ground. "Heed me, salt-creature. You are a fool to believe that serpent's lies."

Mother Nature took Nodin's hand. "Let me speak to Pillar."

Though Nodin believed that was actually a very bad idea, considering the amount of venom Pillar frequently spewed about Mother Nature, he merely shrugged.

Mother waded into the river, her long green dress trailing behind her. She stopped halfway. "I shall be the intermediary. Pillar, what is your purpose in bringing our enemy to this place?"

"He will help Nodin's people. Drive away invaders."

"At what cost?" Nerida charged, moving toward the water's edge.

"This does not concern you, Nerida. Nor does it concern you, Mother." Pillar flicked a hand in a shooing motion. "This matter is between Nodin and I."

"Mother Nature, so nice to see you." Quint bowed like a Victorian viscount. "You look ravishing, as always."

"I do not wish for help from Quint." Nodin ignored Quint's gracious greeting and glared across the river at the woman he loved. "How could you ever believe I would?"

"He came to me offering an olive branch, which I accepted. You are not the only one who can make new alliances."

"He came to you when he knew you were weak and heartbroken." Mother's typically lyrical voice now held an edge of warning.

"And what do you know of the heart?" Eyes narrowed, Pillar turned to Mother. "You do not understand passion for a man. You keep these Elementals under your wing, controlling them, but they do not need you. Nodin and I have done well without your interference and will continue to do so. We'll have Quint handle the problems on this land, and then we'll move on...we always do."

"And what does Quint want in exchange?" Mother arched a brow, trailing her fingers through the calm water.

"Nothing," Pillar responded.

Nodin couldn't believe what he was seeing. The woman who had stood at his side for years, whom he had trusted with his very life, was now consorting with their worst enemy. His heart turned even farther away, because she wasn't the woman he'd believed her to be. He might love her, but based on this reckless decision, along with many others over the past couple years, he finally accepted what his mind knew and his heart had failed to realize—they *had no future together.*

"I don't believe her. Quint wants something." Nerida glanced over her shoulder, meeting Nodin's gaze. "He is a deceiver."

"Actually, Pillar, I do want something." Quint carefully made his way down the bank and stopped near the water's edge.

"See? Get ready." Nerida shook her head.

"In exchange for helping stave off the coming invasion by the French, Spanish, British, and more...I shall become the next Earth Elemental. You've been without one—"

"Because of you," Nerida shouted, water pouring from her fingertips. Hard waves splashed against Quint's feet.

He remained in place. "As I was saying, you've been without one for many years, and I can fill that role."

"An Elemental's duty is to protect the earth and its inhabitants. You only know destruction and death." Mother walked backwards toward Nerida.

"I'd like to change." Quint grinned.

"No, what you'd like is the power that comes with controlling all four gifts." Nerida forged farther into the river. "Earth is the strongest Elemental. Quint knows this." She glanced back at Nodin again. "Earth is our grounding force. If Quint were at our center, we would fall into chaos."

"Nerida, your past prejudices blind you to what could be."

"Past prejudices?" Nerida now stood beside Mother. "Your only purpose in being here is to catch us all together. Pillar, if you wished to keep Nodin there were other ways. Now he'll never trust you."

"I've always known of your pathetic desire for Nodin." Pillar braced her hands on her narrow hips, her white-blonde hair loose around her shoulders. "You're embarrassing yourself."

"You know nothing." Though, Nerida didn't turn to face him.

Mother wrapped an arm around Nerida's shoulder.

Overwhelmed by all these revelations, Nodin focused on Pillar. "Leave, and take Quint with you. I do not want his assistance. Whether you choose to stand beside me or not, I will fulfill my duties as an Elemental and to my tribe."

"Now, Nodin." Quint shook a finger. "We've never been properly introduced, have we?"

Nodin clenched his jaw.

"Regardless, you and I have no quarrel. I like it here." Quint waved his hands out at his sides. "The coming carnage of your people should prove entertaining for years."

Nodin's stomach lurched. What did that mean?

Inky black slithered across the river.

"Quint, what are you doing?" Pillar charged down the bank and stopped at his side.

"You wanted all those negative influences out of Nodin's life, so we'll start with the two who cause the most trouble."

"No." Pillar gripped his arm. Her fingers quickly turned black.

"Too late." Quint punched Pillar square across the jaw, knocking her down. Then he stomped his foot against the river's muddy shore and more dark matter shot across the top of the water.

Mother landed at Nodin's side.

But Nerida held her ground.

Quint dove in and drew her under.

Nodin jumped in after her, diving down, searching for the fighting figures in the muddy water.

Nerida surfaced, but Quint held her face in his hands, his mouth locked over hers.

Nodin had never experienced such cloying darkness. Quint's matter surrounded him, filtering into his lungs, blocking his breathing.

"Nodin, lift her away."

Mother's voice seemed far away, muffled. Nodin blinked, getting his bearings before whipping out of the water, drawing Nerida away from Quint. Once free, he landed beside Mother.

But so did Quint.

Mother stepped in front of Nodin, but Pillar's spinning salt-funnel swirled around Mother's form and carried them into the forest.

Nodin blew a great gush of air to assist his kick against Quint's side.

Black ooze pouring from her mouth and nose, Nerida lifted her arms to

Nodin. "Take me to salt water. Hurry."

Nodin lifted her in his arms, all while bracing for another attack. Glancing around, he discovered Quint was nowhere to be seen. Where had he gone?

Mother rushed toward them, her long legs eating up the distance, but she was knocked down by an onslaught of salt pellets.

"Pillar." Though weakened by the dark matter, Nodin ran toward Mother with Nerida. "Enough."

Pillar landed as her human form between him and Mother, her slim body visible. The body he'd spent so many nights exploring did nothing for him now. If anything, he felt a wash of pity for this sad woman before him, and only a small remnant of love.

"It'll never be enough, Nodin. She's taken you from me." Pillar jabbed a finger at Mother Nature, who now stood, almost camouflaged, between two cypress trees. "You say we shall continue, but more and more you turn to her, and soon I will have nothing."

"I offered you everything. You are the one who turned to the one who offers nothing."

"I'll show you nothing." Pillar ripped Nerida away and dispersed into salt, covering the water-girl's entire body.

"Pillar, no!" Nodin tore Nerida free and twisted them both into the air. The water-girl's body was like an over-dried prune.

Quint's evil thread still coursed through her. Pillar's salt took a further toll, because while salt absorbed water, too much could destroy, especially if Nerida couldn't process it though her body fast enough.

Quint's dark vein flowed under Nodin's skin. How had Flint and Nerida survived so long against such a foe? And how could Pillar not have known how this meeting would end? Quint was never selfless.

"Hang on, Nerida. Not much farther."

Rotating through the crisp air, he breathed deep but again choked. This time, salt lined his tongue and throat and burned his eyes.

Pillar spun at his side and bumped against him again and again, trying to dislodge Nerida from his arms.

"Stop this." Nodin sent Pillar a mental message.

"I saw you with that woman. You betrayed me, so I betrayed you. You said we had a future, but I turned my back for one minute, and you were already in the arms of another."

"You've never truly known me." Once more, his heart ached at the loss of their love. Where had he gone wrong? Hadn't he cherished her enough? He'd forsaken so much to remain by her side...and yet, here they were, once more at odds. *"You betrayed my trust today, and if Nerida dies her final death due to your deeds, I don't know that I'll ever forgive you."*

Regardless of his pleas, Pillar continued to work against him as he journeyed closer and closer to the ocean.

Later, he would wonder if he'd fought hard enough. If perhaps he couldn't truly hurt Pillar as she'd hurt him. Wasn't she simply lost? Her heart shattered just as completely as his own.

He finally touched down near the Atlantic Ocean and carried Nerida into the water. Knowing he was too late, he still let her go, hoping against hope her element would renew her body.

Pillar landed at his side. *"You took from my heart, so I took from yours."*

"How could you do this?" Nodin fell to his knees, clasping his head in both hands. *"I explained to you over and over. I asked you to come with me. I begged for your understanding and love, and this is what I get in return? Why?"*

"You betrayed me with another woman, and I will never forgive you."

"I betrayed you with no one."

"You think I mean that simple girl and her ridiculous attempt to seduce you? No, long before that you chose Mother. That was your betrayal."

"A sickness has entered your mind." He glanced at her. Her long blonde hair flowing with the ocean breeze. Her beauty in complete contrast to her vile actions. *"When Flint discovers what you've done, he will destroy you, and I will not be able to stop him."*

"He can try." Pillar shrugged.

"Then we are truly enemies." Shoulders slouched, Nodin tried to catch his breath, tried to understand how he had come to such an end.

Pillar took one step toward him then, after a moment, disappeared with *a swish.*

Nodin gripped the sand in his hands, and as it poured through his fingers, he screamed out all his rage until his throat turned raw. Though his Elemental body was eased by the wind stirring in from the ocean, his heart and mind remained broken.

For hours, he stared across the water but saw no signs of Nerida.

Two days passed, but the Water Elemental never returned. At a loss on how to continue, he simply flew back to the lands that had once been his home.

But, as he circled the sky above what had once been a thriving Chickasaw village, he swirled away in a rage, blocking his vision from the black swath of destruction brought on by death.

By Quint.

And a woman scorned.

CHAPTER 1

Oklahoma – Present Day

Nodin couldn't breathe.

He didn't belong.

Not now.

Not then.

Not when he'd been born with unusual sky-blue eyes in a culture that believed in omens.

Not when, in 1615, Mother Nature had visited his Chickasaw tribe and altered his future from skilled warrior to nothing but air.

And now, centuries later, standing in a tiny diner's parking lot on the southern edge of Oklahoma, he still felt adrift, unsure of when and where he'd gone off course. He'd lived the past five years in virtual solitude while considering why those he loved always painted him the villain for taking the righteous path. He understood part of his distress was due to recently losing Pillar, a woman who, from the very beginning of time, represented the personification of the salt of the earth. A woman who had been a part of his life since he was a human teen. Though he'd always have an ache in his heart for Pillar, he acknowledged she'd made her choices.

And today, as with most Elemental duties, he couldn't say

the same of himself. He had no choice but to return to his tribe after putting off this task for far too long.

Due to his transformations, he shed all his clothes while travelling as his element, air, so he got creative when obtaining new ones. Creative—stealing, really they were the same thing…sort of.

Once dressed in his new duds, pilfered from a local farmer's closet, Nodin drifted to the café situated along I-77 between Marietta and Thackerville, Oklahoma. The former was home to World Star Casino, the second largest gambling facility in America and likely the reason this old diner still existed.

The fall breeze stirred with the smell of freshly cut alfalfa, a crop the farmers used as hay for livestock. A large assortment of RVs added exhaust to the air as they left the campground next door and headed south toward the shiny lights and tinkling coins of the casino.

Nodin noted a rusty pick-up truck with Oklahoma plates, the diner's metal porch overhang, the ancient air conditioner barely hanging on to the café's front window, and the handwritten note above the Open sign that said, Help Wanted.

And that was why he was here, to find help.

The Elementals believed the girl inside would aid in their fight against the malevolent dark matter being, Quint. Although, Quint hadn't surfaced in the five years since Violet, a witch with the power to control the electromagnetic spectrum, had minimized his existence.

Quint's eventual return was why Nodin now sought the aid of a woman barely twenty-one…or was it twenty-three? He couldn't recall. He only knew she was an innocent who'd probably never left the reservation.

Breathing deeply past the conflicting emotions that always surfaced when he returned to his people, he pushed against the metal handle on the wooden door, warmed by the afternoon sun. The tinkling bells on the door released a hypnotic chime that caused all the occupants to stop and stare.

"Let's do this," Nodin mumbled to himself. Halting in the doorway, he searched for her—Kamali.

Sitting alone at a table for two, Kamali turned, and her gaze seemed to bore straight through him. He took in the fall of her long black hair, her defined cheekbones, sharp nose, red-bronze skin, and this time *he* gasped as something dusted across the fallen ashes of his heart. A sense of recognition—of fate, whipped through his mind, and with it, the icy chill of a cold hand wrapping around his heart and freezing him in place.

Not often, but at times with his additional elemental gift, he could foresee snippets of possible future events. And the picture was never very clear. The visions played out with hazy imagery, and he had to figure out what each portion represented, like some symbolic puzzle with pieces that rarely fit. Regardless of what his visions revealed about the future, humans always had a choice and sometimes, though rarely, the person would choose a path that changed what he foresaw.

Standing at the threshold of this diner, with the thick, greasy scent of French fries and grilled burgers in the air, what choice would he make? Should he step inside, or turn on his heel and abandon his duties? Fly away and return years from now, when she was ready? Or was he the one on unsteady ground?

This internal pull toward Kamali was based on what? Curiosity? Or was his increased heartbeat due to an attraction? Whatever the overriding emotion, he couldn't move.

Hadn't this assignment always blustered across his senses as something much more personal? Something that would blow him far off course? The pull to his homeland had grown stronger and stronger until he could no longer deny the call. Yet, as he gazed into Kamali's clouded eyes, he knew...somehow *she* had been the one issuing the command.

Half in the door, half out, he shook off all fear and prepared to take that final step toward destiny, even as he wondered why he'd never foreseen this moment.

Suddenly, a sharp tingling sensation shot down his fingers and then zinged through the tip of his nose. Gripping his head to fight off the dizziness now erupting through his mind, he glanced around the diner.

A strong wind blew napkins off the tables.

What the hell?

This couldn't be, but the fact was—the breeze came from him.

Clenching his fists, he fought off the beginnings of his body's transformation into air.

Did I lose control of my elemental gift?

"Stay solid. Don't switch. Don't." Nodin closed his eyes and concentrated on maintaining his human form. Perhaps the trauma of returning home was manifesting by altering his body without his will. "Breathe, just breathe."

Nodin glanced at Kamali. She now stood at the side of the table, her head tilted to the side as if listening...as if *seeing*...but...was she in danger? Was someone else aware of her gifts? Could there be an outside force pulling him away? Or was Kamali somehow altering his will?

A dog's low, deep growl rumbled across the diner.

The current swelling within his body only grew stronger.

He had to leave.

But first, he used his Elemental gleaning gift to detect any malicious thoughts in the diners' minds. Why was the dog on alert? And where was it? Unease drew goose bumps across his skin, and he gazed at Kamali once more while clutching the inside of the doorframe. "Kamali, you must come with—"

A sharp tug, like a vicious vacuum, centered from his chest, as if sucking all his outer extremities inside his body. For the first time in forever, he couldn't rely on the air. Couldn't trust his element.

Cursing, he tumbled back and fell to the ground, knocking an elbow against a concrete parking block. After rubbing his elbow, he glanced back at the diner. "H-how is this…possible?"

Struggling for control, he clawed at the ground. "No. Not here. Move. Move." The most important rule rushed through his mind—humans could not witness an Elemental's transformation. Using what little control he had left, he shuffled closer to the side of a parked car and tried to huddle underneath, but his body was already converting.

Someone else had taken over. He'd become his element—Air.

"Stop. Mother Nature, are you doing this? Eamon? Your magic tricks are not welcome."

Fear surfaced, unlike anything he'd faced since leaving his human life behind. Who was in control, and where were they taking him? The internal draw ceased. Then, with what felt like a hand winding up with a pitch, the force propelled him slightly back before firing him forward through the autumn sky.

"Stop. Where are you taking me?" Nodin tried telepathically reasoning with the energies now in control of his element. He considered using his gleaning gift to send a message to his Elemental partners, but, being unclear of the danger, he refused to put them in harm's way. He'd known returning to this place was a mistake. With every visit, his good intentions were dismissed, and now his own body was betraying him.

In four hundred years, this had never happened. Why now? How real was this threat? Was Kamali in danger? Once more, he tried to return to his human form.

To no avail.

Without his direction or will, Nodin continued as a crisp breeze through the gray sky, flying over Oklahoma City then west until he hit the corner where Colorado, New Mexico, and Oklahoma met. Past the border, he felt the grip loosen. Once in control and aware of his surroundings, he mentally mapped out the quickest route to his safe haven—Terran and Maya's cabin deep in the woods of Colorado's Monte Vista forest.

But first, Nodin halted and then slowly spun to the ground, heading for a copse of trees. Beside a ponderosa pine, he reformed into his human body and sank onto a bed of dark yellow-green needles. As a test to see if he was in control, he transformed back and forth from human to air four times.

"Flint." Clenching his hands into fists, he sent a mental message across the earth's frequencies to his partner, the current Fire Elemental. *"Meet me at Terran and Maya's as soon as possible. A new threat has surfaced."*

CHAPTER 2

"Tell him what you just told me." Perched on her kitchen barstool, Maya turned and gestured toward Terran, her thick blonde waves bouncing around her shoulders.

Nodin shook his head. "If you had waited until he arrived, then I wouldn't have to repeat everything." He ruffled Maya's hair then sank beside her.

Maya and Terran's Colorado cabin was homey and open, with all the requisite nature décor and colors. Dark brown marble countertops, flecked with gold, highlighted their black kitchen appliances. A few carrots on the counter and a teapot surrounded by various containers of loose-leaf tea were likely the only food in the house. Elementals were sustained by their element alone. The only one who still used food for nourishment was Terran, and he could only eat root vegetables. Nodin couldn't remember the taste of anything other than air.

The living room beside the kitchen was set up with a green couch and two recliners. Terran did consultant work for the EPA so they had enough money to sustain this small place.

Terran wrapped his arms around Maya's shoulders before kissing the side of her head. "She isn't known for her patience."

"Arnold H. Glasow says, 'The key to everything is patience. You get the chicken by hatching the egg, not by smashing it.'" Nodin winked at Maya.

"Listen, ya dunderhead." Maya huffed and punched Nodin's arm. "Will you quit speaking in quotes? I can't make heads nor tails of anything that comes out of your mouth. Smashing chickens? What does that even mean? I don't have the *patience"*— with two fingers from each hand, Maya threw up air quotes—"to decipher all your philosophical ramblings."

"Maya, let's get you some water." Terran patted her shoulder then pulled a glass from the cabinet, filled it with tap water, and handed it to her. "Okay. Now, Nodin, explain, please."

"The long and short of the story is, for a moment, someone else controlled my elemental gift. One minute I was approaching Kamali, the *supposed* answer to all our problems." He was the one tossing air quotes this time. "And the next moment, I flew out the door. Full-on air-mode, without consciously shifting form."

Terran rubbed his temple. "So, due to this, you believe someone else controlled your elemental gift?"

"I don't believe it, I know it." Nodin drummed his fingers along the countertop, waiting for Terran to work this new problem through his analytical mind. The Earth Elemental had recently transformed. During his human life, he'd been an environmental scientist, so he tackled problems using facts and figures. Nodin tended toward more philosophical explanations, so he believed the two leveled each other out. Flint and Maya, the other two Elementals, they were another story all together. Flint fired through life. Literally. And Maya, though she always meant well, tended to leap without thinking.

"I never would have changed from human to air in front of so many witnesses." Nodin shook his head, bracing his forearms on the counter. "But, I had no control over my transformation."

"Have you mentioned this to Flint?" Terran paced the cabin's tiny kitchen.

"I contacted Flint before arriving." Nodin met Terran's brown-eyed gaze. "I thought this development required a full Elemental council."

"Someone else controlling our gifts...hmm...quite disturbing." Terran stared out the back patio door for a moment. "So, your loss of control only happened for a short period of time, but what if it lasted longer?" He tucked his hands in the pockets of his Dockers and rocked back on his heels. "What if, like Quint, someone else wished to control our bodies, and therefore our gifts? Did you sense Quint's presence? I need to understand how you felt, where you were. More data is necessary to fully understand this event."

"No. This wasn't Quint." Nodin shook his head. "This felt...it felt...more like a warning than any sort of fight for absolute power."

"I'm curious if this has ever happened to Flint." Maya tapped her empty glass against the counter. "He's lived longer than any of us. And we should contact Mother Nature."

"I didn't go into detail with Flint." Nodin rubbed two fingers over his temple. "Regardless, I'm not going back to see Kamali until we figure out what happened."

"You've already put off meeting her for five years, Nodin." Maya nudged his arm.

"Maya, not now," Terran chastised.

"He has to talk about it sometime." Maya flicked a hand in the air.

"Pillar is not an *it*." Hissing out a breath, Nodin closed his eyes for a moment, wishing he could escape his past. "No matter what you may believe, Pillar's death is not the only reason for my...stalling." Frowning, he crossed both arms over his chest and met Maya's aqua gaze. "Five years and nary a sight of Quint meant we could concentrate on our initial duties. Cleansing the environment. Helping the earth's inhabitants. We've made positive strides during this quiet time. Who knows how much longer this stasis will last?" Nodin tugged the leather cord from his hair and shoved it in his pocket, letting his black locks fall free. "Terran, you and Violet have done what you can to prepare for Quint's eventual return, but we still need Kamali to detect his presence."

"Let's backtrack a moment. How and when did you regain control?" Terran opened the patio door, allowing a cool fall breeze to filter inside. Multi-colored leaves danced and crackled across the back deck.

"I was out of Oklahoma." As Air, Nodin had flown over America so many times, each area's landmarks were etched into his mind. A large rock, a winding river, an empty stretch of road—all markers indicating his location.

"Have you felt anything since?" Maya clasped his arm. "Are you able to change with no problems now?"

"Yes." Although, there was another problem—the way his heart had strummed a hard beat when he'd glimpsed Kamali for the first time. His senses had peaked and formed one word, one feeling—*Mine.*

And just before he'd transformed, he swore she'd whispered, "Finally".

"Let's assume Kamali has a protector." Maya tapped a finger against her upper lip. "Or maybe a spell cast around her as a sort of sphere of defense."

Another protector? Just the thought had Nodin scowling and fighting the urge to zip back across the country, grab Kamali, and prove he'd be her only man.

"That's a very real possibility, Maya." Terran shifted from the door to behind her and ran his hands up and down her arms. "I think we need more data. I vote we send another Elemental to visit Kamali. If the same result occurs, we'll have more information. Is Quint responsible? Or, as Maya suggests, is this simply a protection spell?"

"This is my mission. *My* duty." Nodin glared at Terran. "Violet's grandfather, Eamon and Mother Nature said a tribal shaman had been blocking their efforts to study Kamali's gifts." He waved a hand in the air. "That's likely all this is."

"Kamali has been your *mission* for years." Maya straightened from her slump at the counter and jabbed his arm with her index finger. "Don't get all proprietary over something you've neglected for far too long."

"Did you ever consider I was giving Violet and Flint time together?" Nodin countered.

A heated breeze brushed across his skin.

Shooting off his bar stool, Nodin whipped to the back door.

"No worries, Nodin." Flint strode through the open entryway, dark brows waggling over his amber eyes. "Violet is *filled* with plenty of Flint...time."

Maya yipped and hopped off her seat to embrace the Fire Elemental before smacking his shoulder. "Quit talking about Violet that way, or I'll tell her to burn your bum."

Nodin greeted his fiery friend with a couple hearty slaps on the back. "Good to see you."

After rustling up spare clothes for Flint, they gathered around the kitchen table and caught up on events.

"Flint, we may have a problem." The Earth Elemental raked his fingers through his thick brown hair.

"There's always a problem, Pigpen." Flint shoved Terran's shoulder. "But...what's the problem today?"

"Someone else controlled Nodin's element." Maya poked her finger against Flint's chest. "Bet ya didn't see that one coming."

Flint's gaze shot to Nodin. "What's this?"

Nodin relayed the story. Again. But, he refrained from mentioning his possessive feelings toward Kamali. Why *did* he feel such an intense yearning to return to her side? He knew nothing of her other than what Mother Nature and Eamon, a great wizard, had indicated. They knew only her potential. So why, with all her supposed significance, was she alone at that diner? Didn't the woman have an assistant? A guard?

"Nodin." Flint punched his shoulder. "Pay attention. I asked if you were high on peyote or something?"

"Are you serious?" Nodin rolled his eyes. "If anyone is

blowing smoke, it's you."

"No, not since that San Francisco opium den. When was that...the 1850s? Hmm...you were with me, remember?" Grinning, Flint clapped Nodin on the back. "We had those two robust redheads. Now that was a—"

"Shut it." Maya covered Flint's mouth with her hand. "Violet wouldn't appreciate your trip down memory lane. Where is she, anyway?"

After dislodging Maya's hand, Flint said, "She's at this Illinois Cancer Institute, discussing the use of ultra-high frequency radio waves as a cancer treatment...or something." Flint shifted in his seat. "I just nod and say, good luck with that, babe."

"I'd hoped some of her intelligence would rub off on you." Terran shook his head.

Flint flashed a grin. "Well, I believe it was more *her* rubbing off—"

"And back to Nodin's issue." Terran stopped the conversation from taking an innuendo-laden turn, which usually occurred any time Flint was involved.

Nodin chuckled and high-fived Flint. "Good man."

"Moving on." Terran heaved a sigh. "I vote we take another trip to Oklahoma. Maybe we'll glean a mental pattern we could use to tie back to the person issuing the transformation command. We need to test the strength of this force. Can it control two Elementals, or just one? Or, was this something specific to Nodin due to his Chickasaw past? At this point, too many variables exist to provide a solution."

"I'll go." Nodin stood and started braiding his hair. "I have to consider the possibility I transformed due to my reluctance to return to my home lands. They say your subconscious mind is 30,000 times more powerful than your conscious mind."

"Who says that?" Brows narrowed, Terran gazed at Nodin.

"The Internet." Nodin shrugged.

All three of his Elemental partners gaped at him like he'd lost his mind.

"What?" Clearing his throat, Nodin studied a stray tea leaf on the countertop. "It's probably true."

Terran started to speak, paused, and then glanced at Flint, who simply shrugged. Heaving another sigh, Terran nodded. "All right. I'll agree, in the context of everything else that happens in this Elemental world, Nodin could be correct." Head tilted, the Earth Elemental tapped his lower lip. "In any event, revisiting the area is warranted. We must test this further, and soon, because if people *are* guarding Kamali, they'll know we were there. And if they know enough to control our gifts, they know who we are." Terran kissed Maya's cheek. "I should go, too. We can't have Flint turning into a fireball, or you flooding people out of house and home."

"I'll stay here with your woman." Smirking, Flint drew Maya into his arms. "And I'll check on my own. I'm sure Violet would love to discuss her theories on what happened."

"It's settled, then." After wrenching Maya from Flint and kissing her thoroughly, Terran headed for the front door. "No time like the present."

Nodin clasped his shoulder. "I'm right behind you."

Terran met his gaze for a moment then nodded. "Let's go." He opened the door, but he stumbled back.

"What the—" Nodin glanced over Terran's shoulder.

This time someone else wasn't controlling Nodin's gift, but the air whooshed from his lungs, anyway.

Kamali stood just outside the door.

CHAPTER 3

"Kamali?" A strong hand clasped her upper arm. "What are you doing here?"

Tingles shot through her body from that simple point of contact.

As an Empath, Kamali Kiwidinok could detect through colored auras a person's physical, emotional, mental, and spiritual being. This gift was the only way she'd ever seen color. With her cousin Waya's help, she'd had to learn what lay behind each hue. Her blindness had kept her world dark, yet when meeting new people, these vibrant glimpses gave her a clearer perception of their character.

Until Nodin.

She could actually *see* him.

Twenty-three years had passed without any true concept of the human form, so when he'd come to the diner and she'd finally *seen*...she'd had no words.

Kamali doubted people actually walked around with bright auras outlining their bodies, but his did. There he'd stood—a beautiful vision. Afraid to blink, to move, she'd taken in as much of his form as she could. Her entire body shivering with fear and joy—so much joy.

In that moment, everything in the diner had gone silent.

Until Maize, her guide dog, growled, and then the air stirred with something.

A negative energy.

Suddenly, Nodin's aura had changed from bluish-purple to orange before fading from her vision.

Darkness had once more descended before her eyes…and in her heart.

And in that moment, she'd decided she would see him again. She had to know if she would once more receive the gift of sight, even if she only saw him. Even if…

So she'd come to Colorado, because she never backed down from a challenge. And now, standing at this door with a deep brown aura blocking her vision of Nodin, she bit her lip to keep from crying. She'd done enough of that after he'd left, but then she'd received a visitor. One who'd taken her hand and explained where she was needed, if only she were brave enough.

She was.

The flight here was more than worth any repercussions because…she could see—him. She gripped Maize's handle until she worried it might break in two under the pressure. And even if her eyes dried in their sockets, she refused to blink in case this was all a dream.

"Nodin, quit yanking on her arm." A soft, female voice carried through the door and a new aura appeared, this one surrounded by a wavy turquoise blue, similar to Nodin's. This woman's voice was calming, rocking through Kamali's senses as if she were floating on waves.

"Maize." Shoring up her nerves, Kamali waved her arm along her side, palm open and out. "Forward."

Her Labrador Retriever—guide dog and best friend—stepped forward. And with that one step, Kamali knew her life would be forever changed by the events that proceeded from her choice to keep moving forward, never back.

So many emotions flickered within the room, so she focused

on Nodin and what she could see. A broad smile spread across her face and she couldn't refrain from laughing, even as happy tears slid down her cheeks.

"How did you get here?" Nodin asked. "And why are you laughing and crying at the same time?"

Every expression, from his furrowed brow to his hands on his hips, was fascinating. His body was a bit hazy, shifting within his blue aura sparkling with bits of yellow, but she could see his long black hair and sharp facial features. "I need to sit, please. Could someone guide me?"

"Oh, I'm so sorry." The woman spoke before a small hand grasped her elbow. "I'm Maya. I don't know how you got here, but I'm happy you came. Let's sit you down."

Maize moved forward as Maya led them farther into the room before pressing Kamali into a soft chair, likely a recliner.

"May I get you something to drink?" Maya spoke from close by. "I have tea."

"Yes, please. I'd like that." Kamali closed her eyes, seeking a moment of comfort in the shadows. The familiarity of nothingness before she accepted this moment as real. Wiping her wet cheeks, she once more opened her eyes and shifted her gaze to Nodin. This phenomenon was too amazing. She gripped her hands tightly together in her lap to keep from shooting out of the chair, walking across the room, and touching his face and body.

A rush of warm air brushed across her skin.

Flicking her gaze to the side, Kamali noted a bright red-orange aura beside Nodin, and then another great energy at his other side, coming from the same person who had answered the door...how odd...this being's aura was now a mixture of every shade of brown she'd ever detected, and yet, it too, exuded heat.

"Maize, sit." After taking a deep breath, Kamali decided she should answer Nodin's initial question. "I'm sorry to intrude." She cleared her throat. "I am Kamali Kiwidinok. Mother Nature told me where to find you. She came to me in a sort of dream. I woke and remembered everything. She left me with a sense of calm, and a choice. And, as you can see, I chose to be here. To help you. I'm not sure what I need to do, but she said you'd explain further." She smiled and ran her fingers through her guide dog's fur. "This is my girl, Maize."

An earthy smell, like fresh-cut grass, settled across her senses as the brown aura shifted closer. The color was so vivid, so very soothing, not a dull, hazy filter but a deep, earthy brown.

"Welcome, Kamali. I am Terran." His warm hand engulfed hers. "Maya is my...is my..."

"The love of his life, soul mate, one and only." Maya's chuckle followed her undulating turquoise aura then stopped at Kamali's side, along with the comforting scent of peppermint tea. "Flint is also here, as is Nodin." Maya removed Terran's hand and replaced it with a warm cup's handle. "Here is your tea."

"Thank you." Kamali took a small sip. The temperature was perfect. After taking a more substantial drink, Kamali felt Maya's hand return, and together they settled the cup on a side table to her right.

Nodin shifted away from his Elemental partners and moved to stand before her.

Kamali studied his face, biting her lip to hold back any additional tears. Was he considered a handsome man? His body was a bit like Creed's, her bodyguard, full of defined muscles. Muscles she could now shape with more than just her hands, as Nodin did not wear a shirt. Though, she believed his form was trimmer, maybe a bit slighter than Creed's.

How very intriguing.

"Where is Mother, Kamali?" Nodin's curt tone suggested his displeasure. Was he angry she had come? Did he not wish to see her again? Oh...she hadn't considered that.

"Don't tell me you travelled here all alone?" Nodin continued his interrogation.

"Fine." Kamali shrugged. "I won't tell you I travelled here all alone."

Maya giggled.

"I am blind, not helpless." To hide her shaking hands, she buried them in Maize's soft fur. "Though I rely on others to help me travel, I can and do complete many things on my own. My blindness does not hinder my life."

Same argument, different day. Explaining she wasn't somehow "less than," infuriated her. In some ways, not seeing a person's outside helped her better gauge what was on the inside, and that, Kamali believed, meant so much more.

And though she had travelled before, this was the first time she'd ever gone alone. Not that she'd divulge that to anyone, especially frowny-face Nodin. Plus, escaping her bodyguard had been tricky. Luckily her friend, Sawni, a hopeless romantic, had helped plan this journey and had someone waiting at the airport. Sawni was "totally positive" Nodin was her destiny.

Kamali bit her bottom lip, unsettled by her current circumstances and from receiving numerous phone messages from her uncle. Furious was too mild a word to describe his opinion of her, in his words, "ill-considered flight."

Her uncle had never appreciated her daring side. And explaining that Mother Nature had come to her during a dream and directed her to Colorado to help a group of Elemental beings wouldn't fly. Regardless of the old ways and their fundamental belief in the Great Spirit and the power of the elements, Kamali knew her uncle would think this all some elaborate hoax to kidnap and ransom her. A legitimate worry, as her uncle owned World Star Casino, the second largest casino in all of North America, which was nestled in a southern Oklahoma town.

After her parents died in an auto accident, Kamali became her uncle's ward. When he'd learned she carried a special gift from her mother's side, he'd become extremely overprotective, because this same gift had driven her mother to addiction and ultimately caused her death in a drunk driving accident.

Relegating that old pain to the back of her mind, Kamali focused on the point of her visit. "I'm afraid I don't have a lot of time. I need to know what I can do to help." She ran her hands up and down her thighs, trying to stop her body from rocking back and forth. A nervous habit she hadn't fought since childhood. Her psychologist said this motion was a frequent issue for blind persons and was theorized to be a way to gain more information about their surroundings. And, being overwhelmed by all the vibrant auras and actually visualizing a human for the first time, was it any wonder she attempted to absorb more? Kamali tightened her grip on her knees. "I don't fully comprehend my purpose, or yours, but I'd like to help. Mother Nature believes I'm capable of detecting the presence of this evil being named…Quint. Is that correct?"

"Yes," Maya answered. "Though, I don't believe she gave you the full scope of what we're fighting against. I'm not sure you'll agree if you—"

"Why don't you have any time?" Flint interrupted.

Kamali cleared her throat. "I work security at my uncle's casino."

"How can you work—"

"Flint." Terran's brown aura flickered with reds.

"What?"

"She's a guest in my home, try not to insult her," Terran ordered.

"I may be blind, but I can still hear." Kamali chuckled, noting the brotherly interaction between the men, so similar to her cousins back home. "Flint, my duties are more specialized. Much is at stake in both the casino and politically. My uncle must choose his employees, and his allies, wisely." She let her gaze drift to Nodin's face. "I help with that." Could he tell she was staring? Would his skin feel warm under her hand? Were all men's skin the same color as his? And his eyes…"Are your eyes blue, Nodin?"

"Yes, why?" He met her gaze.

A warm shiver breezed through her body. So this was attraction. She reached for her tea and swallowed a big gulp, stalling while she considered how to answer his question. Should she tell him she could see him…and only him? "I-I…I don't think I introduced you to Maize, my guide dog."

"You did." Nodin folded both arms over his chest. "Explain these duties you do for your uncle."

"We don't fully understand the extent of your gifts, Kamali." Coming from Kamali's right, Maya's voice was calm and even. "Mother and Eamon only said you can detect things in the darkness. What things? What can you…um…see?"

"And what do you get in return?" Nodin sat on the edge of the coffee table.

Close. Way too close.

"What do I get in return?" Kamali repeated Nodin's question. Was everything and anything he could give her an overly desperate answer? And those lips, every time he spoke she became mesmerized by their movement. She touched her own and watched as his gaze flashed to her fingers.

Leaning forward, he lifted a hand as if to touch her.

Her breathing halted as everything inside her stilled.

If she reached for him, then he'd know she could see, and that frightened her. Her comforting ebony blanket fluttered with a thin, narrow opening—an escape, yet, she craved the familiarity found within the darkness.

The spell broke as his hand returned to rest within the hazy blue aura lining his side. Yet, in the middle of his chest, she glimpsed a faint pink pulsing within.

CHAPTER 4

"The woman seated before him was gloriously beautiful in a fully natural way. For centuries, Nodin had seen women in various cultures and races, so many lovely faces over his vast lifetime. But Kamali's features were perfection—and represented everything he'd left behind. A descendant of his Chickasaw tribe. In the deepest recesses of his heart, he'd always wished for a woman who came from his people. He'd been pulled from adolescent dreams of maidens in his tribe by Pillar and his transformation, but he'd always wondered, what if? What if he'd remained human and lived with his tribe? What if he'd had a wife? Would she have looked like Kamali?

At her height, she'd fit right under his chin, and for some reason, he wanted her there. He should be comforting her and asking if she was aware of what happened at the diner. He should feel an edge of suspicion, yet nothing about her screamed guilt or malice. Still, he had a duty to fulfill and here was his chance. Why was he so tense? Why did he feel like he was flying out of control again?

"Why are you so frightened?" Kamali turned to him.

And once more he had the faintest tingle that she could *see* him, yet..."I am not frightened." He shifted forward on the coffee table.

Maize rested her head on his knee.

Nodin ruffled the dog's soft fur and questioned her owner. "You can detect my emotions, correct? If so, you have them backwards. Any fear within me is for you. You seemed frightened of your uncle."

Kamali stiffened. "I don't need a protector."

"Everyone needs a protector and a helpmate." He took her hand. "Seeking or needing companionship is not a weakness."

"Why can I...I-I don't understand." Her voice wobbled, and her hand trembled in his.

"Do not be afraid." She bit that full bottom lip, and he fought the urge to take that plump pinkness himself. To taste her and comfort her with soft kisses.

Terran cleared his throat. "Kamali, we, too, have been told your particular skill set will be critical in defeating Quint."

The Earth Elemental had, until now, remained quiet, likely analyzing each word. He and Flint stood behind the couch. Nodin kept his gaze on Kamali as Terran continued. "We will need to speak to Violet, Flint's mate and a very powerful witch, in order to further understand your place."

"Am I to stay here until she arrives?" Kamali tightened her grip on Nodin's hand.

"Yes." Nodin rubbed his thumb back and forth across her soft skin. "Maya and Terran will keep you safe. I'll keep you safe."

Maize licked their joined hands.

"I'm not sure how long I have," Kamali whispered.

"Why?"

"My uncle will come."

Nodin moved closer until her knees rested between his. "He will come and do what?" He reached up and tucked a stray hair behind her ear.

"Take me home." After heaving a sigh, she raised her head and met his gaze.

Again. Could she see? How could she look him straight in

the eye and not see? He kept her gaze, unsure yet, something, if only ingrained manners, kept him from doing anything but meeting her directly eye-to-eye.

What did his aura look like to her? And how was her uncle "using" her? Though that thought didn't sit well, he couldn't help but note the correlation in his own need to use her gifts. But what did *she* want? "You will not go anywhere you do not wish to go. And, if you'd like, please consider this your home while you stay. Maya and Terran are willing hosts."

"Yeah, they don't use their bedroom for anything fun, anyway." Flint finally added to the conversation in his usual manner.

Maya rolled her eyes. "Kamali, ignore him. I always do. But just so you understand, it's true Elementals don't sleep. Although, Terran and I do have a very large bed, for obvious reasons." She chuckled. "We have a spare bedroom, and you may stay as long as you need."

Maya hadn't had a true place to call home until she'd settled with Terran. Nodin had never seen her so happy, and she did love when people visited, especially since she had a very limited circle of friends. He took a deep breath and, since he never held back what he felt, he admitted, "I want you to stay." He stopped short of making any demands. He refused to own her. Protect her? Yes. But never stifle her inner strength.

And she was strong—a remote island. Yet, even an island welcomed a tropical breeze. A brisk wind rustling across its isolated shores, scattering up sand across the lonely surface.

An elemental connection flowed between them, wrapped in their linked past, yet unraveling in the future and, in that moment, he knew she wasn't leaving—him or their mission.

CHAPTER 5

Unable to concentrate on the many demands of running his flourishing casino, Adler startled out of his daze when his cell phone buzzed on his desk. Creed's number appeared on the screen. Though the man was on his shit list, he tossed aside his spreadsheets and answered. "If you give me another excuse, Creed, I'll slice you to pieces with my great-grandfather's knife."

"We've located Maize, sir."

"I assume you're en route." Adler held the phone away from his ear as Creed had yelled each word into the phone. Was the fool standing right beside the plane's engines?

"Not yet, sir. The beacon is signaling from Colorado."

"After you extract Kamali, make sure those Elementals understand what happens when they take something that is mine."

"Understood."

Adler doubted Creed really understood. He was basically a mound of muscle with a tiny head and an even tinier brain. The lug only did as he was told. Still, he was loyal and willing to get his hands very dirty, so Adler kept him around, like a tamed pet viper. "Is *she* with you?"

"Er...um...yes."

Creed's hesitation did not bode well. His 'yes' came across as more of a question than a statement, though the dunce must have finally moved to a quieter area.

Adler sighed. "Is she prepared to do as I've asked?"

"Yes." The line went silent for a moment.

"Creed?"

He cleared his throat. "Er...um...she wishes to speak to you."

"I tire of her wishes."

"Sir, she won't let the pilot leave."

"Fine." Adler pressed his index finger and thumb against the bridge of his nose. "Put her on the line." Rustling, then he heard a short muffled argument before Creed shouted and a woman shrieked.

A clanking, likely from her gaudy rings, sounded against the phone before a throaty voice spoke. "Why, Adler, you deign to speak to little ol' me?"

"Raven, I tire of your games." The treacherous, though gifted, woman was his sister-in-law, a manipulative bitch who had him by the balls, because they shared too many secrets. In her case, the old adage of keeping your enemies close had never rung more true.

"Is that so, dear Adler? I find that odd, coming from a man who is surrounded by games." She laughed. "Speaking of being tired, I am very tired of performing all these little favors when our business finished years ago. We both got what we wanted, but you continually drag me back into my niece's life. I care not for her welfare. Retrieving her is your goal, not mine. Your continual errands are beginning to bore. Understand this, if not for Creed's...charms, I wouldn't have left my home."

"Going soft on me?" Rounding his desk, Adler paced before his office's one-way mirrored wall and stared down at the gambling patrons. "You enjoyed your last visit to Oklahoma. I figured you'd consider this next trip a continuation of that fun."

Whatever wild notion had Kamali fleeing without a word to her family was not anything that would generally cause Adler concern. She'd had flights of fancy before, yet Creed was always at her side. But now, he worried those Elementals could hold sway over her. Take her away from him and his plans for her within his organization. He refused to conduct business without her. She was his shield against those wishing him harm—the cheats, liars, and gamblers without a conscience.

And his Kamali had caught the eye of a congressman's son. This marriage would create a connection outside the casino world. His little "spirit guide" would do more than guide his spirit, she would transport them into a political realm they had long tried to exploit. His sons would inherit his casino kingdom and so much more.

Just last week, Adler had the politician's son vetted. A bit of an entitled twit, not attractive in the least, but as long as the man was kind to Kamali, Adler didn't care. She never judged people by their outside appearance anyway, and this man, though arrogant, would treat her well enough.

Lost in thought of everything he could lose, he gripped his phone tighter and concentrated on cajoling the woman who could ease his burden. "Nothing to say, Raven? Well, I have plenty. We've used Malachi to block that wizard, Eamon, and Mother Nature's efforts into learning more of our girl. We both know she's too valuable to risk in their endeavors. You will bring her back, and you will make sure the Elementals understand not to seek her out again. Creed will handle Kamali. I'll have a separate car on scene. Do not fret, you won't have to deal with her."

"You make this whole rescue mission sound simple, but you are betting against forces you've never understood, Adler."

"I understand power, and I'm the one with the upper hand. Never forget who holds the ace, Raven."

Her chuckle came quite clear across the line. "I'll let you continue to believe that."

"Maybe we could ask Malachi. Or, better yet, how about we let Kamali unleash that savage side our medicine man has blocked?"

"Fine, tamp down your threats." She sniffed. "I'm doing as you wish."

The line went dead.

Near the office's doorway, a cough sounded from his second son, Waya.

"Damn it. Never enter without knocking first." Spinning, Adler narrowed his eyes. "I thought you were getting that cough checked out?" He sneered, waving a hand in the general direction of the door. "I don't need your cold or whatever illness you're currently spreading throughout my office."

Waya shrugged, his ebony eyes covered by dark shades. "Have you found Kamali?"

"Why are you wearing those ridiculous sunglasses indoors?" Adler shook his head. "We tracked her using Maize's locator chip." Raking his fingers through his hair, he stormed back over to his desk. "Why aren't you out on the floor?"

"So, you've sent Raven to fetch her." Waya cleared his throat before hacking into a white handkerchief he'd pulled from his jacket pocket.

"Yes." Done discussing his wayward niece, Adler pulled up his private email.

"Good." Smiling, his son gazed out the one-way mirror. "I'll look forward to her return."

"Why should Kamali's return matter to you? Sure, you were close as children, but you've abandoned her of late." Of his three sons, this one was most frequently in trouble and well-known by the local police. A wild child who cared not for consequences.

Apparently, his son needed a reminder about stepping into his domain without an invitation. Shoving away from his desk, Adler tugged down his shirtsleeves and approached then clutched Waya by the throat, holding him against the glass. "I know you've worked with Kamali. Perhaps you believe she is your ticket to my throne, but I'd be careful of your games, Waya. I know just how feral you are. You are *my* son, after all."

His son didn't sputter, didn't make a sound, though his face turned beet red. His children showed no pain, and certainly no mercy. Ever. Though, Adler was sure, under those mirrored-lenses, his son's gaze was cold and hard. *Good.*

Adler tightened his grip and stood nose-to-nose. "She is my tool." After a final squeeze, he shoved away. "Get back to your station and send Malachi to me."

"As you wish." Jaw clenched, his son mock saluted.

Turning his back on the boy, Adler sank into his leather office chair. "Don't come back until that cold is gone."

At the door, Waya turned and smiled. "It's not a cold. I believe it's more of an…infection."

A cold chill swept down Adler's back. Seeking security, he gripped the .45 he kept secured under the desktop.

Waya tipped his glasses down his nose and winked.

After watching his defiant son leave with a cheeky slam of the door, Adler toyed with the gun in his hand while he considered his upcoming meeting with Congressman Blake Turner and the man's son, Tosh. Actually a social occasion, a dinner he planned to attend with Kamali on his arm. He needed her to charm the boy and to gauge the congressman's honesty.

Taking a deep breath, he coughed against what felt like a bombardment of dust particles shooting up his nose and down his throat. Gasping, he clutched his throat and fought to breathe. Buckling over, he fell onto the plastic carpet protector under his desk chair.

Had his son left behind a poisonous gas? Or had his worst nightmare snuck into his domain? Damn that medicine man, his defensive walls were waning. Malachi and Kamali were strongest when together. One more reason to get the girl back where she belonged.

Blinking against the particles now blanketing his vision, he reached for his cold coffee and poured it over his face. Rising onto his knees, he grasped for the phone on his desk. After wiping a hand across his face, he blinked. Vision now clear. Throat raw. He frantically punched numbers on his phone and choked out, "M-Malachi, he's returned."

CHAPTER 6

Snuggling under the fuzzy blanket in Maya and Terran's spare bedroom, Kamali reflected on all she had learned the day before. After the flight, and staring all afternoon and evening at every one of Nodin's movements, she'd drifted easily to sleep.

Her phone chirped again with Creed's ring tone, and though she wanted to forget the outside world and concentrate on her new-found vision, she had to answer. Allowing her uncle to continue worrying was unkind. She reached for her cell, which had voice-activation. "Answer phone." After the click, she said, "Hello, Creed."

"Kamali." Her bodyguard's hard tone practically vibrated across the line. "I'm waiting outside."

Sighing, she leaned back against the pillows. The rustling of her hair brushing back and forth was the only sound in the room. Rubbing her eyes, she considered how to deal with Creed. Direct generally worked best. "You shouldn't have come. Maize and I are staying."

"Uncle wants you home."

Maize's collar jingled at the mention of her name. Her cold snout nudged Kamali's hand.

"Creed, I need to stay here."

"No. I have my orders. Uncle Adler needs you for the

meeting with Senator Turner tonight."

Shoot. She'd forgotten about that. The senator's son, Tosh, always turned from violet to a muddy pink. His aura reflected a clear sense of superiority, which switched to lustful passion, childlike emotions, and critical judgment in her presence. Still, based on her uncle's implications, she understood this man liked her. But she found that hard to believe as Tosh rarely spoke *to* her, more *at* her, and he treated her like being blind also meant she was mentally deficient.

"Kamali, please," Creed pleaded. "Just let me come in and get you. You've had your adventure. It's time to come home now."

Knowing Creed was likely suffering for her secret departure, Kamali conceded. "Fine, I'll go to the dinner tonight, but then I must come back." While she believed she owed her Uncle Adler since he'd raised her and provided all the comforts and education she could ever need, in this one instance, she felt reluctant to participate. The thought of entertaining someone she had no attraction to—especially now that she understood that real heat, that true chemistry she'd only read about between two people—she rejected the notion of toying with another's heart. Though, for her uncle's sake, and in order to explain why she must help the Elementals, she would return with Creed.

"Maize needs to go out." She used her guide dog as a stall tactic, since she couldn't detect any of the Elementals' presences. "I'll come, but I need time to get ready and say goodbye to my friends."

The bedroom door slid open, ruffling across the carpet fibers.

"Kamali, who are you speaking to?"

Nodin's voice offered a sense of comfort, like being curled up beside a roaring fire after being lost in a blanket of snow for days.

Staring at his form—which she could still see—she smiled

and temporarily forgot she was on the phone until Creed rumbled her name in her ear. "Uh...I'll be out soon." She sat up, keeping the covers over her body. "Bye, Creed."

"Who's Creed?"

She gasped as Nodin sat on the bed. His bright blue aura swirled with streaks of yellow, representing intelligence, and white for self-awareness.

Heart pounding, she considered asking if he'd stick by her side. Forever. Could he, in the smallest sense, grasp how monumental vision was in her blank world? She wished she could see more of his body, though not necessarily in a sexual way, even considering her overwhelming physical attraction to him. What did he look like bare? Naked?

"I thought I'd come in and wake you, but I see you're already up." Nodin's smile faded when his gaze shot to the door. "Listen, Kamali, a car is outside. The man in the car, well...I'm gleaning some pretty hostile thoughts from his mind. He wants you to leave in a very bad way."

"I know." She reached out and patted Maize's soft ears, but let her hand fall so it would brush against Nodin's thigh. "His name is Creed. My bodyguard. I-I have a-a...duty tonight, for my uncle." She cleared her throat and then covered her mouth, sure she needed to rinse with a gallon of Listerine. "I must go with him, but I promise to return."

"Kamali, once you leave, that man out there has no intention of ever letting you come back." Standing, Nodin jabbed a finger toward the front of the house.

"How can you say that?" Frowning, she watched, fascinated, as he tapped his temple. Body language was foreign to her. Reading about their intricacies was one thing, seeing them another.

"I'm an Elemental, remember?" He rested both hands on his hips. "I can glean his thoughts. He's ready to storm in here and take you away. However, he won't even reach the front door. He knows that, too. Seems he's aware of who you are with. Your uncle is, too."

"Leave him be." Kamali shot out of the bed, wearing one of her long T-shirts. She noted Nodin's gaze sweeping over her body. For some reason, that simple glance made her hot all over. Made her forget her anger at his seeming threat to Creed. Was that how a man looked at a woman he desired? Oh, she certainly hoped so. Lost to her impetuous nature, she fingered the edges of her T-shirt, wondering, just wondering what would happen if she ripped off the shirt and revealed her body to this man. Dear Lord, she almost swooned like some silly starlet at the lust shooting to every corner of her body and centering between her thighs.

"Kamali? What are you—" Frowning, he reached for her, licking his lower lip, but just before he touched her face, he jerked back and shook his head. "Terran will speak to Creed."

Her stomach sank. "No." She gripped Nodin's arm. "Creed is...he tends to react physically. I won't have him hurt."

Nodin chuckled, and this time when he raised his hand, he brushed her hair over her shoulder. "Pakali, my little flower, as the Earth Elemental, Terran has all four elements at his disposal. Creed won't even make it out of the vehicle."

"Please, don't hurt him." She took Nodin's hand. "He's only doing his job." Though Creed sometimes frightened her with his dark aura, she knew he was only concerned for her safety. Plus, besides her cousins, he was her only friend. Sometimes his aura turned darker, and she would catch him slipping into her room to lie beside Maize and sleep. She didn't understand why he did that, but maybe he sought solace in this gloomy world, as well.

Someone knocked on the door, and then Terran's brown aura appeared beside Nodin. "Kamali, it's Terran."

"Um...I feel I should be honest." She chewed on her thumbnail. "I know who you are by your auras."

Nodin tilted his head. "You can see me?"

"Well..." Should she tell the truth? Sighing, she ventured

forward, all while wondering how much longer Creed's patience would hold. She flicked a hand toward Terran. "Terran, you are a deep brown, which denotes you as a manager and an industrious person. At times, you are intermeshed with reds, which indicates you are a leader. Flint is all red, vital and warm. Maya transmits an aura of calm and is very turquoise, though she also puts off green, which could indicate a gift as a healer." Chewing on her lip as she considered that revelation, Kamali shifted her gaze to Nodin. Then, losing her nerve, she closed her eyes for a moment before opening them again and taking in all of Nodin's form. His legs were clad in a fabric of some sort, likely sweat pants, and he wore a long T-shirt, which had words on the front she couldn't read because she only knew Braille. She wiped at the tears falling down her cheeks.

"What is it?" Nodin held her shoulders.

"You. It's you." Smiling through her tears, she reached out and cupped his face in her hands. "I see you."

Nodin opened his mouth and then closed it as he held her wrists, locking them in place.

"Nodin…you are blue, as well. But"—pulling from his grip, she rubbed her temple—"I can see you within your aura."

"Interesting." Terran's aura drew closer. "But then…why can you see him and not me? How can you be sure what you are seeing? What does he look like? I assume you've always been blind, so…well…I don't know what to say." He paused for a moment. "Are you all right?" He placed a tissue in her hand.

After wiping her nose, she crumpled the tissue. "I'm a bit overwhelmed and, though it makes me very angry, I'm a little afraid."

"Why?" Nodin tipped up her chin. "Look at me."

"I *am*." Her heart thumped so hard, she had no doubt he could feel the vibration, surely the beat was shaking the walls. Tears continued to pour down her cheeks as the reality of her situation lay open and aching at these two men's feet.

Nodin wiped away each tear with his thumbs.

Then, her breath stuttered and her heart edged closer to explosion as he leaned closer...*oh, dear God*...and lined his lips with hers.

A soft kiss. Once, then twice, before he pulled away. "Don't cry, Kamali. I think I am starting to see you, too." Nodin smiled, but it didn't reach his eyes. "Why do you think you can see me?"

"I don't know, but I want to stay here...with you...until I figure it out."

Nodin kissed her forehead this time. "I don't understand either, but I'd like that, as well. Kierkegaard said, 'Life is not a problem to be solved, but a reality to be experienced.' Something ancient exists between us—a thread. Perhaps, in another life, we were destined to become one, but we were torn apart before fate got her due." He gazed into her eyes, brushing his hands up and down her arms. "For a long time, I was off course...and I have continued along that vein for far too long. But with you, there are no rustling winds, no call to fly, no stirring to search out someplace new. My element is suspended in this moment."

After caressing her cheek, he shook his head "Why? How can you come along and change everything? I don't like it. I don't trust it. But I'll see this through, because after living all these years lost in the wind, I need someone to see me, just as you need someone to see you."

With those words, he leaned closer and once more lightly pressed his lips to hers, shaping and dancing across their surface until she responded in kind, wrapping her arms around his neck. Losing herself in his skilled caress, because his words were too close to her own yearnings.

Would she have time to make sense of everything before being drawn back into her uncle's world? Was she stifled there? She'd never thought so before, but with Creed waiting impatiently outside, she now wondered how much of her life was her own?

Terran cleared his throat.

And then, Maize nuzzled her hand.

After one more soft press, Nodin pulled away, brushing his thumb across her damp lower lip.

The moment passed, but the residual heat remained on her lips.

Her first kisses. And she'd absorbed each caress with open eyes, memorizing the flutter of Nodin's lashes as he drew close, the tilt of his head, the short puff of breath against her lips. The way his gaze remained on her lips as he'd pulled away.

Did he realize how beautiful a kiss could be? How much was revealed by that simple act? How much that small touch meant to a girl who hadn't felt the loving embrace of another since her parents had died twenty years ago? She craved more. Craved everything this man could give.

Her dreams of finding love had come to life and now, not only in her mind's eye did she see every color of the rainbow, but her body burst with every hue, as well. Too many emotions stirred…could Nodin glean her thoughts? Could Terran? *Oh, sweet biscuits.* She stuttered out, "C-can you r-read my thoughts?"

Nodin turned and glanced at Terran, whose aura still lingered in what must be the doorway.

"I'll confess Maya delved into your mind last night, but all she detected was a gray wall." Terran answered. "She said it seemed ethereal, hazy, but she couldn't get past whatever you've built up. Nodin?"

"The same for me." He tilted his head as he studied her.

Maize whined and brushed against her side.

Kamali chuckled. "I need to let Maize out, and if you wouldn't mind, I'd like to speak to Creed alone for a moment."

"I do mind." Nodin shook his head. "If you go out there, you don't go alone. We still don't know who controlled my gift, and we believe you are at the center of that mystery. So, I'm going with you."

Usually, she didn't like people hovering or telling her what she would and wouldn't do, but she liked the woozy, soft feeling fluttering through her body in Nodin's presence.

"Fine." She rose to her feet. "Let me get dressed. Would you mind guiding me to the bathroom? I don't—" She gasped and tumbled back against the bed as a roiling burst of hatred crashed against her empathic senses.

Terran's aura turned bright red, churning with smoky, gray circles. "Something's off."

Nodin stilled. "I sense it, too, but I can't lock down where..."

"No. Please, stop." Kamali screamed and grasped her head in her hands. "I've never felt such sinister energy. She...she means you great harm." Another sharp pain shot through her temples. "Go." She shoved at Nodin's arm. "Leave this place."

Terran's aura disappeared quick as a flash.

At her side, Maize growled and barked.

Nodin gasped, his gaze locked on his fading fingers. Eyes wide, he clutched her shoulders and gave her a shake. "Are you doing this?"

Terran's shouts sounded from outside the room.

A door slammed.

"Nodin, what is happening?"

"I'm losing control again. Transforming." He clenched his jaw. "We need to get you out of here."

Echoes of Nodin's fear and stark terror ricocheted through Kamali's mind.

And still, that wicked presence teased her brain, taunted her with something...something that seemed almost familiar, but at the same time, gleefully delivering shards of piercing pain through her every pulsing vein.

Maize barked madly and pushed against her knees.

Nodin's body flickered in and out. He grabbed her by both shoulders. "Do you trust me?"

"Yes."

"Come with me." He lifted her in his arms and carried her

out the door.

"Where are we going?" She tugged her T-shirt down over her legs.

"Once outside, I'll create a whirlwind and carry you to safety."

A large pop sounded then glass splintered before tinkling to the ground.

Outside air whipped against her skin, joining the robust breeze pouring from Nodin.

She had no chance to enjoy the comfort of his arms, because smoke filled her lungs and burned her eyes.

"Oh, please no." Nodin halted. "What has he done?"

"What's happened?" Coughing, Kamali gripped Nodin tighter, wishing she could see what had to be a blazing fire.

"It's Flint. He's become his element. He's burning."

Kamali glanced at Nodin. His mouth gaped open, and his gaze was riveted on something to his left. "He's destroying everything."

Crackles and pops exploded nearby. The scent of burning wood wafted through the air.

A woman's insidious tone hissed through Kamali's mind, *"Go home, little girl."*

"Nodin." More frightened than she'd ever been in her life, Kamali gripped his face in her hands. "We must leave, now. She's close." She glanced over her shoulder, sure the woman would descend and commit some heinous act against them.

He met her gaze. "Flint doesn't know what he's doing. He doesn't know. When Maya sees this…she'll be…she'll be—"

"I'm losing you, Nodin. You're fading in and out. Please, we need to leave."

"I need to stop him before he starts on the house. Stay here." He released her legs and set her on her feet.

"No." Kamali wrapped her hand in his T-shirt. "You can't. She'll just control you, too."

"She who?" Nodin glanced at his flickering body. "How is this happening?"

Kamali nudged against his chest. "That doesn't matter right now. We must go." She blinked against the smoke stinging her eyes.

"Give me a minute." She watched him turn from her, his shoulders rising and falling, over and over again. The crackling stopped, and no longer did she have to blink away smoke.

"There. The fire's out." Glancing over his shoulder, he smiled before his gaze landed on something behind her. "No, Flint, don't!" He frantically waved a hand back and forth.

The smell of burnt hair filled the air, and her neck flushed hot.

Nodin leapt toward her and beat against the back of her head before lifting her in his arms. "Hold on."

The jangle of Maize's collar rattled at her side, drawing her attention just before her feet left the ground.

Nodin had done as she'd wished, lifting her up and away, but at what cost? His Elemental partners remained behind, lost in a haze of smoke and fiery destruction.

Dizziness clouded her mind, and she couldn't catch her breath as the day's trauma coalesced. No longer gripped in Nodin's hold, she floundered for a moment, succumbing to her natural instincts to return to stable ground.

Higher and higher she swirled through the sky, her entire body shivering from the icy air. No longer physically or mentally able to endure these unreal circumstances, she opened her arms and closed her eyes, letting her body drift.

Just before she lost consciousness, one word screamed across her mind.

Raven.

CHAPTER 7

"What do you mean you don't have her?" With his index finger and thumb, Adler flipped his great-grandfather's bone-handled knife over and over on his desk to prevent him from plunging it into Creed's chest.

Crossing her legs, Raven smirked.

"This big dude went crazy, lighting everything on fire." Creed rested his elbows on his knees. "My driver just took off." He flicked at a piece of lint on his shirt, his gaze unfocused. "You wouldn't understand unless you were there. I've never felt such heat. Like…a…blowtorch or something, but the blowtorch is inside your body, and your skin starts to bubble." With a shaky hand, Creed sipped his Mountain Dew. "I didn't wanna, but I knew you'd want me to, so I went back a couple hours later. The house…" he shivered. "Burned to nothing."

"Damn it, Creed." Adler sighed out his curse.

And damn Raven. He knew better than to let that genie out of her bottle. He may get three wishes, but they were never without a price. If the bitch wanted to play games, then he'd be the one setting the pieces on the board. Mischief-making when Kamali's welfare, and his own, were at stake was not a time for playful diversions. He may live in a world of gamblers, but some things were too precious to risk on a toss of the dice.

He shouldn't have beckoned Raven so soon after sending her to deter the Air Elemental during the blowhard's visit to that diner Kamali frequented.

He glanced out the glass encompassing an entire wall of his office. The lights from the slot machines flickered across the walls, hypnotizing his patrons with their bright colors and, for a moment, himself as he considered his predicament.

Kamali gone.

Dinner plans cancelled.

Creed a mess.

Raven out of control.

Elementals on alert.

Fucking fantastic.

Taking a deep breath, he asked the one question he really didn't want answered, especially with his rage on the verge of boiling over the top. Feigning calm, he rested his hands against his stomach before leaning back in his leather office chair. "Do you know...did Kamali escape, or is she dead?"

"She is not with the Great Spirit," Malachi responded as he sauntered into the room. Though descended from a long line of medicine men, he chose to dress in excessively expensive couture. Business suits of only the finest cut, and always all black, except for his tie, which exhibited his tendencies toward a more colorful flair. In his late fifties, his hair now peppered with gray, the man's body and face could still pass for much younger. He'd never married. Adler assumed he was gay but had never delved deeper, as he had asked once, years ago, and was struck down with an illness for three-months no doctor could explain.

Pity, as now the tribe's medicine man had no child to carry on his knowledge. Malachi's bag of medicines, or more likely deadly poisons, lay tied around his waist, but hidden at his side beneath his jacket. Adler was sure other, more modern, weapons were secreted away in pockets and sheathed against his skin. Carrying knives and guns, the man was a walking arsenal.

"Kamali escaped with Nodin." Malachi rested his hands against the back of Raven's chair. "Elementals are wily."

"Flint's will was strong, ancient. I focused the majority of my power on lighting him up." Flashing a wicked grin, Raven studied her red-tipped nails. "Eventually, he beat me back, but not before I controlled him long enough to roast that barn and the little cabin." She shrugged and sipped Adler's high-end single malt scotch. "I caught them off guard once, and they'll run to the witch, Violet, and her grandfather. Then we'll have more of a fight on our hands." Raven sniffed. "But right now, the Elementals are damaged. Disoriented. You have a slight advantage, so if you want Kamali back, you'll need to move quickly."

"I'm aware of what I need to do, Raven." Adler glared at the dark-haired menace. "And I'm also aware I wouldn't be in this situation if you had done as I asked, instead of playing with fire." He slammed his blade into the desktop. "Kamali is too innocent to comprehend the snake in the grass these Elementals wish her to fight."

Raven scoffed. "Right…she's always been *much* safer with you."

"You posing bitch. I made you what you are." He jabbed a finger in her direction. "Never forget that. I took on that burden so you wouldn't have to." Half rising from his desk, he removed his knife and whipped it forward so it flipped end over end before piercing the tip of Raven's stiletto, slicing through her big toe. "Understand this—when I ask you to bring me the girl, I expect you to do so."

Raven simply glared, pulled the knife free, and wiped the blood on his leather chair. "Are you finished beating your chest? Because I have places to be." Arching a brow, she glanced at her feet. "And new shoes to buy."

Clenching his jaw, Adler chucked his empty snifter at Creed's head. "Track the dog. Now."

Creed rubbed the side of his head then moved the glass off

his lap, setting it on the coffee table.

As if his office didn't already have enough people, Waya meandered into the room, still wearing sunglasses.

Adler sighed.

Malachi visibly stilled, watching Waya cross the room. Then the medicine man drew a pipe from an inside pocket and lit the end.

Hands lifted, palms out, Raven stood, eyes wide, staring at Waya. "What are you?"

Waya smirked then leaned against Raven's chair.

Malachi began chanting a song to ward off evil spirits.

Stomach churning, Adler gazed at his middle child and stepped around his desk. "No, please no."

"What's wrong, Uncle?" Creed's head jerked back and forth between the room's occupants.

"I believe my dear father has finally figured out he's not the biggest bully in the room." Grinning, Waya tilted his head and ripped off his glasses to reveal pure black eyes.

Suddenly, an unseen force propelled the medicine man against a bookshelf, tumbling photo frames, historic clay pots, and figures found during burial mound excavations off the shelves.

"I tire of your ridiculous chants." Waya rubbed his temples. "They do nothing but knock against my head, Malachi the medicine man. Your smoky potions have no power over me." Waya's gaze shot to Raven. "What's this? You think to journey into my mind? To control me as easily as you controlled those pathetic Elementals? Think again. I'm almost back. Almost ready. I've been waiting, learning, growing for five years."

Adler took a step toward the door, knowing he'd lost this son, but he wished to warn the other two. To escape this dark matter creature now at his leisure in his office...and within his son. Why had he brushed off Waya's illness? Why hadn't Malachi seen the signs?

Detecting his movement, Waya snapped around and then

curved his index finger. "Come back, Daddy. Neither you, nor any of your boys, can escape now."

Heart breaking, Adler studied his son. "What do you want? I have money, this casino. What will it take for you to leave my son's body?"

Waya laughed, slapping a hand against the top of Raven's chair. "You humans always throw around money like financial gain matters to an evolved being like me. Money is not the ultimate power. I am." He huffed out another laugh, shaking his head. "If I wanted your money, hell, if I wanted you, Adler, I would simply take it. As it is, I find your suffering amusing."

"Malachi. Raven," Adler summoned. "Do something. Combine your gifts as you did before? Remove him from my son."

Malachi met his gaze before glaring at Waya. "You are a mere seed, dark creature. Unwelcome on this plane." This time, the medicine man began to chant a song of war.

Raven had settled back in her chair, her legs crossed, one foot swinging as if she hadn't a care in the world.

Waya rocked side-to-side, along with the Malachi's lyrical beat. "Catchy little tune. Needs some drums, though, to bring out the authenticity, don't you think?" With a grin, he met Adler's gaze while tapping his fingers against the chair. "I can see why your people pranced around to that shit back in the day." He glanced at Creed. "So, Muscleman, Flint impressed you, did he?" He cocked an ebony brow and waved a hand before him. "What's one thing you desire? Something you crave above all other things, but you know obtaining it could mean your end?"

"I-I don't...Waya, what's wrong with you? Why are you talking like this?" Creed glanced at Malachi. "And why is he singing a battle song?"

"He's become another, Creed." Actually speaking those words, acknowledging his son was lost, tightened Adler's chest, and he fought for each breath. Clenching his jaw, he considered the foe before him. "Listen, Quint, I'm prepared to cooperate. We both want the same things. I can help you, if you'll help me."

"You dare to believe I need help from a mere human?"

"Take me." Adler spread his arms wide. "You need a host. Someone with the reserves to bring the Elementals to their knees. I'm your man." He edged closer. "Once we get Kamali back, we can use her and Malachi, and even Raven, to attain whatever, whoever you want. I only ask that you remove your presence from my son."

Halting in his chant, Malachi clutched his forearm. "Adler, do not offer such a thing."

Waya tapped his finger against his upper lip before smiling, more of a dark snarl than a pleased expression as he shifted his gaze to Raven. "You're right, Adler. I'm feeling a little itchy in this boy's skin, but *you* are not who I want."

"No, please," Adler begged, falling to his knees before the dark matter creature. "Don't take my son. There has to be a slim chance he'll recover."

"Too late." Recoiling, Waya shifted his legs to the opposite side. "I'm finished with him."

Adler stifled a scream as he watched his son's whole body tremble and shake.

A thick, tar-like substance spilled from Waya's pale lips and nose.

When his son gasped for breath, Adler caught him and held him close. "Fight it, Waya." He peered up at Malachi. "Do something. Say something. You must help him."

Malachi started to chant, holding both hands over Waya's head.

A loud gurgling rumbled in Waya's stomach, and then that tar-like substance streamed from his ears.

Raspy breathing joined Malachi's chants as Adler held Waya tight, though the boy jerked and convulsed in his arms.

Creed dropped to his knees and wrapped his arms around

them both. "He's dying, Uncle." Tears poured down his cheeks. "Let the Great Spirit take him."

Raven laughed from somewhere in the room and a loud thump sounded, as if a body had collapsed against the carpet.

Waya's body arched in his arms then relaxed at the same time a powerful energy wave shot through the office, strong enough to crack the glass wall and topple the desk.

Propelled across the room, Adler maintained his hold on Waya as he hit the corner of the coffee table. He ignored the sharp pain in his shoulder.

Creed braced both arms over their heads as the moose antler light fixture rocked and then fell from the ceiling.

Adler adjusted his body to protect his son's.

Creed took the brunt of the pain, bellowing as the fixture crashed against his back.

On alert for more danger, Adler quickly gazed around the room. Where was Malachi? Or Raven?

He once more studied his son's face, where no expression of life remained. His son's vibrant personality now replaced by a horror-filled glassy gaze and a trickle of black ooze seeping from the side of his mouth.

Stiffening, Waya opened his mouth and gasped his final breath.

Adler closed his son's eyes and kissed his forehead. Then, rocking his child back and forth, he released his people's song of mourning, believing to his very core that with this chant, his son's journey to the Great Sprit would be sheltered during its final voyage home.

CHAPTER 8

In a cave nestled within the tip of Mount Elbert, the highest peak of the Rocky Mountain's Sawatch Range, Nodin studied Kamali's sleeping form, nestled beside Maize. After landing, he'd travelled farther down the mountain to gather enough dry wood to maintain a small fire, though the ground beneath her was likely still frigid.

Snowflakes sparkled and trickled to the ground just outside the old bear den. At these heights, the air remained fresh and untouched, filtered by lodge pole pines, spruce, aspen, and fir, which lined the slope below.

Crouching at Kamali's side, Nodin added more wood to the fire. Hearing a slight rustling, he whipped around and stared at the beautiful creature standing at the narrow mouth of the cave—Mother Nature.

Long red-gold locks tumbled around her shoulders, her lanky frame like a tall, narrow aspen.

"Mother." Nodin dipped his chin. Too many thoughts raced through his head, rendering him incapable of his usual philosophical speeches which would help him simplify how and why he'd landed in such a state. "For once, I am at a loss for words." He raked a shaky hand through his loose hair. "What happened back there?"

She sighed. "Flint was controlled by another."

Nodin refrained from making a biting comment, holding back his impatience at her continually stating the obvious yet never answering the deeper question. Gathering his thoughts for a moment, he broke a few branches in half and added them to the flames before working his way over to Mother. "Is he all right?"

She nodded and stepped forward with a canvas bag full of clothes, food, and water. "Though he is very distressed...and angry at being manipulated in such a manner." She clasped Nodin's hand with her long, spindly fingers.

As always, a calming warmth streamed through his body.

"I'm sorry to say, though...Maya and Terran's home was destroyed."

"No, that cannot be." Nodin's gaze shot to hers. "I blew out the flames."

"You left, but Flint remained." She squeezed his hand, which had formed into a fist.

Nodin stepped away. "I've received a mental message from Terran. He said he escaped with Maya, but he didn't mention anything about his cabin. Do they know?" After rifling through the bag, he slipped on black sweats and a faded gray T-shirt. They were too big and smelled of smoke. Mother must have raided Flint's closet at Violet's family's castle in Kilkenny, Ireland.

"You are correct." Mother's green-gold eyes sparkled. "I *did* just leave Flint and Violet. Your fiery friend was inconsolable." She sighed. "Terran delivered Maya to their Hawaiian island. She's already forgiven Flint. Regardless of their banter, they love each other dearly. She doesn't blame him at all." A sparkling tear slipped down Mother's face. "Still, Maya is heartbroken. That cabin was her first real home in far too long."

Nodin pounded the side of his fist against the cave wall. "What are we dealing with? Do you know?"

Mother folded her hands at her waist. "What do you know of Kamali's history?"

"Nothing." He scoffed and waved a hand in the air. "We just met."

"You know of her gifts. How she can see auras. Detect who people are at their core." Mother spread her arms, and the chill breeze from outside the cave no longer blustered through. "Eamon and I have studied her maternal line. Her mother was a strong Empath, able to control others' emotions and make them see visions. Kamali's full gifts are masked, somehow. Based on her line, she should be...more." Mother paused for a moment, tapping her bare toes against the floor. "A haze surrounds her that Eamon, in all his wizardry, and I are unable to penetrate. We now wonder if we shouldn't find ways to remove the mist, rather than trying to see through it. Eamon is aging and...not well, so he's passed this duty to Violet." Mother flowed closer to Kamali, her long, embroidered hunter-green cloak billowing behind her. "We believe Violet can remove the spell that blankets this child."

Nodin leaned against the cold rock wall, refraining from arguing Kamali was anything but a child. A fact he knew as, he'd held her mature body in his airy clutches all the way to this rugged peak. "Apparently, Kamali has no blanket when it comes to seeing *me*." He raised a brow, meeting Mother's now hazel gaze. "Anaïs Nin said, 'We do not see things as they are, we see things as we are'. Why can Kamali see *me*? How are we connected?"

"Destiny refuses any boundaries, even time."

"I'd considered our link through fate, as when I'm with her, I feel a pull to my past, my human life." He shook his head. "Still, those are considerations for a calmer time. What I need now are facts, a game plan. A way to protect her and the Elementals."

Mother Nature rarely saw the world on a linear scale, her scope too broad to focus on a singular point.

"I'll ask again, who is taking over our gifts, and how?"

"Kamali does not know all of her history."

Refraining from heaving a sigh at Mother's ambiguity, he tried following her train of thought. "And this part of her history is relevant to today's threat how?" He rolled his hand in a circular motion, urging Mother along.

"Indeed, yes." She nodded and knelt beside Kamali.

Nodin fisted his hands at his sides. *Patience, grasshopper.*

Maize jerked awake and her tail wagged like mad as Mother crooned and petted her head.

"They can track Maize."

"How?" Still standing, Nodin bent one leg at the knee, placing his bare foot against the cave wall, and then he crossed both arms over his chest.

"One of those…pet tracking chips. I understand it's standard practice in guide dog training facilities. They inject them under the loose skin over the shoulder." Mother ruffled Maize's head. "You'll need to take her to a veterinarian to have it removed."

"I'm frightened for Kamali." Nodin shifted his gaze to the clear, crisp mountain air swirling just outside the cave, wishing he could lose himself to the wind, yet knowing deep in his core he belonged at Kamali's side. "What do I need to know? About her? About her blindness? How does her history mesh with mine? And who is controlling our gifts? I assume these troubles are related." After living such a long life, he grew frustrated with any weakness of understanding. Shouldn't he have solved all of life's mysteries by now? Know how to act in every situation? Why must life change, ever remain without clear answers?

"Everything throughout all time is related." Mother rose from her crouch. "Kamali is stronger than most, because she's had to be. Too many losses in her life and too many shields. Let her stand on her own, but be there if she falls."

Nodin rubbed his chin. "I find myself…challenged in this task, Mother. Especially since…since…"

"Since she's blind?" Mother provided in her lyrical tone. "Yes, but so are you if you can't see. She can give you everything, and you can provide her even more. Show her the world. You've seen so much, now give her vision through your eyes."

Leaving that stirring her words provoked for another time, he refocused on their current problem. "The threat, Mother? Who is it?"

"As always, many disturbances rumble across my Earth." She flicked her fingers through the air. Dust motes glittered in the firelight and danced around her hand. "The medicine man, her uncle, and an aunt, of which Kamali has no knowledge. These three have plotted against this poor girl and shaped her life to their will. She is merely a pawn in their game."

"What game?" He shoved away from the wall, ready now that his anger had a target. "What do they want from her?"

"The same as ever. Power." Mother shrugged. "A sense of dominance that, in the end, means nothing. Yet, these creatures destroy everything to obtain it."

"Which one is controlling our gifts? This aunt? Her uncle?" Frowning, Nodin paced. "Is Kamali helping them?" Even as he asked, he knew this couldn't be the case, yet the trouble tied back to her somehow.

"Her aunt carries a gift similar to Kamali's. One she inherited from Kamali's grandmother...but her aunt also has another gift, one she stole." Mother's eyes blazed a stormy blue, and a slight breeze flickered against the flames, stoking the fire momentarily higher before she blinked and shook her head. "Her aunt tore this gift from another so it fights to be free, like a caged bird, ripping and gnashing, until it tears apart the cage."

Contemplating the significance of Mother's words, Nodin gazed at Kamali's sleeping form, watching the steady rise and fall of her breathing. She slept on, her dreamy state enhanced and deepened by his small mind-nudge that had lulled her into a worry-free rest. "How do I keep her safe?"

Mother smiled. "You open your heart."

"My heart?" Jolted by her words, he spun and met Mother's gaze, shaking his head. "But, I am nothing but a wisp of air." Searching her sparkling, ever-changing eyes, he silently pleaded for understanding.

Mother wrapped the long fingers of each hand around his shoulders. "Nodin, you know as well as I that the winds change. Do not rely on the steady breeze. Tempests and raging winds wait within." She squeezed his left shoulder then gently stroked the side of his face with her other hand. "On this quest, you need to remain at her side as a helpmate and guide. In time, I believe fate will reveal the path that was torn from beneath your feet so many years ago. Your bond is already building. Allow this. Share one heart, one goal, as time is never guaranteed." She tipped his chin. "Quint has returned."

Nodin breathed deep before bending over to exhale, unable to filter that unwelcome knowledge through his chest. "The others...do they know?"

"Yes."

He straightened and pulled his hair into a ponytail at the top of his head, a sort of faux scalplock similar to the ones the warriors in his tribe had worn when preparing for battle. However, they had shaved the sides and back of their heads, leaving only a long tuft of hair at the crown to bind into a single ponytail. Although his nature had taken a philosophical turn, he still prepared to fight in the old ways. The members of his Chickasaw tribe had been known as the Spartans of the lower Mississippi Valley, after all. "We are ready. Terran and Violet's plan will work."

Mother patted his cheek and then glanced at Kamali. "She will return to her family soon."

"No." Nodin mock-laughed, shaking his head. "I don't think so. Kamali is not going back to her uncle. Not with Quint's return. Not only that, based on what I've assessed from your vague comments, Kamali's aunt is responsible for our loss of control."

"She is, but she is not the only threat. There is another. Quint has learned much in his absence."

"Another? Who?"

Maize ambled closer to the cave's opening then whined.

Nodin pinched the bridge of his nose. "One sec, Maize." He glanced at Mother Nature. "What has Quint learned? As if we need him gaining any additional evil skills." He huffed. "Evolving from dark matter into a sentient being that can insert itself into a human host is enough to perplex me for one lifetime."

"Camouflage."

"Camouflage?" Nodin arched a brow.

"Yes."

"But, he already did that." As he shook his head in disbelief, the tip of his ponytail brushed against the back of his neck, making him shiver.

"True, but now he's made detecting his presence inside a human host even more difficult."

"How?"

"He is ever evolving."

Scoffing, Nodin shook his head. "How I wish that wasn't true. John Polkinghorne said, 'Evolution, of course, is not something that simply applies to life here on earth; it apples to the whole universe.' At times we forget the vastness above, how we are but a blip in a cosmic plane of endlessness. And dark matter and dark energy make up ninety-five percent of the known universe. How can we defeat such an entity? The thought of Quint evolving into something even more insidious sends shivers down my spine. We must halt what he's become."

Quotes no longer soothed his soul. Kamali was his responsibility now.

His to protect.

His warrior nature always soared just beneath the surface, waiting for him to beckon it forth and once more clasp his bow and arrow. He pounded a fist against his palm. "How can I protect her?"

"Hope." Mother's eyes flickered green-gold in the firelight as she studied Kamali's slumbering form. "Kamali must see."

"And how is she supposed to do that?"

"By opening her eyes."

Great. Once again, Mother's words came across as clear as mud.

CHAPTER 9

Inside the waiting room of a small-town Colorado veterinarian's office, Kamali breathed in the earthy smell of frightened pets, dog food, and pine-scented air freshener, which created a falsely fresh environment.

Finally warm in a hooded sweatshirt and a pair of slightly-too-short jeans Nodin had stolen from a local thrift store, Kamali remained stationed by the space heater just inside the door. Nodin had explained that the care center was composed of a pole barn, which housed sick livestock and injured rodeo animals and also had an attached building for the treatment of smaller animals.

Upon entering the vet's office, she'd been amazed at how quickly all the auras turned a similar hue to Nodin's. The Elemental had delved into each mind and moved Maize's surgery to the front, his urgency at removing the locator chip quite apparent.

Nodin remained with Maize during the vet's removal of the GPS chip. This was not the norm, but before the assistant could argue her case, Nodin had tweaked the doctor's mind and gained his consent. Knowing Nodin was watching over her beloved pet offered a modicum of relief. All their crazed flights and quickly altered environments probably confused the poor pup. They rarely spent any time apart, so she was grateful Nodin understood her worry for her furry friend.

Kamali rubbed her hands together, encouraging blood flow to her fingertips. Her chilled nose twitched and she sneezed. The person beside her must have a cat. She covered her nose and sneezed three times in a row. "Excuse me." She turned to her left. "Do you have a Kleenex?"

"The box is right beside you," a female voice huffed.

"Oh, sorry, I couldn't see it." Though she'd love to embarrass the snappy-woman by adding, because I'm blind, she refrained. She patted out her hand until she felt the cardboard box then tugged free a handful of tissues.

Rubbing her itchy eyes, Kamali bit her bottom lip and covered her flushed cheeks while remembering what had happened in the cave that morning—the fulfillment of her wish. Nodin naked. A bout of nervous laughter followed the memory. *Oh my!* Were all men as comfortable with their nudity? She didn't believe so, but after twenty-three years of wondering she could now define what a man's thighs, knees, and ankles looked like, and as her gaze had scaled higher and she'd openly stared at his...at his...he'd caught the direction of her riveted gaze and laughed.

Then he'd taken her hand and asked, "Have you never seen a naked body before?"

She'd replied in the negative, very confused as to why he'd even ask such a question. Had he forgotten she couldn't see anything but him? He'd smiled and squeezed her hand before adding, "Nothing but beauty in the human form. We put our own shame on it." He'd spread his arms wide and said, "Look all you'd like."

Now, as then, Kamali shook her head while considering how shamelessly she'd done just that, and even asked about...about...Good Lord, sometimes she wondered at her nerve. She'd wanted to explore more of the feelings he evoked in her heart and her libido, but he'd been in a hurry to leave, so she refrained from making more brazen requests.

Something nudged against her leg, followed by a loud purr.

"Why hello, little kitty." Kamali felt for the cat winding between her legs and rubbed the soft fur, though she'd regret her actions when her eyes puffed up and she sneezed a zillion times.

She released a deep breath and considered another irritant—Raven. Something deep within said this Raven was the root cause of all the chaos. Who was this woman? And why did Kamali feel a connection to her? As if a missing piece of her soul, which she hadn't known she'd lost, was fighting for reunion. *Very odd.*

After closing her eyes, Kamali jumped when her cell phone rang with Creed's ring tone, the fourth call of the day. In addition to Creed's calls, there were three or four from her uncle. Since she wasn't sure how much longer Maize's procedure would take, she had her text-to-talk app read her messages out loud. At the end of her uncle's distressing message, she listened to it again then hunched over in her seat, fighting to breathe.

Waya had died.

Waya. Her teacher. Her counselor. Her friend.

As the middle child, her cousin was the mischief-maker, always seeking attention from his father. Being the same age, they were inseparable, causing trouble and creating unforgettable memories. Waya had fought off her bullies, bandaged her knees, and spent hours, days, weeks teaching her which colors went with which emotions so she could better understand auras. He'd shaped her childhood, given her a future, and now he was gone.

With a moan, she slid off her chair and crumpled to her knees. Tears fell, yet she didn't wipe them away.

"Miss?" Cat lady tapped her shoulder. "Are you all right?"

"No." Kamali shook her head. "I wasn't there. I didn't keep him from danger."

"May I call someone for you?"

"No, thank you." A moment later, Kamali gasped as pain lanced across her chest, and a searing wash of orange flashed before her tear-drenched eyes.

A deep, pulsing red-orange, like rage, like madness.

No light. No escape.

Trembling overtook her body as the fury of another human slithered into her empathic senses.

As arms wrapped around her from behind, Kamali screamed and fought. "No, no. Don't touch me." She pulled free of the constraint, hearing nothing, seeing only a muddy red-yellow dripping down a curtain of black. "Something is coming. Dark…so dark…has no soul, only an empty hollow." Chest heaving, she floundered for something solid. Arms waving, she cried, "Nodin. Nodin."

"I'm right behind you, Kamali. Turn around. It's okay."

She focused on his form resting within his blue aura. "You must leave. She's coming."

"Who?"

"Raven. Her name is Raven. She is pure evil," Kamali sputtered, clutching at Nodin's chest. "There is no light within her aura."

"Where?"

Scuttling backward until her back hit what felt like a wall, she slithered down before wincing when another wave of pain shot through her temples. "Get everyone out of here." Wrapping her arms around her churning stomach, she opened her eyes and locked her gaze with his. "Call the Elementals. Bring them here." He only stared, so she pounded her fist against the floor. "Now."

"I don't have to say anything out loud." Nodin crouched by her side. "I call them mentally. Do you understand? And the lady with the cat left. She was the only other person in here besides the employees. I gleaned their minds and told them to go out for lunch."

"I understand." She reached out and seized his hand. "The Elementals must come. I've never…it's never hurt like this before. What is happening?" With her free hand, she gripped her hair in her fist and pulled. "Make it stop." Another sharp pain fired across her temples. Her grasp of the world went fuzzy, and she slumped forward. Tumbling, screaming into a black void. No color. No heat. Empty space.

She blinked, trying to focus, trying to stop her descent, but the plunge continued. "Not real. Not real. Get out of my head."

A sliver, a bright speck of light blue, twinkled before her eyes. Nodin would ground her. She would not become lost in the dark. She focused on that and fought her way back to the surface. "This isn't real. Isn't real."

The pain receded, and she released a great gush of air, as if she'd been deep within a murky pool, fought to surface, and could now breathe. She heaved in and out, striking against the hands forcing her back down. "No. I won't go."

"Kamali. Shhh....shhh, It's okay." Nodin gripped her face in his hands. "Stay calm. I'm here."

Whole body still trembling, she slightly opened her eyes, afraid of what she'd see. Was he just an illusion? What had attacked her mind? She'd never delved that deep into an aura before, and she'd be happy never to travel there again. "Wh-what?" She held Nodin's wrists, locking his hands against her cheeks. "You're here now, right?"

"Yes."

"I'm not lost." How had he become her grounding force? Independence was a quality she valued, but right now, she needed his strong hands, needed to know he'd lead her to safety. She'd deal with the true meaning of this foreign, and quite unwelcome, reliance on another when her head wasn't about to explode.

"I've got you." He sank beside her and pulled her onto his lap.

She kept her gaze locked with his and ran her hands over his jaw, refusing to blink. "Nodin," she spoke in a shaky whisper. "Something is waiting for us outside."

He nodded. "I sense it. I need you to calm down. The Elementals are on their way. I won't go outside until they arrive, all right?"

Shivering, she buried her face against his neck. "I don't want to go back there."

"Where?"

"The darkness."

"Then stay in the light with me." Nodin grasped her chin and kissed her. Delving deep this time, lingering longer, brushing the tip of his tongue against her lips before she opened, allowing him inside physically and emotionally. With each sweep of his tongue, he washed away the chill of emptiness, of drowning. Eyes wide, she pulled back. "I-I want...I'm not sure..."

"Relax." He traced his thumb over her lower lip. "Follow my lead."

And for a moment...a long moment, she took, selfishly, hungrily, and she was sure, quite sloppily of his seeking, expertly delivered kiss. Overcome by the moment, she nudged him, bumping them both backward as she kissed him with full fervor. Wanting more, so much more.

With a gentle touch, he drifted his hand up and down her back, prodding her with his hips. When she felt his hard desire, she reveled in the fact she affected this man.

A dog yipping in the distance jolted her to the present and where they were—on the floor of a vet's office.

She jerked backward then cringed when that red rush of malice screamed through her mind once more, but in Nodin's arms the effect seemed diminished. Shuddering, she pulled away and squeezed his biceps. "Keep me here. Don't let her take me away."

"I won't." He kissed her forehead. "Kamali, how do you know the one upsetting you is a she?"

Maize barked from somewhere behind her.

She turned toward the sound. "How is Maize? Can she leave with us now?"

"Kamali." Nodin coaxed, tipping her chin with an index finger. "Tell me."

She sighed, whether from frustration or lust, she didn't know. "She told me."

Nodin stood and pulled her to her feet. "Who told you?"

"Raven." Though a bit unsteady, she steeled her nerves, clenching her hands into fists at her sides and rose to her feet. "I don't know who she is, but this ends now. I'm tired of her messing with everyone's heads. Who does she think she is?" Kamali barreled toward where she'd heard the door opening earlier.

"Whoa." Nodin held up a hand. "Where do you think you are going?" He shifted between her and the exit.

"I'm facing that terror, and then I'm going home to face another."

"Kamali, what are you talking about?" Nodin's tone softened.

He spoke to her as if soothing a crazed horse just stung by a bee, but this threat wasn't a bee, just a stupid ass bird. "We are going outside and confronting Raven." She jabbed a finger against his chest. "Aren't I supposed to help you see toxic energy? Isn't that the plan?"

"Well...yes." Nodin ran a hand over his mouth.

"Then lead me to the door."

"I don't know think that's wise."

"I don't always do what is wise, Nodin." Kamali met his sky-blue gaze. "That woman...whoever she is...is connected to me somehow. She has something that is mine. I can feel it." She clutched a hand against her chest, right above her beating heart. "I want to know why. Right now."

Hands on hips, he studied her a moment before offering a single nod. "If there is too much danger"—he shook a finger—"I'm taking you away."

"All right." She shifted her gaze to his feet, unable to look in his eyes as she delivered her horrid news. "After this is over, I need to go home."

"That won't happen. But I'll let you explain why you feel you should return to that nest of vipers."

She bit her lip to hold back tears. "My cousin is dead."

Nodin tugged her into his arms. "I'm so sorry. How did he die?"

"My uncle said…he said…Quint killed him."

He rocked her back and forth. "And so it begins."

CHAPTER 10

Stepping outside the vet's office, Nodin breathed in the pungent, yet not unwelcome, smell of the open livestock pens. Scents of raw nature meshed with memories of horses he used to own. More loyal creatures he had never known.

Though leery of what awaited him outside, he glanced at the shaggy horse standing on the other side of the wooden fence. Poor creature was shaking, its body ravaged by whatever disease ailed it.

His people had relied on canoes and foot for travel while living east of the Mississippi, but then they'd moved south to Tennessee and Alabama. Horses weren't used until his tribe traded with the Shawnee in the mid-1700s. Nodin remembered with pride the Chickasaw Horse, once known for its long stride and endurance.

Sensing the disturbance within their midst, a horse bucked and kicked. In another pen, a passel of cows bundled together, snorting and grunting, pawing in the dirt with their hooves.

All due to her.

He didn't require Kamali's aura-reading abilities to glean the evil in the air.

A dark-haired woman, obviously of Native American descent, stood in the parking lot. Dust from the dry gravel stirred and billowed around her long legs, clad in black leather pants.

Raven.

Nodin tried gleaning her thoughts but was blocked by a vision of the ocean, as if he were really there. The sand between his toes. The sun warming his skin. He closed his eyes, whispering over and over, "This isn't real. Just an illusion."

The woman's cackling laugh broke through the mirage. "Now that you and the Elementals have witnessed my abilities, I'd stay out of my head, Nodin, or I'll send your mind to a place from which you'll never return."

A flicker of heat sparked through the air as Terran, then Flint, landed behind Raven. Then a light mist trickled against his skin just before Maya appeared at Kamali's side. All three Elementals were naked as the day they were born. Good thing Nodin had evacuated the premises using his gleaning gift.

Would there be a repeat of the time at the cabin? Would Raven send him away, leaving Kamali to face her alone? Could this woman control all four of them at once? Raven hadn't sent him off as quickly when they were at Maya's cabin, but perhaps she'd focused primarily on Flint and his fiery fingers.

"Is this welcome party for little ol' me?" Raven made a show of glancing around the parking lot, rocking her hips back and forth with each word.

Maya stepped in front of Kamali. "I intend to have a party…after I kick your ass for destroying my home."

"Maya." Kamali reached out toward the water-girl, gripped her arm, and then stepped to her side. "I have questions for Raven. Please, give us a moment."

Nodin kept his gaze on Raven, hoping the woman didn't harm Kamali again as she had inside the vet's waiting room.

"Fine." Maya nodded, glaring at Raven. "But know this, I've dealt with tricksters like you before. I've lived a very long time, and I'll continue to do so. You, on the other hand, will end." The tips of Maya's hair turned blue, and water dripped from her fingers. "So feel free to give me your best shot, because I'll learn all your weaknesses and keep coming back for more, until one day"—Maya shrugged—"I'll finish you."

"Maya." Terran spoke from behind Raven. "As you say, we have time. Let Kamali ask her questions."

Raven laughed. "Yes, blondie. Do as you're told."

A wave of water knocked the woman off her feet.

Nodin grinned. *Round one to Maya.*

Standing, Raven brushed off her pants then flipped Maya the bird. "Very mature."

Maya chuckled. "Gotta be quick on your feet around here."

"Kamali, I suggest you control your friends, or this won't end well."

Nodin blew a breeze through Maya's hair. *"I know you're angry, but put a lid on that impetuous nature for a moment."*

She glanced over her shoulder. *"Whatever."*

"I want to know who you are." Kamali's tone held no quiver of fear. His woman held strong, stepping right into the breach. "You are familiar to me. Why?"

"I've never introduced myself, have I?" Raven swept her arms open at her sides. "I am Raven. Your mother's sister." She mock-bowed. "I was banished long before you were born, so I'm sure I was never mentioned. An unfortunate fact, as there is a lot to say."

"My mother was light." With her head slightly tilted, Kamali took another step toward the leather-clad menace. "Your aura is black, glowing with crimson red, full of hatred, malice, and an infection of something rooted very deep…something you are desperately trying to hide, but it calls to me." She leaned forward. "I see a sliver of pure white screaming to be free. Something that wishes to be mine."

"You see nothing, little girl." Raven tossed her hair over her shoulder. "As for you, water witch, I might not be able to destroy you, but I can certainly destroy her." She glanced at Kamali and then winked at Nodin.

He stiffened, stepping forward and drawing Kamali to his side.

"Get out." Kamali swiped her hands before her face as if swatting at a swarm of mosquitos. "You are not welcome in my head."

"What is your business here?" Flint shifted from side-to-side, the tips of his fingers glowing red. "We are ready for your tricks this time, Raven."

"No, fireman, your little...*hose*...is no match for me." Raven licked her lips. "How did it feel to have me inside you? You were so...hot." She laughed. "Where's Violet? Not here? How unfortunate. Quint is very excited about seeing her again."

With a roar, Flint fired forward.

Terran gripped his arm and held tight. "Enough. Tell us why you're here."

Raven shifted her gaze to Kamali once more. "I'm here for the girl." She rolled her eyes. "Her uncle wants his widdle niece to come home."

"She's staying." Nodin took Kamali's hand.

Shrugging, Raven arched a perfectly sculpted brow. "She'll come on her own."

"No." Nodin paused, bracing his stance. "She won't."

"Waya is dead, Kamali." Raven sniffed. "Dear God, it reeks out here. I can't believe I agreed to come to this foul place." She glared at the barn before focusing on Kamali. "Anyway, your uncle is inconsolable. Now come along, your little play date is over."

"I will go, but not with you," Kamali answered from directly behind Nodin. "I do not wish to be near you."

"Oh, Nodin, she's hurting me. Make it stop." With a mocking tone, Raven clasped her hands to her head before laughing. "Too bad your gifts are so weak. We could have had fun together." With a shrug, Raven sighed. "I suggest you make heading home a top priority. And don't worry, you won't see me again." She flicked her red-tipped fingers in the air. "I had my fun and now I'm bored."

Kamali stepped toward her aunt.

Nodin held her arm. "Kamali, I don't think—"

"I must. She has something that is mine."

Maya glanced at him before sending a message. *"Don't let her go over there alone."*

"I know my duty."

"I must discover the answer on my own." Kamali patted his hand.

Nodin released her and tightened the battle-ready knot on his head. Letting his woman face off against Raven went against everything in his nature, so he stayed two paces behind her as she moved forward.

All was silent except the crunch of gravel under Kamali's feet.

Even the animals in the pens stopped shuffling, as if aware something momentous was about to occur.

Maya's and Flint's anger rolled together through the air as a mix of heat and mist, as if a blanket of steam had descended.

The ground rumbled, and a tiny fissure split between Raven and Kamali.

Frowning, Nodin glanced at Terran.

He winced. "Sorry."

"Stop, please." Kamali held up her hand, palm out. "I will do this alone. I see you, Raven." Somehow, she accurately reached out and grabbed her aunt by the arm. "You've stolen an ability that belonged to another."

Raven ripped her arm free.

Nodin glanced at Terran, the most levelheaded of the bunch.

He nodded in return, silently declaring he was ready to strike.

"You stole something from my mother," Kamali accused with a hard tone.

Raven gasped and shoved Kamali to the ground.

After blowing Raven down with a stiff wind, Nodin whipped through the air to kneel at Kamali's side.

She flailed, gripping his arms, tears pouring down her cheeks. "Sh-she killed my mother." Rising to her feet and facing her aunt again, she cried, "Why? What did you do to her?"

Back on her feet, Raven's eyes widened. "You do indeed see." Flinching, she took a step back. "Understand this—what happens next is all *your* fault. You just had to dig, so..." She turned and glared at Flint.

"Oh, shit." Terran tackled Flint just as the Fire Elemental burst into flames, hot enough to scorch the wooden fence line beside him.

Nodin quickly blew out the smoldering fire, unwilling to let the pole barn burn to the ground with all the helpless animals inside.

Maya surged forward, a wall of water aiming for Flint.

Raven smiled. "Good. I'm feeling a bit parched."

In an instant, the water-girl dissolved from a high wave into a gush of liquid that ended in a puddle, spreading across the dry lot.

"Maya." Terran lurched to his knees then transformed from human to water.

Whether Terran did this consciously, as he could control all four elements, or due to Raven's influence, Nodin was unsure.

Contemplation time was over as Raven turned her black gaze on him. "And so we meet again. You should have heeded my warning that day at the diner."

"No," Kamali cried, now on her knees by the Maya-puddle. "Stop hurting them."

Nodin broadened his stance, knowing he was the last line of defense against this woman, yet feeling the change coming, blowing air around him, sucking him into the nothingness surrounding them.

Dust stirred at his feet and whipped through the air, coating his body with a thick layer of dirt.

Kamali coughed, and tears streaked down her cheeks. "Raven, I'll do as you ask. Just leave him be."

The tips of his fingers tingled then disappeared, but he could still deliver his warning. "As Maya said, we've learned much today and we will return, smarter and stronger." He clenched his hands into fists, closed his eyes, and focused all his energies on staying whole.

Solid.

To no avail.

As his element, he drifted farther and farther from earth. Still, he focused on changing, on returning to his human form. To protecting Kamali. His air-filled heart collapsed as he heard her cry, "Nodin, no!"

"Why, Kamali, haven't you heard?" Raven mocked. "If you're going to date a man, you need to know what he's made of."

Raven's stark laugh was the last sound he heard as he drifted across the land, at one with the breeze, yet completely out of synch with his element.

CHAPTER 11

Kamali focused on the car's hum, straining to hear any significant sounds outside. A car that had to be a limo since her aunt sat across from her, not at her side. No frequent stops occurred, so they must be traveling along a highway. An empty highway, as she hadn't heard the swoosh of another vehicle passing in quite some time. "Where are you taking me?"

Raven sighed. "I already explained I'm taking you home."

"Quint is there."

"Is he?"

"Yes. Uncle said Quint killed Waya."

"Hmm...well, I think Malachi ran him off."

"I hardly think Malachi has any sort of power over a creature composed of dark matter and dark energy."

"Why worry about such things, girl?" Her aunt sniffed. "Not as if a blind person can do anything about such matters, anyway."

Kamali gripped her hands together in her lap, refraining from choking the life out of this unwanted relative. How this woman could be her mother's sister was beyond her...but when Kamali considered what she remembered of her mother, perhaps she had sugarcoated her memories.

Still, she refused to appear weak, even though her temples

pounded and her stomach was on the verge of losing all its contents due to her aunt's repulsive aura, not to mention her putrid perfume. "The Elementals will return." Kamali heard an unladylike snort, followed by her aunt's acid response.

"They are worthless. I reduced all four to their elements quite simply. Really, they are no match for me, or for Quint."

"You just said Malachi ran him off."

"Did I?"

Kamali half-growled, and then sank against the plush leather seat. Were her aunt's words true? The Elements *had* seemed easily overcome. So what did that mean for the future? Could they, as Maya and Nodin indicated, learn and defeat her aunt during the next confrontation?

What was the full scope of her aunt's powers?

And, since they were related, what did that mean about her own abilities? For the first time, Kamali considered using her gifts for ill. She'd always had a clear direction. Her uncle's guiding hand leading her down one path. But what if there were others? Could she fight her aunt? Could she win?

She'd consider that later, as she didn't know if Raven could delve into her thoughts. Instead, she focused on Nodin and the way he made her feel. Was he simply offering comfort to the poor blind girl? Or was there more behind his kisses? What possible future could they have? He had his Elemental duties, and she had her own.

While they might mesh for a time...then what? Could she walk away from the one person she could actually see? Return to murky emptiness? Live in a world filled with momentary flashes of color followed by periods of nothingness? *No.* She was stronger than doubt, than fear of the unknown. No more questions. As long as she was able, she would rejoice in her moments with Nodin.

"Pining over that man?" Raven nudged her leg with what felt like the tip of a pointed shoe. "While I understand the allure, I can't believe you'd honestly think he's interested." She snorted out a half-laugh. "Men like him, they play. Not only that, he's peri-mortal, and you, my girl, are mortal. How long do you think you could hold him? He's Air, always blowing from one woman to the next."

Kamali watched her aunt's red aura draw nearer then felt her cool finger brush a stray hair over her ear.

"Your mother isn't here to tell you this, so I will. You are stronger on your own. You don't need a man. All they do is control you. What you are...your ancestry...you are so much more." She paused for a moment. "Your mother let your father take everything. Let him drag her down until she became a shell of her former glory. A straining simpleton who only craved one thing. And look where that got her. Dead."

"My mother is dead because you killed her." Kamali wasn't sure why she believed this was so, but she knew deep in her heart that her aunt was directly responsible.

"Your mother is dead because she was a drunk."

Though Raven's tone remained harsh, her color softened from roaring red to deep pink. "Do not speak of my mother." Narrowing her eyes, Kamali pointed a finger. "I saw your guilt meshing with memories of her. You are harboring something, and I will figure out what it is."

"And how do you know what it is you're really seeing?" Raven scoffed. "You are blind, after all. Perhaps I killed another."

"No." To keep from striking out and likely missing her target, Kamali dug her fingers into the leather seats. "What did you do, and why?"

"I'm not on trial here. And after today, we will never be in each other's presence again."

"My uncle will see you punished."

"Your uncle." Her aunt laughed. "You're so naïve. He's even worse than I am, and that's saying a lot."

"You make the mistake of underestimating me, Raven. I

have seen the darkness in Uncle's aura at times, but he is nothing like you." Kamali refused to consider the implications of her aunt's statement. Refused to believe her vision of her uncle had been manipulated somehow. And why would that thought pop into her head? Maybe out of a sense of debt she had blocked her uncle's negative traits from her mind. After all, her uncle was nothing but supportive, and while she realized not all of his business dealings were legal, she refused to fault him. Not after he'd raised her as one of his own. "You will not turn me against Adler. He and I will discuss who you are and what you've done after Waya's funeral. I won't disturb him with thoughts of something as foul as you during this time."

"I see you've found some bite."

"I never lost it. Plus, I know something you do not."

"And what is that?"

"Nodin will come for me."

"Oh, I hope so. I quite enjoy making them realize others are more powerful."

"You aren't. They'll figure out how to defeat you."

"I think the past hour says otherwise."

Realizing the fruitlessness of rational conversation, Kamali quieted.

A short time later, the car slowed.

She both heard and felt the rumble of jet engines.

The limo halted then slowly eased forward into a series of turns.

Though she didn't want to leave Nodin, she'd known she would have to return home. Mourning Waya, her friend and confidant, was essential, regardless of the threats surrounding her. Though worry for Nodin added to the ache still rocking like jagged bricks through her head, she believed the Elementals would recover and come back stronger than ever.

During the melee outside the vet's office, she'd felt a strong wash of heat against her skin and then water splashing at her feet, just before she'd watched Nodin disappear into his element. Fury and helplessness had crashed through her spirit. But now, she steeled her spine. She would overcome Raven. Would discover this woman's devious deeds and make sure she was punished. Somehow, some way, this was her vow.

Finding strength when Maize, her source of guidance, was gone was hard to come by. Poor thing was probably worried sick.

Kamali straightened and gazed right at her aunt's aura. "I want Maize back."

"We'll get your stupid beast."

The sound of Raven's nails tapping against something plastic clicked through the car.

"I have no idea why people get pets. They are filthy animals, bringing in their shit-covered paws, spreading their grime across floors. Not to mention they spend half their day licking their ass."

Kamali rolled her eyes. "Maize is a highly-trained service dog."

"Ass-licker."

"Someday, I'll get a litter of St. Bernard puppies, tie you down, and then release them so they can lick your face and jump all over you."

"Oh, I'm shivering in my stilettos." Raven laughed. "Such a creative persecution. Seems we are related, after all."

"That we are, and I can guarantee I'll take back whatever you've stolen from my mother." Kamali leaned forward, unbuckling her seatbelt. "Even now, I sense you're desperately trying to conceal something within you that's calling to me, but I'll find out what it is."

"Your loyalty to your mother is unfounded. She was more likely to drink from a bottle than to give you one."

"I'm well aware of my mother's faults." Instant memories flashed of times she'd been left alone, locked in her bedroom. Her only friend a Barbie with one set of clothes. That doll, that plastic toy, had kept her sane. Her pitiful early childhood was not something she ever dwelled on, yet other memories existed, happy ones. Her mother and father had tried, when they were sober. But, was there more to the story?

In her mind, present and past clashed together, offering nothing but an overriding sense of the unknown. A place she lived in daily, but this was so much more. Her fears included others now. The Elementals, Maize, Quint, her aunt. And she couldn't bury her guilt over causing her uncle additional worry while he was also mourning the loss of his son.

What would her cousins say? They would not let their brother's death go unanswered, and they could not defeat Quint. Fear for their lives added a cherry to the top of her worry sundae.

Was Malachi working on magical wards to keep Quint at bay? Was her involvement with the Elementals the reason Quint had chosen her family?

Kamali felt the car slow again. "If Quint covets those bearing extra gifts, then you should be leery, Raven. You could be next."

"Ah, such familial concern." Raven hummed out a laugh. "If Quint came calling, he'd find a willing ally. Besides, I believe he seeks stronger prey. He covets the witch, Violet. I'm sure he'll attain her this time."

The car finally came to a stop.

"And how would you know?" Kamali didn't get an answer because the door opened, and Creed's aura greeted her.

"Kamali, your uncle's been worried sick." He tugged her out of the car. "Please, don't leave like that again."

Wrestling free of Creed's arms, Kamali turned toward the sound of heels clicking against the pavement. "Raven, you didn't answer my question. How do you know of Quint's plans?"

"I never said I did." Her smarmy tone was accented by an aura that turned full black.

Interesting. Was her aunt attempting to hide something by masking her aura? "This is true, Raven," Kamali whispered. "But, you never said you didn't know, either."

"What are you saying, Kamali?" Creed squeezed her arm at the elbow. "And where is Maize?"

Kamali coughed after breathing air teeming with jet exhaust and Creed's musky cologne. She stepped away, searching for a modicum of fresh air.

"Kamali, we need to go."

"Creed…just give me one moment…I need to breathe. I've been locked in a car with that woman for what felt like hours, and I need to cleanse my nostrils of Raven's perfume, Eau du Wicked Witch."

"What are you talking about?" Creed nudged her shoulder.

"Nothing." She chuckled and shook her head. Poor Creed never got her jokes.

Drifting farther from her friend, she closed her eyes and focused on the cool fall breeze brushing against her skin, dancing stray pieces of hair across her face. In the deepest recesses of her heart, she gloried in the purity, appreciated each soft caress and each crisp rush through her lungs.

Though she may not have a gleaning gift, she sent a mental message across the sky and hoped the Great Spirit delivered her plea. *"Nodin, return to me. You are the only air I need."*

CHAPTER 12

On the grounds of the Irish castle, Nodin paced within the ancient ruins, stifled by his friends' indecisive dialogue, lack of direction, and the fact they were stalling, instead of developing immediate plans to secure Kamali.

The fresh air in Kilkenny never failed to entice and feed his senses. Pure air. Unpolluted, wild, and untamed. A return to nature both he and the animal at his side craved. And today he'd never felt more feral.

He'd been overtaken—again. Lost within his gift.

Stopping along the path, he kicked at a stone peeking from beneath two tufts of grass. Maize trotted along at his side. She'd been moping around the house, sitting by the back patio doors as if awaiting Kamali's return, so he'd brought her outside for a walk through the fields surrounding Violet's family home.

Nodin crouched and patted his inner thigh.

Maize came immediately, tail wagging, and her entire body circling round and round between his bent legs.

"We'll see her again soon, girl. I promise."

Maize licked his face, almost knocking him over.

Maya strolled through the grass, barefoot and wearing an odd combination of oversized T-shirt and a skirt that looked like it came from the castle's attics.

"What are you wearing?"

"I know." Maya settled her hands on her hips. "It's hideous, but I have nothing here. Actually, nothing anywhere because of that stupid bitch, Raven and her apparent giddiness at playing pyro-girl."

"I'm sorry about the cabin." Nodin patted Maize's side before standing. "Go on. Explore." He flicked a hand toward the field.

Maize barked then took off, gamboling through the tall, vivid green grass.

"Thank you." Maya ran the tip of her big toe through the grass, avoiding his gaze. "Terran has plans for building a new place, and I'm trying to be excited but...it won't be the same." She sighed and shook her head.

He understood; that cabin had come to represent home for him, too. Giving them both a minute, he watched Maize bounding through the fields. "What did you want to speak to me about?" He detected her unease and blatant masking of her thoughts. They could block each other, but if he wanted, he could breeze by her barriers. A skill he'd developed but rarely used.

"Nothing." Maya shrugged. "I just needed some fresh air. All that talk of spells and strategies isn't for me. I'd rather charge in and bring Kamali back. But, as Terran says, her cousin has died. We must respect that. Plus, you said she and Waya were close, so she'll need time to mourn."

"I'm worried she'll do something reckless." Nodin leaned against a faded stone pillar. A remnant of Irish history, likely tied to some ancient Celtic ritual.

Maya chuckled. "That's what I like about her. Brave and fearless, regardless of her supposed barriers."

"She isn't you, Maya." Nodin stared at the blonde beauty, his friend and confidante for decades. They'd weathered many a storm together and would continue to do so—no matter how this current tale ended. He fought back memories of another blonde who'd once stood at his side. A woman whose passing still pinched against his heart—Pillar. He'd lost her at this very castle.

Quint had taken her body.

Death had taken the rest.

No matter their past trials and tribulations, he hoped Pillar was now at peace.

"True." Maya nudged his arm. "Kamali isn't me, but she isn't Pillar, either."

Shaking his head, he glared. "Stay out of my head, water-girl."

Maya laughed. "I didn't need to glean your thoughts. That look, the one I haven't seen in five years, and honestly, hoped to never see again, was on your face." She hugged him, quiet for a moment, resting her head against his chest.

He ruffled her long, wavy locks. "Terran will get jealous."

"If he were here, he'd likely hug you, too. Bit of a softy, my earth-man."

"Ah...I don't think someone who singlehandedly fought Quint is a softy." He left his arm around her shoulder and glanced across the field, locating Maize still romping through the grass.

Maya gripped his hand. "It's so beautiful here. Peaceful. Too bad we can't stay right here. This castle is perfect for all of us...except Flint...and that's not such a bad thing." She burst into giggles, bending over at the waist. "Oh, that wasn't nice."

Nodin shook his head. Maya loved Flint, but she loved teasing him even more, like a rambunctious little sister picking on her older brother.

She wiped a tear from the corner of her eye before clearing her throat. "Ah...hum...anyway, all kidding aside, Kamali's a fighter, and like us, she wasn't given a choice in this gift she carries. Imagine what seeing only the deepest core of each person must be like. Their hidden secrets, their true selves. Sure, we can glean that information, sometimes it screams across our minds, but we can block it. She cannot." Maya stepped out from under his arm and turned to face him. "Imagine how completely disorienting seeing you, and only you, must be. Her whole life, she's had nothing but auras and feelings, until you."

"Until me." Nodin scratched the back of his neck. His world had literally spun out of control since meeting Kamali, but he took this moment to absorb Maya's words and all their implications.

A broad smile broke across Maya's face. "Until you." Her gaze trailed up and down his body. "Well, if she was to see a man for the first time, golly-gee buckets, the lucky girl got a whole heaping of scorching hot man."

"Coming from someone who's basically my sister...that's a little"—he wiggled his hand side-to-side—"creepy."

"Oh, hush." She smacked his arm. "That whole situation"—she waved a hand toward his crotch—"is old news. How about we change the subject?" Uncharacteristically nervous, she gathered her hair into a bun then tugged it down again before braiding a section. Then, she cleared her throat. "So...um...Kamali has made herself indispensable to her uncle."

"She's being used." Nodin tensed a little, knowing they were approaching the real reason Maya had ventured outside.

"And we'll use her, too." Maya leaned against a flat stone altar then shot upright. "Yikes, there's some kind of witchy juju going on with that rock." Shivering, she glared at the offending piece before meeting his gaze.

"Maya, I love you, but get to the point, please."

She arched a blonde brow. "Kamali will help our cause, and we need all the help we can get." She paced closer to the field then stopped and focused on the castle. "I have one worry, my dear friend." Her shoulders hunched, and she didn't turn to meet his gaze. "Now that Quint has returned, I'm not...I just don't know how much help Flint will be. If Quint is destroyed, the spell that keeps Violet immortal will be broken, and she will begin aging again. And up at the house, he's shooting down every one of Terran's ideas. I didn't know what to say or do, and seeing Flint like this…it's breaking my heart. I didn't want him to glean my pity, so I left."

"I see." He followed her train of thought completely. "We have to put aside our own desires."

"We may try to set aside what we want, but do we ever really?" Maya wrapped both arms around her slim waist. "I fail quite often at this. Terran is always scolding me."

"We can only try. Edmund Burke said, 'Nobody made a greater mistake than he who did nothing because he could do only a little'."

Maya glanced over her shoulder before turning to face him. "I know since Pillar's death, you've"—she huffed out a long breath then shrugged—"well, you've had a hard time understanding the whys of everything, and if your philosophical quotes bring you comfort that is fine, but you must stop blaming yourself for Pillar's downfall. You tried to steer that salty-shyster in a different direction, but she wasn't like you. Pillar didn't sacrifice for others."

"In the end, she did." He'd done his best to forgive Pillar, and himself, but returning to this castle brought everything to the forefront. Pillar was part of his life even before his transformation. Years of memories didn't simply drift away, they remained, constantly billowing through his mind.

Maya took his hand. "You're right. I suppose she did. It's just…I see Pillar from the perspective of hurting you, and that is something I'll never tolerate."

"I understand, but how about we focus on the future now?" He tugged on a lock of her hair. "What's the consensus up at the castle? Did Violet find a way to block Raven?"

"She did, but…well…the spell demands a sacrifice." Maya sniffed then looked everywhere but at him, rubbing her upper arms. "It's chilly out here. Maybe we should go inside. Where did Maize go?" She jetted toward the field as if chased by angry bees.

Nodin, while not sure he really wanted an answer, caught up

with her anyway and grabbed her arm. "Maya? What aren't you telling me? What kind of sacrifice?"

Sighing, she shifted back and forth before blurting out, "We need blood."

"Fine." Shrugging, he tugged her through the grass toward the castle. "We'll get some."

"No." She halted at his side and took a deep breath. "In order to keep Raven from controlling our gifts, we need Kamali's blood."

"Fine, prick her finger, or whatever the spell entails."

"It's a bit more involved than that."

He arched a brow. "How much more involved?"

Maya winced before answering in a barely audible voice, "We have to drink it."

"What?" Nodin halted, feeling as though nothing but air wafted between his ears, as he could not have heard Maya correctly. "Drink her...you want me to..." After pacing, he shook a finger at Maya. "Absolutely not. We aren't vampires. I don't even have blood. Neither do you. Our internal systems don't work that way."

"The spell serves as a ward. The ancient Celts—"

"No." He slashed a hand through the air. "I won't."

"Blood is the strongest ward. Raven's powers extended to all of us at the same time." A slight mist stirred through the air before Maya pounded a fist against her palm, and water splashed from her hand. "We must fight her back, and in order to do so, we must be protected."

"I hardly believe Kamali's blood will serve as some sort of warning, as if we're living in ancient Egypt and avoiding the final plague."

"I came out to explain what we *are* doing." Maya's sharp tone brooked no further discussion. "We need Kamali in order to remove Quint once and for all. You know we must do whatever is necessary. I'd prefer not having to drink blood, either. I'm rather repulsed by the idea, but in this, neither of us has a choice." Frowning, she met his gaze. "He's already killing people." Jaw clenched, she braced her hands on his shoulders. "We just said personal feelings must not interfere with our goals. Plus, you know as well as I do that when asked, Kamali will freely offer her blood."

Nodin inhaled deeply though he no longer found refreshment in the cool Irish air. The smell of blood now tainted his senses. Many times he'd practically choked on that copper scent, and now to think of drinking it, of taking that life force from Kamali. He shook his head. "Please, ask Violet to look for another spell."

"I have. She did…to no avail." With a huff, Maya tugged up her loose skirt at the waist. "Listen, we have the spell and the plan. Two days from now, we're going to that Oklahoma casino, and one way or another, blood or no blood, Kamali is leaving with us." Maya combed her hair back from her face. "Come back inside. Please." She took his hand and lightly squeezed. "I'm worried about Flint. He needs you."

Nodding once, Nodin closed his eyes and saw only black for a moment, but then light broke in, creating a hazy glow behind his lids. He would never truly understand Kamali's blindness, but he did comprehend his duties. "I'll be along. I just…I need a minute." Opening his eyes, he squeezed Maya's shoulder then whistled for Maize.

The dog raced to his side then wiggled against his legs, tongue lolling out her mouth.

Leaning down to ruffle Maize's fur, Nodin watched Maya until she disappeared inside the castle. All the choices he'd made in his vast lifetime, those before and after his elemental transformation, had led him here. Last night, he'd called upon his other elemental seer gift, looking into the future. But nothing came.

Once before he'd chosen duty over love. Was he doing the

same now? Yet, he didn't love Kamali, did he? Something about her made him recall the human he used to be. Made him long for days spent racing across open fields, hunting to survive, swimming in the muddy Mississippi, ceremonial dances, and sitting around the fire listening to his grandfather speak of the past.

He was Nodin Osi descendant of the Eagle tribe. And at times, even before his transformation, he'd sit silently at the top of a hill or upon a rocky crag and spread his arms, reveling in the wind pouring over his skin.

Yet from his perch he hadn't seen everything, hadn't felt the changes coming. He hadn't sensed the moment fate stepped aside and let nature control his course.

Sinking beside Maize in the grass, he closed his eyes and prayed to the Great Spirit for the safety and happiness of his friends.

Because Maya was right, spell or no spell, he'd not let Raven control his element again. "I control the wind, Maize. It does not control me. I will remember that, and I promise, I'll get Kamali back."

CHAPTER 13

"Well, look who's come to visit." Moving through the medicine man's entryway and into the living area, Quint made sure to emphasize her name. "Good afternoon, *Raven*."

The bold woman had slipped into this apartment, lying in wait. Her mind abuzz with confidence in her charms. Not a drop of fear. He'd change that. Quickly. "Where did you get that name, anyway? Were you born with it, or is it something you've chosen to call yourself?"

This unwelcome visitor annoyed him.

Being inside this apartment annoyed him.

Using this medicine man's old body annoyed him. Though he had to admit, the man had one hell of a wardrobe. "What's the matter, black bird? Cat got your tongue?" Quint slid up against the back of Raven's lounger, gripped her long black hair, and yanked so her neck snapped back.

She didn't wince or blink.

Interesting. Maybe this one could replace Pillar. He did miss that salty blonde bitch, but she'd changed. They all changed. Only he remained constant.

Another constant was his reliance on these worthless humans to sustain his form. He'd entered this medicine man's body, hoping to gain usable magic or spells, but discovered only chants and incantations. God forbid he'd break out a drum and start beating the damn thing. Still, some of the herb mixtures could suit certain purposes, and the man did have an extensive stash of weapons.

"Would you mind releasing my hair?" Raven arched a sculpted brow.

"What?" Quint glanced down into pitch black eyes. "Forgive me. I was lamenting the lack of power within this meat suit."

"You cannot harness his powers, because you do not believe in the spirits and energies necessary to bring forth his gifts."

"Is that so?" Quint scoffed. "What shall I do, wipe my ass with lavender? Pray while wafting sage about the room? Make a shrine to a sun god?"

The minx shrugged.

"I find it comical you do not fear me, Raven. Know this. I will use you and, when I'm done, I'll dispose of you." He released her hair and moved around the chair to sit on the coffee table before her.

Raven studied him for a moment, tapping her red nails along the leather chair. "I've sensed something since you've taken over Malachi. He was the only thing keeping Kamali's other gifts hidden. Now that he's...gone, I'm worried she'll become...more."

"Ah...the one thing you do fear." He fluttered a hand by his chest. "Oh, Quint, my niece is stronger than me. Destroy her for me, will you?" Quint spoke in a whiny female tone. "That's why you're here, isn't it? To ask my assistance. To offer your body, such as it is, in exchange for my help." He gripped her knees and wrenched them apart. "Will you fall on your knees and show me how good you can make me feel? I've been with more practiced whores than you, I doubt I'll be impressed." He ran both hands along her inner thighs. "But do not fret, my sweet dark bird. We'll come to some sort of understanding. You'll learn not to enter my domain without paying a price." He shifted backward again, but kept her gaze. "As for Kamali, I'd be entertained by a cat fight.

My focus is not on helping you but on obtaining Violet. Do you understand the power that witch holds over the entire electromagnetic spectrum? Radio waves. Infrared. Ultraviolet. Gamma rays."

Quint stood and shoved back the table, pacing. "All that slipped through my fingers, but she will not do so again because, you see, they have a weakness. They won't sacrifice everything to destroy me. I know this now. They had their moment and they let me go, choosing to survive rather than assuring my destruction."

"I can help you." Raven rested her hands in her lap. "I can control the Elementals while you go for Violet."

Quint shoved her onto the floor and wedged his black dress shoe under her chin, pressing on her throat just enough to have her gripping his ankle. "*You* don't control anything. Understand that now. If you think they haven't already devised a way around you, you're a fool." He eased the pressure a little then sank down, locking her between his legs so that his knees sat on each side of her head.

"Let me up."

He easily deflected her attempts to control his mind. He sighed, letting her struggle to break free while glancing at the bar, wishing he had a drink. He'd been at the casino all day, having a bit of fun messing with gamblers and the machines. One wrinkled old lady had won thousands. He'd waited until she'd left, followed her to her car, and then, waving a gun around, he'd stolen every penny. *Oh, fun times.*

After the last battle at Violet's Irish castle, he'd returned and needed a little fun. Perhaps tomorrow he'd find a sports car dealership, take a car for a test drive, and then prowl for ladies who liked the darker aspects of sex.

Curse words lit up his ears and reminded him another was in his presence. These humans just never shut up. "Quiet. Your incessant shrieking will get those wings clipped." Quint pulled the shiny Smith & Wesson revolver from the holster at his back and shoved the barrel between Raven's lips. "Are you ready to listen?"

Eyes wide, his captive nodded while attempting to jerk aside her head.

After removing the gun from her mouth, he tapped her on the forehead with the barrel. "Stay still."

Raven clenched her jaw and glared.

"Wipe that look off your face. You came to me." He pulled back on the hammer and fired right by her ear.

Once the smoke settled and the ringing in his ears ceased, he ignored the neighbors banging on his door and glanced down. "Now, where were we?" He tapped his temple with the end of the gun. "Oh yes, your niece. Kamali *does* interest me. You say she'll be stronger than you…well then, I might have a use for her. Right now, she is bait. They'll come for her. They always do."

"I've had enough. I came here to help you, and what do I get for that? I'm deaf." Raven shoved against his knees, her voice a decibel above a shout. "Get your dick out of my face."

Quint laughed. "But, my little black bird, isn't that why you're here? To be my partner, in all ways?" Using the barrel end of the gun, he shoved a strand of hair off her sweaty forehead. "Partners promise so many things when all they want is my power." He shrugged and shook his head. "So being a gracious creature, I grant their wish, but none are strong enough. It's quite tiresome really." He sank back on his heels, resting his bottom on Raven's torso. "I don't have anyone. Never have. I've been alone on this earth, but no more. I will capture my Violet and she will remain at my side forever."

Pounding sounded at his door again, jolting him back to his current situation.

The woman between his legs still struggled to break free. She wasn't his glorious witch but another worthless stand-in.

Still…the night was young. He slid down Raven's body and ran his nose along her neck. "You want to be free of your cage, black bird. Let's test the limits of that wish, shall we? But first, a little foreplay. Let's dispose of those nosy neighbors. Consider it a test of sorts. How comfortable are you punishing those outside my door, curious about a wee thing like gunfire?"

For the next half hour, he evaluated her usefulness after observing her ruthless tactics, and then he spent the rest of the night unleashing his own brand of pain mixed with pleasure. In the end, she scored a solid B+.

CHAPTER 14

At the same funeral parlor that had handled his wife's ceremony, Adler clenched his jaw as the minister lit the bundle of sage meant to purify the soul from pain, grief, anger, and sadness.

The man continued, asking, "Those who wish to be smudged and cleansed, please come forward now."

Though he'd done so at his wife's funeral, this time, Adler remained seated between his two remaining sons, Caddo and Isi. He had no desire to be purged of the turmoil roiling within his mind and heart. Though, he had vented some steam once Kamali arrived.

She'd tried explaining why the Elementals needed her. Words that meant nothing, as he'd needed her here. She could have stopped Quint from entering Waya if only she'd been around to sense the dark creature's presence.

Again, Adler searched the room for Malachi. The man had texted earlier saying he was ill. He'd better be close to death to miss this funeral.

After the prayers to the Great Spirit, Kamali stood to blow the eagle's bone whistle to help carry away Waya's spirit.

When she finished, his sons stepped to the back of the funeral parlor where drums were set up.

Adler remained, staring at the urn holding his middle child's ashes. The thumping rhythm of the antique instruments and the tribal mourning songs did nothing to soothe his soul.

Kamali stayed seated, as well. Without her guide dog or walking stick, she was helpless to move freely about the room.

Adler moved from his seat to sit next to her. "Kamali, I will not apologize for my harsh words. You must understand we are at war with this Quint. He chose to strike this family as a warning against your involvement with the Elementals."

She wiped her nose with a crumpled tissue. "I know my duties, Uncle."

"As I know mine." He refused to offer her comfort when he had none of his own. His wife had died in childbirth after delivering Isi. He'd raised his children by himself. Part of his fury stemmed from knowing he was powerless against Quint. But maybe, just maybe, Kamali and Malachi could keep them safe. Though, in order to do so, the medicine man would have to drop the barriers he'd put in place around Kamali's gifts. She'd likely be hurt they'd altered her in such a way, but Malachi believed putting restraints on some of her abilities was best. Adler glanced at Kamali. "I will not let that beast rip another son from my side. You will stay and help us fight."

"A swirling of color is present within your aura I've never seen before, Uncle." She pulled another tissue from her mini-pack and whispered, "Do you despise me so?"

"I cannot help but feel this is your fault." He choked back tears. "Waya would be alive if not for your selfish endeavors. But, I've already made that clear. You are the one who must carry that guilt, not I." He stood, eager to be away from her and all she could see.

Kamali reached for his hand and pulled him back down beside her. "I must say something."

"Make it quick."

"Something evil writhes along the edges." Releasing him, she bent at the waist, clutching her head in her hands. "A thick red wall, teeming and screaming with black, drip-drip-drips." Heaving in a deep breath, she gazed up at him, eyes wide. "Quint is here, surrounding us even now."

Heart pounding, he grabbed her shoulders and lifted her half out of her seat. "Where is he?"

"Not in this room, but he is very close." Kamali's hands trembled as she placed them palms out, as if touching a barrier. "The wall grows stronger. Impenetrable." She met his gaze, her eyes no longer opaque but clearing enough for him to see glimpses of her natural dark brown. "Even while reading the dark auras of the foulest of your associates, I maintained a faint sense of optimism, but with this...with Quint, I sense nothing but a stark and empty malevolence."

Each strike of the drums, still beating in the background, felt like an end note to each gut punch delivered by Kamali's words. They must find a way out of this madness. He would *not* lose another son. "We will speak to Malachi. He will help us."

With tears free-falling down her cheeks, Kamali shook her head. "No, Uncle, he will not."

# # #

Though Kamali spoke the truth, she braced for the moment her uncle would lash out again. She'd already received a harsh slap across the face the moment she'd been brought to his office by Creed.

"Explain." Adler jabbed her shoulder with a poke of his finger. "Why won't Malachi help?"

"You already know." She hated to alert her uncle to another loss, but he needed to remedy his misguided notions of her and Malachi working together.

"Shall we go back to corrective measures, Kamali?"

Adler's tone slithered through her ears. Unaware she'd been soothing herself by swaying side-to-side, she shivered at the thought of the bindings her uncle had used in the past to stop her from a motion that embarrassed him. "Malachi has been overcome by Quint."

"I suspected." Adler paused for a moment. "He would never have missed this funeral, as Waya was his favorite."

"Waya was my favorite, too." Shifting in the hard chair, Kamali continued with her submissive tone and posture, though very much against her nature. Yet, since leaving Nodin, she'd been sinking. Down, so far down. How had he become her champion in such a short time? Hadn't she stood on her own? Fought her own battles? Still, she wished Nodin was here. After losing her dear cousin and friend, she needed the comfort she'd find in his arms. Calling on some of Nodin's strength now, she straightened her shoulders. "Uncle, are you still there?"

"Yes." He blustered out with a long-suffering sigh.

"Malachi screamed across my dreams last night. He fought against the takeover, but he lost. Then another voice, I believe it was Quint's, warned me of what is to come."

"And what is that?"

"Destruction, pain, the walls of your casino crumbling. More death."

"I won't allow it."

"None of us have a choice. He's bent on revenge and he covets the witch, Violet. She is his end game, and he'll tear down the world until he has her. The only thing standing between that creature and unbridled chaos is the Elementals."

Her uncle heaved another heavy sigh. "I cannot hear this right now. Stay here. I will retrieve you once the ceremony is over, and we'll discuss this further. Right now, I must join my people in mourning my son."

Kamali nodded, not allowing his blatant emphasis on "my people" to rip against her already shattered heart. Her uncle needed a target for his pain, and she was strong enough to endure his barbs. Although the ferocity of his words did sting, especially when he blamed her for Waya's death.

Could she have saved her cousin? This question would torture her forever. Her gifts did allow her to detect Quint, but she doubted her ability to perceive energies could halt this dark matter creature from entering host bodies. She'd sense when he was near, just as she did now, but that was the extent of her powers. As far as she understood, once Quint entered a host, that human wouldn't survive, no matter what. Waya had been doomed the minute Quint chose him as his next human shell.

And, though alerted to Quint's dark presence, she knew he wasn't in the immediate vicinity. The throbbing ache in her heart and the pounding in her temples occurred more from sadness over her cousin's death and worry for the Elementals than from Quint's proximity.

Was she truly the reason Quint had attacked her family? How much did he know about her? And now that she was aware of her aunt, how much of her own history was hidden? Upon her return, she had asked her uncle about Raven, but he'd declared her questions were not a priority.

Rubbing her swollen eyes, Kamali leaned back in the metal chair and tried to lose herself in the sounds of the beating drums.

Suddenly, a vice squeezed her throat and a wall of orange, the color of power, soaked her senses like a too-bright sun, burning the very skin from her body. She slid from the chair to her knees as the hostility, greed, and arrogance of the dark creature ripped across her soul.

Quint drew close.

So very close.

The pain from Raven's mind games was nothing compared to this drilling through her brain. Kamali dry-heaved, as she hadn't eaten since yesterday, and once more she tried expelling the wretched villain overshadowing her mind, but nothing stopped this being's pure madness.

Malachi was with him, or had become him.

A scratchy voice, the same one from her dream, strummed across her mind. *"Welcome home, Kamali. I know you can sense me, but I'm not disturbed by this notion. I'm quite pleased, because that means they'll come. The Elementals will try to help you escape, and when they do, I'll have my revenge and a new host."*

Heart pounding almost louder than the drums, she stumbled wildly to her feet, bumping into someone. "Please, forgive me. I-I'm blind. Would you help me to the restroom?"

A soft female voice answered. "Of course."

"Thank you. Take my elbow, please." Clenching her jaw against Quint's mental bombardment, Kamali put one foot in front of the other.

The drumbeats drifted farther away as the woman led her from the room.

Kamali heard a door creak open and the normal odors of a bathroom wafted through her nostrils. "Thank you."

"Are you all right? You're shaking." The woman remained at her left side.

"Waya was my cousin. I just need a few moments alone, please."

"Here you go." The woman took her hand and placed it upon a stall door's handle. "Shall I wait outside?" Her aura was filled with pastels, the colors of kindness.

"No. I have my phone. I'll call someone to come get me. I'm just a bit overcome with…everything." And by everything she meant the oncoming embodiment of death. Would Quint dare show his face at this funeral? Shouldn't she be strong enough to face him if he dared?

Without warning, the woman drew Kamali into her arms.

This compassionate embrace helped remind Kamali of what was real and good in the world.

The woman tightened her arms just slightly before pulling back and taking both Kamali's hands. "Take your time, dear."

"Thank you." Kamali waited until she heard the door open

and close before plopping down on the cool tile floor, uncaring what germs lay beneath as she fought for calm. Resting on her side, she recalled something Malachi had screamed across her consciousness during her nightmares. *"I release you from your bonds."* As those words whispered across her mind once more, she closed her eyes.

Liquid fire shot from her heart to the tips of her fingers and toes. She convulsed and arched in pain. As a kind of heat seared through each vein, she momentarily lost consciousness.

Gasping, she opened her eyes and blinked. Then blinked again. Her vision was blurry, not all black. She made a fist and brought it before her face then wiggled her fingers. They moved. She waved them again and the same phenomenon occurred. These were *her* fingers. This was *her* hand. "What happened?"

"I release you from your bonds."

Bonds? Was this the release Malachi meant? A veil lifted from her eyes. But why? Who had put her in these bonds to begin with? She studied her hand again. The color unlike any aura she'd ever seen, close to brown, but not quite. What did this mean?

Answers. She needed answers. Even if Quint was holding court over everyone in that funeral parlor, she'd shove aside his evil ass and find out just what the hell was happening with her vision.

Clear in her mission, she pushed off the floor then wobbled as her eyes adjusted to everything they could see. "Oh, dear, what did Malachi do to me?" Closing her eyes, she breathed deep. "Take a minute. Breathe, just breathe. Waya, my friend, I need you more than ever. I don't know what anything is. I need your help." Tears slid down her cheeks, but she wiped them away. "No. I will not cry. I won't."

Glancing around the room for the sink to wash off her face, she glimpsed something bright red. After stepping closer, she stuck out her hand and felt the soft, cool color. "A flower." She bent and inhaled the beautiful fragrance. "A rose. This is a rose."

So many emotions whipped through her heart as the reality of the situation clarified. She bit her lip to hold back the torrent of tears. "I can see, Nodin," she whispered into the air. "Not perfectly, not clearly, but blurry images. How will I see *you* now?" This thought led to another, and she lifted her gaze. Didn't they have mirrors in bathrooms? Could she finally see herself?

There. An image right before her. Kamali reached out and touched cool glass. A face, though indistinct, surrounded by dark waves. With a shaky hand, she touched her hair and watched the vision in the mirror do the same. *Oh, Great Spirit, is that really my face?*

"Why is this happening?" Again, she considered the fact she hadn't eaten as a blessing, since she'd have discarded her stomach contents all over the floor. A cold sweat coated her body. "Don't do this. You can handle it. You'll find answers. Nodin will come. He'll come."

Kamali felt around for the sink, found the faucet, turned it on then splashed her face with water. A baptism of sorts, for a new beginning. A cleansing of the old to welcome the new. And what was the new? Would her vision fade again? Could she still see auras?

Now that Quint used Malachi as a host, had she regained an ability the medicine man had stolen from her, because he'd lost his hold over her?

The door opened, and a muddy yellow aura entered. Well, at least one question was answered—auras were still visible.

Kamali jolted as a woman's voice spoke inside her head.

"What is wrong with her? She looks quite savage. Has she been rolling around on the floor?"

"What's wrong with who?" Kamali answered.

"I'm sorry, what?" The woman spoke out loud this time.

"Oh my goodness...I think I just...I think..." Could she hear thoughts? Overwhelmed, Kamali swayed. Reaching for the sink, she missed and knocked over the roses. The vase crashed to the floor, and a wash of wetness poured across the tip of her right shoe.

"Miss, are you all right?"

Her unwelcome visitor took her arm. The door opened again and the woman hollered, "I've got a woman in here high on something. We'll need an ambulance."

Kamali huffed out a laugh at the absurdity of her doing any sort of drugs. The laughter turned hysterical as the reality of her situation became too insane to comprehend.

With the door propped open, she could hear the drum beat reaching a crescendo, and the singers' piercing wails echoed from the room. The repetitive sounds did nothing to prevent the sudden bombardment of each and every human thought.

Lust, sadness, loss, fear, greed, hunger, and impatience all mixed and churned together in her mind. With a cry, she clutched her hands to her ears, muffling the madness. "Stop. Just stop."

A flurry of hands groped then held, locking her in place.

"Let me go. Please." Shoving free, Kamali burst forward, colliding face first into a narrow wall. Blinking, she shook her head as the scent of copper filled her nose. "So, yeah, I didn't see *that* coming." She crumpled to the ground and once more her world went black.

CHAPTER 15

The next sound Kamali heard was a low moan, and as she opened her eyes, she realized the sound came from her. Tilting her head, she flicked at the coarse, thin blanket covering her body—a blanket she didn't recognize.

"Kamali, are you awake?" Her friend, Sawni's voice sounded from somewhere to her left.

After breathing a sigh of relief over the familiar voice, she croaked, "Yes. Water, please."

"I'm not sure. I should probably get a nurse."

"No." Kamali gripped the bedcover in a fist and glanced around the room. "Am I in a hospital?" She heard water splash against a cup.

"Oh my gosh, Kamali, you've been out for three days." Sawni squeezed her hand. "You scared everyone half to death."

"Out how?"

"Like comatose or something, I don't know." Sawni held the straw to her lips. "Take it slow."

Kamali straightened. Her entire body was weak, but her mind began to focus.

She could see the cup.

Sawni's blurry hand.

Light pouring into the room.

She wiggled her toes and laughed when she detected their movement under the blanket. Was this how a butterfly felt when shedding its cocoon? A freedom. Seeing the world from up so high, soaring, absorbing each facet from its new heights. While she couldn't fly, she still exulted in this new view.

"Why are you laughing?" Sawni hummed out an accompanying laugh. "You're high on drugs, girl."

After sipping her water, Kamali studied her friend's gold-brown aura, which indicated worry. This color was much different from her normal pink, which represented kindness and joy. "I'm all right now, Sawni. Everything will be fine."

So, this was her friend. Her hair seemed dark, too. And, though Kamali couldn't clearly make out each facial feature, she noted Sawni was biting her lip.

Her friend tilted her head. A voice travelled through Kamali's mind. Sawni's voice. *"I doubt she'll be fine. I probably shouldn't have given her that water. I should tell Adler she's awake."*

"No. Please, don't." Kamali was in no way ready to face her uncle, not when she had no understanding of why she could now read her friend's thoughts and somewhat see. Would her vision improve if she got glasses? Her heart pounded at the thought. Did she dare hope?

"Please don't what?" Sawni leaned forward.

Studying her friend, Kamali momentarily forgot everything. "What color are your eyes, Sawni?"

"Brown, why?"

"Just trying to get some clarity." She shrugged, squinting at her friend. "What color are my eyes?"

"They are the same. Why are you asking all these questions?" Her friend lifted her hand and bit her thumb. Her nail was painted red, just like those roses.

At the thought, a sharp pain shot through Kamali's head. "I remember now. I think Malachi had something to do with it."

"You're not talking sense. Maybe you should get some sleep."

"No." She straightened. "I want to see as much as I can. I

don't know how long this will last." Kamali pointed to her right. "Is that the door?"

"Yes." Sawni took her hand. "Kamali, are you feeling all right?"

Looking at the open doorway unleashed another opening in Kamali's mind, allowing a bombardment of voices to pour inside. "No, no, no. I don't want to hear you." She clutched her head. "Not all at once. I don't know how to do this. Sawni, shut the door. Shut it!"

Sawni jumped from her chair and slammed the door. "It's okay, Kamali." Her friend hustled back to her side. "Why are you so scared?"

Somehow, the action of shutting that door allowed her to close the door to her mind, as well. She really needed Nodin. He knew all about gleaning minds.

Sawni took her hand. "Listen, I'm not trying to freak you out more, but this nurse with a really crazy purple dye job just left. Kinda weird. She wouldn't talk to me, and she took a lot of blood."

"My blood?" Breathing deeply, Kamali focused on the colors within Sawni's aura.

"Yes."

"Wait." Kamali straightened. "She had purple hair?"

"Yeah, bright purple, almost violet."

"Oh, thank goodness."

"Why? Do you know her?"

"No, not really. Not yet." Kamali tried controlling her excitement. This purple-haired girl had to be Violet. The witch. But why would she risk coming here with Quint so close? "I need to go." Kamali shoved away her covers and sat on the side of the bed. "Can you help me?" She glanced at her friend.

"I don't know, Kamali. I got in so much trouble when you left last time. Your uncle came over to our house, mad as a hornet. I thought he was going to kill me."

If only Sawni knew there was a worse bully in town. Was her friend in trouble? She should leave. Now. Before Quint picked up on their connection. Anything that mattered to her was fair game in his sick mind. And now that the Elementals were here, a battle would likely occur. "Sawni, listen to me, you need to...to..."

A wave of empty darkness choked her. Fighting through the muck, Kamali tried to narrow her focus on Quint's location. She jumped and shrieked out a curse when hands gripped her shoulders.

"Kamali, what's wrong?"

She couldn't answer. The dark matter beast raged closer. Her blood moved like sludge through each vein, and ice coated her heart.

Violet was close.

Quint was close.

Everyone else needed to get the hell out of Dodge.

"I-I need to go." Kamali shuffled to her feet. "Sawni. Get in your car and go home. Now."

A beacon of blue tore through the black wall of malice.

Nodin.

"Kamali, what is going on? You're pale as a sheet. I think you should lie back down until I get a—" Sawni gasped as the door banged open. "Who are you? I don't believe you're a nurse. Get out before I call security."

Kamali stared at the bright amber aura a few feet from Sawni's. Intermixed with orange, this aura was full of inner strength, intellect, and power. The woman stepped farther into the room, a bright purple halo of hair around her face. "Violet," Kamali whispered then shook her head. *No.* She needed to leave. They all did. "Violet, you can't be here. Quint is here and he wants you. Go. Now." She shot out of the bed, wobbled after a wave of dizziness struck, and then approached the petite woman. "He's right outside. Call Nodin and have him jet you out of here. Quint has used me as a trap."

"I'm so happy to finally meet you. Be at peace." Violet simply hugged her, as if she wasn't moments away from becoming a madman's captive. "Quint will not take me today, or any day."

Kamali's hair crackled. All the monitors in her room popped then fizzled.

"Give me your arm. As you say, we've not much time. We'll get you more suitable clothes when we return to Castle Nemon."

"Kamali, who is this woman?" Sawni spoke from behind her.

"I am Violet Levina." The witch moved to shake her friend's hand. "Please know that I will take care of Kamali."

"Where is she taking you?" Concern radiated from Sawni's tone.

"Where I belong." Kamali smiled. Would this be the last time she saw her friend? She turned, rushed across the room, and held her friend tight for a quick moment. "I cannot tell you how many times you helped me escape the loneliness." She brushed a hand across Sawni's cheek, blocking all her friend's thoughts from her mind. "Please, go home now. I'll call when I can and answer your questions then."

Sawni held her at arm's length. "Be careful."

A floral scent drifted through the air as Violet approached.

Sawni nodded at Violet then left the room.

Kamali blinked away the tears, sad to say goodbye to her friend, but grateful she'd be away from the melee.

"Your friend loves you dearly." Violet took Kamali's hand and led her to the door.

"I love her, too. She's stood by me since forever."

Violet halted for a moment. "You've become stronger, and you can see me. Am I right?" Piercing purplish-blue eyes studied her face.

"Yes, how did you know?" Had this witch woven some kind of spell? Could she read minds?

"Let's just say, I'm in…well, I'm in tune with you right now." Violet tugged her down the hall.

Was that a draft at her back? Kamali glanced over her shoulder. Was the hospital gown covering all her parts?

"Violet, do you think you could block everyone from seeing us, because my bum is hanging out of this gown."

"Already covered."

"I wondered why I hadn't detected any shocked thoughts about your colorful hair or my pale butt."

"About that, the Elementals will teach you to control your gifts, and my hair, well…this is a remnant of my last battle with Quint." She sighed. "It used to be a beautiful shade of red."

"I'm sorry that happened." Kamali quietly followed Violet for a moment before focusing on her own changes. "I believe my gifts were somehow masked by our tribe's medicine man, Malachi. I don't know why I was stifled, but I'll find out somehow, someday."

"But not today."

"No, not today."

An elevator button dinged.

"I'm not sure I could lead you down the stairs properly," Violet admitted. "I'm sorry."

"I understand." Kamali shifted back and forth. "Is Nodin…is he all right?"

"No, he's distressed, to say the least, at not being the one to swoop in and rescue you from this hospital. But you and I aren't as mobile as the Elementals." She chuckled. "Just imagine him flying down the corridors with you."

The elevator dinged again and Violet led her forward. "My grandfather can space jump, but I haven't mastered that task…yet."

"Thank you for coming." Kamali closed her eyes. "I see Malachi, or Quint, rather. He's in the parking lot." She gripped Violet's arm. "What if Raven is with him? What if she takes over Nodin's powers again?"

"Kamali, don't be afraid. We'll get you somewhere safe." The elevator stopped, and Violet drew her out.

Kamali followed but pulled Violet closer. "I don't sense her, but if Raven *is* here, everyone is in danger. If she controlled you, especially in a populated area, she could wreak all kinds of havoc."

"We've handled Raven." Violet met her gaze. "I worked a spell earlier that will serve as a ward against her powers."

Trembling at the thought of what that entailed, Kamali gritted her teeth as the dark menace's presence overwhelmed her senses.

With each step across the hospital lobby, they drew closer to Quint. Somehow, he was the only one in her mind. She still had no idea how her mindreading skills worked, or why Quint could block out everything, but hopefully they'd escape and she'd find her answers. If not, she wished she could at least see Nodin one more time before she died an excruciating death.

"Stop, Kamali. You will not die, though you are right about Raven. Quint will use her." Violet led her outside. "He's absorbed and retained all of Malachi's memories, so he knows what Raven is capable of. He'll use her to strike against us."

"We shouldn't be out here. You should go." She tugged free of Violet's grip and stepped backward. "Please. Just leave me here."

The cool fall mist raised goose bumps on her skin.

Kamali bent over at the waist as a wash of torment flowed through her body.

"Do not let him win." Violet cupped her elbow and urged her upright. "Have faith. Terran and Nodin are just down this aisle. We move forward. Believe you can defeat him. You are stronger than your fear."

Strengthened by Violet's words, Kamali focused on one thought. Nodin.

A vile madness swirled in her head, speaking, jeering, "*A flower delivery. For me,*" the mocking voice exclaimed. "*Thank you, dear Kamali. And for this gift, I just might let you live. The others...well, they won't fare as well."*

With each word, she felt an insidious pollution blanketing her lungs, making her gasp for each breath. "Enough. I refuse you."

"Kamali," Nodin shouted. "Run to me."

After scanning the area, she saw him, standing by the back of a red truck. Every facet of him clear, so clear. "I see you. I'm coming." She ran, for the first time, sure of her destination. Not afraid she'd stumble over things she couldn't see.

Only Nodin existed, until she heard Maize bark. Her knees buckled, but she regained her balance quickly. "I will not fall." Gaining strength from Nodin's presence, she broke free of the ebony aura seeping through her mind.

Her will to live. To survive. To fight. Just two steps away then one. With a loud whoop, she jumped and wrapped her arms and legs around her source of hope.

Nodin released a quiet, "Ummpf", then toppled over.

Maize joined in their happy frolics, madly licking their smiling faces.

CHAPTER 16

"Obviously, Maize and I are happy to see you." Nodin finally breathed freely without the worry that had coursed through his heart the entire time Kamali was away. He braced her face in his hands and kissed her, showing how much he'd missed her with each soft caress.

Maize continued to prance around at their sides.

Yet, he remained focused on the woman in his arms. Gripping the back of her neck, he pulled her closer and delved deeper into the kiss, needing only to breathe in her scent, her presence,

Violet cleared her throat.

Reluctantly, Nodin broke their connection. "I've been so worried about you. Are you all right?"

She gazed at his mouth. "What?"

He chuckled. "Let's get you out of here."

"Wait." Kamali clutched his bicep. "Quint is here."

"I know." He stood then helped her up.

As if emphasizing his words, the lights in the parking structure exploded.

Holding Kamali at his side, Nodin quickly blew all the glass under a grouping of trees before it hit the pavement.

Quint, fully immersed in Malachi's body, stepped from

behind a large SUV, blocking them from Terran and the escape vehicle.

No matter, there was always a Plan B.

Hands braced into fists at his side, Terran paced just behind Quint before slowly moving forward.

Quint sneered and, without turning around, said, "I know you're back there, Earth-man." He rolled his eyes before smiling at Violet. "Where do you think you're going, dear? I just returned, and you're leaving without a word? I'm heartbroken."

The ground rumbled beneath their feet.

"Terran, too many people are around." Nodin sent a mental message to his Elemental partner. *"Pull it back."*

"Get Kamali out of here, Nodin," Terran commanded.

"Yes, Nodin. You never know what's in the air these days." Quint lifted his hand, opened his palm, and blew.

"No." Violet shoved Kamali from the dark particles' path.

But Nodin had already blown away the piercing shards before any could reach Kamali. He spoke right by her ear. "Be ready to fly." He gazed at Quint and drew a deep breath before expelling a raging wind.

Quint toppled and tumbled through the lot, but then disappeared.

Violet tensed. "What? Where did he go?"

"Violet, move!" Kamali screamed. "He's right in front of you."

"It's the camouflage, Terran. He's—" Nodin blinked as he was struck right between the eyes.

Violet grabbed Kamali's hand and spoke a quick spell.

"Through the vision of one who can see,
reveal what is hidden to me,
with the power of earth, wind, air, and sea,
as I will so mote it be."

"Terran, I can see him." Violet blinked a few times then cried, "We must act now."

"Go." Terran waved Nodin away. "Violet and I have our plan. We'll give it a test run."

"No." Frowning, Nodin rubbed his forehead. "You won't be able to see Quint if Kamali leaves."

"Yes, I can." Violet glared straight ahead. "The spell worked and you forget, I've had her blood."

Nodin shivered at that thought, hoping Kamali was too overwhelmed to completely grasp the meaning behind that statement. He glanced at the woman in question. She remained at Violet's side, both women moving in tandem as they sidestepped as if dodging someone.

Quint was making his move.

Nodin spurred into action, grabbing Kamali and calling Maize to his side before spinning into a funnel. Though he didn't want to leave the Elementals behind, he knew where his duty lay…and his heart.

As his element, he lifted Kamali and Maize higher and higher, until they were hidden within the clouds. Maize fought against the flight, so Nodin gleaned into the dog's mind and calmed her.

For two hours, he carried his shivering quarry across the continent and the Atlantic Ocean before landing at Violet's castle. After touching down, Nodin whipped Kamali and Maize closer to the fire, as both were covered in ice crystals.

"Eamon!" Nodin called for Violet's wizard grandfather.

"I am here, son. No need to shout." Leaning heavily on his cane, the gray-haired man toddled closer.

"Can you help them? I had to take them quickly through the sky, but now they are practically icicles."

"Bring them closer together." Eamon shuffled over. "Help me down."

Nodin helped the frail man to his knees.

Eamon placed one hand on each, whispering a spell.

Their shivers quickly subsided. Kamali's cheeks turned pink

once more, and her breathing went from rasping pants to a smooth, quiet rhythm.

"Grab those quilts beside the couch then head to the kitchen and ask Enda to heat some soup." Eamon ruffled Maize's fur before grasping Nodin's arm. "Help me up."

Nodin pulled him to his feet and led him to a rocking chair set before the roaring fire.

"I shall sit here with them."

Nodin hesitated, unsure of his next move. He hadn't felt this way for a woman in a long time, and now that she'd returned, he didn't want to leave her. He stared down at her slumbering form then jolted when Eamon's voice broke the silence.

"Well, boy, do as I said. They need to be warmed from the inside. Enda will know which herbs to use. Now be quick about it."

Smiling at a man who acted like his elder but hadn't lived as long, Nodin knelt beside Kamali and kissed her cheek. "You will be safe here. Be well." He stood and blinked, wavering as he felt the dark stain left behind from Quint's sucker punch.

Maya scuttled through the doorway. "Nodin, where are..." She came into the room then stopped, wide-eyed. "What has happened? Where's Terran?"

"I must remove Quint's dark matter from my vision." He shook his head. "Please care for Kamali and Maize until my return."

"But, Terran..."

"He is with Violet. I have absolute faith he will return."

Maya visibly swallowed then nodded. "I will see to Kamali's care. Go. Rejuvenate."

After one more glance at Kamali, he drifted through the door and swirled with the air out to sea. Far away from all inhabitants. Elementals were peri-mortal, not immortal. They could die. Many had.

A "peri" was a spirit who had been denied paradise until they had done penance three times. Though, in Elemental mythology, this wasn't entirely accurate. Mother Nature chose them and their mortality was perpetual. Round and round, unceasing, relying on their element to survive. If he were placed inside a vacuum for days on end, he would cease to exist. And, if he so chose, he could ask Mother Nature to return him to human form. As far as he understood, if he were to convert, he wouldn't remember much about his Elemental life. That thought whispered through his mind a lot of late.

After all, Kamali was human, and in order to remain by her side, at some point he'd have to make a choice. He'd stay with her until the end of her days. After losing so many loved ones, he'd drifted as a solitary breeze, never allowing his heart to open to those who would not remain. With Kamali, he had no choice, but...he didn't know the depth of her feelings. Her life had changed so drastically, how could he ask her to remain with a man who couldn't give her a family, a normal life?

Mind spinning along with his airy form, he stilled and landed on a rock in the Gulf of Lyon, outside of Aude in Southern France. This location hosted a windsurfer competition each year, the Defi Wind Event. Nodin spread his arms, allowing the balmy breeze to cleanse him. He breathed deep before sinking to the ground, crossing his legs, and resting his hands on his knees.

Kamali had changed since he'd last seen her.

Subtle, but something was different.

Terran's voice broke across his mind. *"I am returning Violet to the castle. I'll join you shortly."*

Nodin nodded, though no one could see, grateful his Elemental partners had escaped, but aware they still had a long way to go before they could stop running.

CHAPTER 17

After settling in a rocking chair beside a fire now freshly stacked with wood and blazing courtesy of Flint, Kamali nestled under a quilt as Maya asked question after question. *Why was she in the hospital? What had her uncle said? Was she able to mourn her cousin?*

Flint's red-orange aura flickered right beside the water-girl. Kamali could make them both out now. Maya's wavy blonde hair, curling over her shoulders, her expressive aqua eyes. Flint's dark short locks, though she couldn't see the color of his eyes as he was too far away and remained blurry. She squinted to bring him in focus.

Maybe someone in the castle had glasses. She'd love to see if wearing them would improve her vision.

"Flint, will you stop pacing?" Maya huffed.

Maize rested with her head on Kamali's lap, nudging her every time she stopped petting her soft ears.

"So, you believe Malachi was somehow masking your extra gifts?" Maya had settled on the same ottoman where Kamali rested her feet.

"Yes." Kamali clenched her hands together in her lap, provoking another poke from Maize. "Although, I'm not sure what I can do. I can see, but everything is blurry. I have no basis of understanding what I'm seeing. I'll admit to being overwhelmed

122

and a little frightened." She considered the truth of that statement. She'd never seen a blanket before, but now she understood this object that covered her was one. And earlier, when she'd gotten a good look at Maize, she'd burst into tears over the dog's golden fur and black nose.

Unwilling to ride that emotional roller coaster again, she focused on answering Maya's question. "I can also hear voices in my head. I don't like that so much. I'll have to learn to block it. Will you help me?"

"Absolutely." Maya took her hand. "I will help you with everything I can."

Flint cleared his throat. "Do you think Malachi is responsible for your blindness?"

"I considered that, but I believe he more masked what I could see, not that I see much." Kamali shifted in her chair. "I still cannot completely see you. Yet now, you are more than an aura. I recognize the colors that were strongest in the aura spectrum, but some colors, like the hue of my skin, are hard to define." She sighed and fought for a way to explain her changes not only to Flint, but also to herself. "Before, colors simply existed as a way to define a person's character, but now I see your shape and your aura." She rocked side-to-side then, realizing the nervous gesture, she clenched the chair's armrests instead.

"Nodin is complete to me now." She smiled. "Not shrouded, but quite clear." A hazy version of Nodin was a lot to absorb; having an unhindered view of the man would likely give her the vapors. She giggled. No vapors, more like sheer lust.

"As far as my ability to read minds, I don't know why Malachi would mask that gift. Perhaps I'll never know, as he is no longer alive, but dead inside Quint."

"Try to read my mind, Kamali."

"Maya." Flint laughed. "Just because you can't stay out of everyone else's mind doesn't mean Kamali wants to delve."

"Hush." Maya placed her hand over Kamali's on the armrest.

"I'll let you in. Go ahead."

"All right." Kamali gazed at the blurry blonde, staring directly into her blue eyes. Suddenly, she detected thoughts of water and sand. "A beach," she blurted out. "Is that right?"

"Yes." Maya lifted a hand and pressed it toward her, palm out.

"Why are you doing that with your hand?"

"High five."

"Oh," Kamali nodded before tapping her palm against Maya's.

"We'll have to work on your body language skills." Maya chuckled.

"True." Kamali smiled and then shook her head, quickly sobering. "I'd also like to conceal my thoughts from Raven and Quint. You'll have to help me."

"Nodin is the most talented at working through the human mind. When Terran and I first met, I let Nodin alter his thoughts, since I refused to change his gorgeous mind." She sighed. "I miss him. I hope they get back soon."

Maya was quiet for a moment.

The fire popping in the background and Flint's feet padding back and forth across the hearthstones were the only sounds in the room.

"I believe you can see Nodin, because he is your destiny." Maya broke the silence. "Even before Terran became an Elemental, he and I were connected. He called to me, and I answered. I believe it is the same for you and Nodin."

Kamali unwrapped from the covers, toasty from Flint's fire and suddenly feeling quite sleepy until jolted awake when the tips of her fingers buzzed like she'd stuck her finger in a light socket. She straightened in her chair and looked around.

"What is it?" Maya took her hand.

Maize's harness jangled, and then she stood at full alert. A low warning growl slipping from her throat.

Kamali reached for Maize's handle, stretching her fingers across the metal in an attempt to stop the buzz tingling through her hand. "It's all right, girl. It's just Violet. I can sense all that energy surrounding her. She really is like a bolt of lightning, but her aura is only one color."

"Which one? White?"

"No. Violet."

She and Maya laughed.

"Where is she?" Flint fired to her side. "Outside?"

"Yes." Kamali closed her eyes so she could concentrate. "She is in a field, near stone ruins." Suddenly, a hot blast of air struck her back and smoke billowed through her nose.

Then a door slammed shut.

"Oh." Kamali sank back against her chair. "I suppose he's gone to find her."

Maya's aura churned with greens and blues. "He's scared to lose her, and honestly, so am I, because if she goes...I don't believe he'll rise from the ashes this time." She squeezed her knee. "Terran sent me a message. He's joining Nodin."

"Terran is unharmed?" Kamali had tried to hide her worry from Maya.

"Yes." Maya passed her a cup of hot peppermint tea. "Drink this. I'm worried you'll catch cold after that frigid flight."

Kamali considered the kind woman before her and all the years she'd been on earth—all the battles she'd fought, all the people she'd helped, all the water she'd cleansed. Maya's life was peri-mortal, yet her own would end. Every minute counted. Quint could arrive here tomorrow and destroy them all. A sense of urgency pulsed through her veins. When death came, she wanted no regrets.

Determined to start her new live-like-there's-no-tomorrow path, she squared her shoulders and turned to Maya. "When they return and everyone is settled, I want to know everything. Past, present, and future plans. I'm all in." She scooted forward in the rocking chair. "Teach me what I need to know, because Quint is growing stronger. I sense his cloying malevolence all around us. His long fingers are seeking to infect and destroy everything in his path in order to obtain one goal. Violet."

"He won't take her." Maya's tone turned steely.

Knowing those words were grounded in hope, not reality, Kamali refrained from comment. Seconds later, she swayed in her seat as a chill of foreboding shivered down her spine. Unexpectedly, in her mind's eye, a vision of Violet's lifeless body lying in a bed of green, surrounded by tall brown figures streamed across her mind. Leaning forward, she gripped Maya's hand and focused on recalling Nodin's handsome face in order to escape this horrid vision.

Dear Great Spirit, what new curse was this?

CHAPTER 18

Sitting in the hospital lobby's coffee shop, Quint studied the humans skittering about. They were like ants, tiny creatures crawling around, carrying ten times their weight in over-priced coffee. Though loath to admit such a thing, he felt odd.

Violet and Terran had some new trick, some new spell they'd performed out in the parking lot. He'd been shocked to discover his essence thinning, as if being drawn through a narrow opening like the thin red straws these humans used to stir their coffee.

What did the pair have up their sleeves?

Terran had created an intense amount of heat then Violet joined in…and, he'd actually experienced a moment of fear.

He crushed the napkin dispenser in his hand, bending the metal in half.

An elderly woman in the booth beside him gasped.

Tilting his head, he met her gaze. "I'm a bit angry. Someone just left with my wife."

"Oh." She covered her mouth with both hands.

Shrugging, he inwardly smirked. "I'll get her back though, even if I have to kill them all."

"What?" The white-haired woman shrank back.

"What?" He mocked before leaning forward and tossing the bent container on her table. "Get out of my face, you worthless waste of skin."

With a shriek, she stood and skittered away.

He laughed, enjoying the moment, but as black ooze trickled from a cut on his hand, he once more considered his loss of Violet—and her brazen science experiment.

He hadn't enjoyed *that* moment—at all.

Luckily, a mother and her passel of children had teetered out of a van, breaking whatever hold the Elementals had over him.

Then, like the cowards they were, they'd scattered. If they truly were able to complete their spell, they'd have continued. Yet, once again, they weren't prepared to sacrifice in order to complete their mission. A weakness he would exploit, because this time they'd conjured something powerful. A niggle of worry settled like a sickness in his brain.

Perhaps Raven could garner more information, read their minds again and figure out what they had done that had him feeling as if he were on the verge of disappearing forever.

This would never do. He pounded his fist against the flimsy table.

Violet would be his…and if they refused to surrender, he'd unleash a world of pain on the inhabitants of the earth. Non-stop chaos. Non-stop death.

These cat-and-mouse games had grown tiresome. As had his continual reliance on lesser humans for his existence. He braced his chin on his open palm and closed his eyes.

Tired, so very tired of everything.

And though the Elementals may hold the weapon to defeating him, he knew with absolute certainty they'd never pull the trigger.

But he would.

Eyes now open, he drew a target on the table with his index finger and in the middle he wrote a capital K and an M, knowing if he eliminated Kamali and Maya, he'd leave the Elementals weakened.

The key to destroying the Elementals lay in destroying their hearts.

Time to let the bullets fly.

CHAPTER 19

In one of the castle's spare bedrooms, Kamali stirred awake. Hot, like she'd never been before.

A loud gasp escaped as she noted an arm resting across her waist and realized the heat came from a body plastered against her back. "Nodin?"

"Yes." His breath blew across the back of her ear.

She turned. "You're here."

"I am."

"I'm glad." Though unsure of his intent at joining her in bed, she'd make clear he was welcome. Carpe diem, after all. Resting on her side, she wrapped her arms around him, bringing them chest-to-chest.

"Not concerned at finding a strange man beside you?" Nodin trailed his fingers up and down her back.

"Are you a strange man?" She raised a brow, her tone flirtatious.

Studying him, she could actually see a tiny scar under his right eye and the clear sky-blue of his eyes. She would treasure this moment—the smile on his face, the fall of his ebony hair, all of his features forever locked away in her mind—just in case this was all a crazy dream.

"You ask if I'm strange?" He tapped her nose with his index

finger. "Absolutely. I can morph into wind, whip up a tsunami, and break down mountains." He chuckled while brushing her hair over her shoulder. "I think most would believe that peculiar."

"Not peculiar, fascinating." She met his gaze. "With all the excitement of your return last night and the discussions regarding Quint, I didn't get to tell you something important."

"What is that?" His deep voice rumbled through her body.

"I can see you much clearer now."

"And?"

"And"—she trailed a finger down his smooth chest—"I want to see more."

"Kamali." He stalled her seeking finger. "You've undergone some drastic changes in the past few days. We need to understand what is happening to you and why. You were comatose for three days before we pulled you from that hospital." He shook his head. "Perhaps, we should develop our relationship at a slow and steady pace."

Taking a chance, she rose above him, supported by her knees. "I'd like a slow and steady pace, but not as you've suggested."

"Wait." He grabbed her hand and brought it to his mouth for a quick kiss. "I came in here to wake you up, not to make love to you."

"I *am* awake, Nodin, in so many ways." How could she explain this need to act now to a man who'd lived hundreds of years and would live hundreds more?

She trailed her fingers up his muscular chest before massaging his shoulders. "When I was three, my parents died. I don't remember much about the time, but I do remember my absolute terror at moving from my small house to the opulence of Adler's home. My parents and I hadn't spent much time with his family. Mostly holidays." She traced a finger along Nodin's collarbone. "Caddo tells me for the first year I searched everywhere for my mother. She may have had issues, but she was still my mother. I wasn't as close to my father. He was gone a lot because he drove a semi."

"Then, I only had Aunt Skye, Adler's wife for a short time. When Isi was born, we lost her." She breathed past the lump in her throat. "The two women who represented motherhood disappeared from my life within a few years of each other."

"I'm sorry." Nodin pulled her against his chest and held her for a quiet moment.

Kamali eased away. "I decided I would love hard and strong for as long as I could because life ends." She nudged a finger under his chin and met his gaze. "Just as you and I will end, so I'm taking this moment of calm and experiencing something I never have before. I want to be touched, held, loved. I know dangers lie ahead, but right now, in this quiet room, I want to shut out everything and leap forward."

Seeking more, she tugged off the shirt she'd borrowed from Violet and massaged her breasts with her hands. "I want you. Only you."

"Kamali." He hissed in a breath. "If I stay, I'll want all of you."

"I haven't asked you to leave." She ran her hands across his taut chest, glorying in his warm, smooth skin.

He tugged her down to lie on her side and studied her face. "Many years have passed since I've felt this pull toward a woman." He brushed a hand over her bare shoulder. "I believe we are caught in destiny's web, brought together to seal a gap in our past. Centuries ago, two young lovers missed their chance. We shall resurrect that moment and make it right."

A light breeze caressed her skin, the silky draft gliding over her neck and through her hair. "What a beautiful thought." Kamali smiled. "Why do you believe we are star-crossed lovers?"

"Because sometimes, when I close my eyes, I see you dressed in buckskin, standing in a field just outside our people's encampment, but your back is always turned and I can't see your face. Still, I know it's you, just waiting to be seen."

Kamali wiped tears from her cheeks. "I was waiting."

"I took a wrong turn, or maybe after all this time, I can finally see I was on the right path all along." Nodin shook his head. "Many years ago, I cared very deeply for another, but after her betrayal, I walked away. She was a crutch. An easy way to escape the Elemental I'd become and all the responsibilities." He sighed before meeting Kamali's gaze. "I was a child, but now I understand the interconnectedness of all things." He brushed a light kiss across her lips. "With you, a sense of finality exists, as if that sunset I've tried so long to reach is now within my grasp. The soft reds and violets, blaring yellows and oranges, are all right here with you." With his thumb, he rubbed a circle on her breastbone before flashing a lopsided grin. "Maybe…I am seeing *your* aura."

Kamali laughed. "If you could see my aura right now, you'd see bright red, representing stimulation and passion." She glanced down at the bed. "I'll admit my changes are frightening. I don't know why I see you so clearly, but I want more and more glimpses. And I want to show you all of me."

He lifted her chin with his forefinger. "May I kiss you now?"

A barely whispered yes crossed her lips just before he drew her closer and kissed her.

She ran her hands along his sculpted chest, eliciting a soft murmur of approval from deep in his throat. Daring and always moving forward, she wasn't hesitant about sliding her hand lower and delving under his loose sweat pants.

He shifted onto his back so she could touch his thick member, but after a moment, he closed his hand over hers. "You understand what will happen if you continue to touch me?"

"Yes, and I want to experience this first with you."

"Kamali, be sure." He squeezed her hand, his gaze intense. "Don't do this out of fear or desperation."

She placed a finger upon his lips. "I am not afraid, but I will admit, I *am* completely desperate." She resumed teasing his erection.

He paid homage to her breasts, stroking each into a beaded tip.

Sharp gasps tore from her throat, and a sensation like lightning rushed to her core.

Hands skillfully shaping and heating her body, Nodin once more captured her lips and pressed their lower bodies together.

Reality was lost with each stroke of his tongue, each enticing plunge.

With a sure hand, he directed her to stroke his cock again. Linking his fingers with her, he taught her what he liked. "That's right, Kamali," he whispered against her neck. "Hold me tight."

"Enough. I want you inside me." After nudging him aside, she shimmied out of her remaining clothes, mounted him, leaned down, and kissed him. The tips of her overstimulated nipples brushed against his bare chest, coursing lust through her body. "I'm so hot right now. Are you sure you aren't the Fire Elemental?"

He held her at arm's length then blew a soft breeze across her wet nipples, her neck, and through her hair.

"Oh, that's nice."

He chuckled and tried shifting her onto her back.

"No." She bent and kissed him, bracing her hands on the mattress. "Let me. Please."

"Kamali, this is your first time." He gripped her upper arms. "I can ease the pain."

She gazed into his sky-blue eyes then gasped as her tears splattered against his cheek.

"Why are you crying?"

"The beauty of this moment, the heat between us, the look in your eye, your burning aura...I can sense everything you're feeling. You really *do* want me."

"And why shouldn't I?" Nodin brushed her hair over her ear. "You're amazingly brave, loyal, and honest. You have tremendous inner strength. Plus, knowing we are connected on an elemental level, that destiny is finally having its due, makes everything more real. So, yes, Kamali, I really do want you." He pulled her down for a kiss, nipping and biting at her lips before laying her on her back and working his way down her body, stopping for what seemed like hours at her breasts, her stomach, her legs, teasing her with pleasure.

He finally drew his tongue across her aching core, and she nearly came. Locking her fingers in his long hair, she moaned when he entered her slick hollow with a finger. Incoherent murmurs poured from her throat as he continued his sensual assault, brushing with his tongue and stroking her insides with that skilled finger. Until...until...

"Nodin. Oh, please." Her back bowed, and she cursed as her entire body juddered and pulsed around his skating fingers. Flying, soaring with pleasure, she gasped for breath before floating down from that orgasmic high, slowly and in a hazy daze of splendor. Though her body still ached to be taken, plundered.

She refrained from laughing, but she did feel like a romance novel heroine laid out on a pirate ship's deck, awaiting her deflowering by the handsome captain. An interesting fantasy for another day.

Fantasy, the perfect word for this moment. She'd dreamed of this day. And now she would become his, in every way. Her heart, her soul, and her body, connected in the past but bonded in the future by the spilling of her blood. Some might think her wanton for surrendering to this man so soon, but he was her mate, and this moment was a consummation of life and love.

"Watching you blossom at my touch, my beautiful Pakali, was the most glorious vision I've ever seen," Nodin whispered against her lips before kissing her again, dispensing any lingering doubt or fear.

Pakali, his flower, and she surely was blooming in his arms. "Take me, now." She arched against him before settling his cock at her slick opening. "I want all of you. Seal us together with my blood upon your body."

He bent and drew her nipple into his mouth while teasing and rocking against her opening. Drawing away, he gazed into her eyes. "I'm usually much more eloquent. Never at a loss for words. But, in this moment, I feel too much urgency. A need to connect. I'm sorry, Kamali, but I want you as I've never wanted another. If I had blood, it'd be boiling under my skin. As it is I'm fighting to stay whole, because you make me want to fly."

And with those words, he bent and kissed her. A passionate kiss that made clear everything he felt. Unrelenting, probing, seeking, and hot, so very hot, his tongue, his lips, his every emotion, boring down against her mouth, and she accepted and returned the intensity.

Breathing heavily, he pulled back, the tip of his cock now resting just inside her entrance. "Look into my eyes, Kamali."

She met his gaze and braced her hands against his shoulders.

"Do you see me?"

"Yes." She fought back tears, as she knew he meant much more than just vision. "I see you as you see me."

"Then in this moment, I claim you as mine." With a single plunge, he slid deep inside her core and murmured words of love in their native tongue. He continued kissing her, gently rocking until she found the pleasure. "Bend your legs for me, Pakali."

She obeyed, on the verge of blooming, like a closed flower bud feeling the sun for the first time. The power of the heated rays warming each silky petal until they burst open, seeking more. "Nodin. I'm...I'm close. There's something...I can't..." She met each thrust until an overwhelming tightness gathered at her core before exploding in a burst of indescribable pleasure.

Shaking and feeling as weak as a wildflower swaying in an open prairie, Kamali fought to breathe as her release breezed through her entire body. Tiny spasms pulsed around his still-thick cock.

He locked his lips to hers and stole her air, replacing it with his own. "Look at me."

Unsure of when she'd closed them, she opened her eyes

"Watch as your body gives me pleasure." Continuing to thrust inside her shivering heat, he met her gaze, his blue eyes intense and his lips a burnished red. "We are one now."

After those words, he seemed to lose control, driving, breaking within her body until after shouting her name, he stilled then…once…twice, with shuddering thrusts, he came.

He kissed her once more softly, reverently, before collapsing half on top of her.

Lost in a haze of bliss, Kamali relaxed underneath him and reveled in his weight upon her body. Her lids grew heavy then as she felt his cock slip from core, she gasped when a thought whipped through her mind. "Oh, no, we didn't use protection."

"What?" Nodin mumbled against her neck.

"A baby. Is it possible?"

"No." He shook his head, his hair tickling her chin. "Elementals can't have children."

"So, what comes out of…you know?"

He chuckled. "Nothing, I experience pleasure but nothing comes out. I have no fluids in my body. Air is my blood."

"Oh."

"Understanding the intricacies of an Elemental body is something I gave up on a long time ago, because the hows and whys of our existence are known only to Mother Nature and she's not talking."

Kamali was quiet for a moment before another thought crossed her mind. "Did you have children when you were human?"

"No."

"I'm sorry." And she was. Still, she refused to let this moment be shadowed by what they couldn't have. Right now she had Nodin, and as she stared deep into his eyes, she understood why love was such a powerful thing. Love could rip your heart from your chest while at the same time be the only thing that kept it beating.

Kamali brushed his long, black hair from the side of his face. Her body on fire, aching for more, and very willing to spend the rest of her days locked in this very room, making love to this man. "Together, we've met fate's decree. You are all I see, until time pulls me from your side."

At her words, he placed a hand over his heart. "Time has no place here."

Overcome by all these new feelings racing through her mind and heart, she pulled him close for a kiss, to seal his words and take them as her own.

Swept away by the heat building between them, she paid no heed to each tick of the clock as once more he led her to that unending stream of love that flowed when two bodies and hearts combined.

CHAPTER 20

Terran leaned against the solid wood table, likely as old as the ancient tomes lining the shelves of the castle's library. "Now that we're all here, we need to discuss our next plan of action."

The smell of old books wafted pleasantly through the room. During Nodin's vast lifetime, he'd spent many an hour, even days, over an open book.

"Kamali needs to eat first." Nodin braced his arm around Kamali's shoulders and kissed the top of her head. He wasn't much of a cook, since all he needed was air, but he could whip up something.

"How did she work up an appetite?" Flint's teasing words fired through Nodin's mind. *"What have you two been up to, Air-boy?"*

Nodin glared at Flint, shaking his head. "Maize needs food, too. Do we have any dog food?"

"Yeah, Pigpen. Some people need sustenance before scheduling destruction." Flint shoved Terran's shoulder. "Kamali needs more than carrots and weeds."

After heaving a heavy sigh, Terran mumbled, "I don't eat weeds."

"I'll refrain from commenting. We'll be back in a few." Nodin bit back a smile before leading Kamali into the kitchen. Though he'd rather ravish her on top of the table, he gently settled her into a chair, all while pushing aside memories of her pleasured gasps and silky skin. He cleared his throat. "What would you like?"

"If there are eggs, Maize and I could eat those. Or we could both eat oatmeal, I suppose…as long as there isn't much sugar in the mix."

Five years ago, after a battle against Quint, this kitchen had been a crumbling mess, but now everything was thoroughly modernized, although the rustic look remained. The stove was still gas and topped with six burners. The butcher-block table set up in the middle was new and massive, checker boarded with various colored woods.

Nodin rummaged through the fridge and decided on scrambled eggs and thick pieces of Irish bread. The biggest copper kettle he'd ever seen was on the stove, waiting to sing and pour its boiled water over fragrant tea leaves. *These Irish love their tea.*

"You cook?" Kamali piped up.

"As you know, I only need air to live, but I've been around long enough to learn a few things." He winked.

"I agree." She blushed and offered a cheeky smile. "You are very, very skilled."

Unwilling to leave that comment unanswered, he sauntered across the kitchen with his hands full of eggs and his pinky wrapped around the handle of a gallon of milk. Stopping before her, he bent and gave her a thorough kiss. "I'd love nothing more than to toss these eggs, lift you up on this table, and show you how very skilled I can be."

With a grin, she eased back and trailed a finger down his cheek. "Will you paddle me with a spatula?"

Lust shot to his groin, and he kissed a path to her ear. "I was thinking the wooden spoon."

Maize wanted some love, too, and placed her front paws on Kamali's lap, licking Nodin's face.

Kamali laughed then ruffled the dog's head. "No spoons and

spatulas, is that right, girl? You want eggs. Is that what you want?"

Nodin kissed Kamali's cheek then headed back toward the stove. He should be grateful for the interruption, because having his Elemental team walk in on him making love to Kamali wasn't something they'd ever let him forget, Flint especially. Too bad his rock-solid cock didn't care.

After clicking on the burner, he dropped a pat of butter in a pan he'd rummaged out of a cabinet. He cracked open the kitchen door. Fresh air would soothe his raging emotions, and hopefully chill his need.

He glanced at Kamali, still gently petting her best friend. "So, you can see me clearer now." He added the mixed eggs and milk to the skillet. "Why do you think that is?"

Maize trotted over to his side.

Poor pup was hungry. "Just a few more minutes, Mazy." After stirring the eggs, he popped two slices of bread into the toaster.

Kamali hummed out a sigh. "I'm not sure about any of these changes. I wish I could speak to Malachi, but we both know that is no longer an option."

While grateful she could better comprehend her surroundings, Nodin wondered why those closest to her had masked her abilities. Wouldn't Adler have gained more with her undiluted gifts? Perhaps by suppressing her, they made her more dependent. But why was that necessary?

The bread popped up from the toaster and startled him from his wayward thoughts. "Maybe you could use glasses." He turned off the burner and then buttered her toast.

"I thought so, too."

His heart broke a little at the hopeful note in her voice. "Then that's what we'll do." He tossed a piece of unbuttered toast to Maize. She caught it in mid-air then swallowed it in one gulp. Nodin sliced two more pieces of bread and dropped them in the toaster.

Kamali sighed. "I don't know."

"Don't know what?"

She shrugged. "As a child, I ran the gamut of eye doctors and specialists. Not pleasant memories."

"I'm sorry for that." He brought her plate to the table before setting Maize's meal on the floor then settled in the seat beside Kamali. "What else has changed?"

"I believe I can read minds now. When I was in the hospital, I had all these voices bombarding my head. I don't know how you can stand it." She bit into the toast.

"Interesting." Realizing Maize needed water, Nodin whisked out of his chair and searched the cabinets until he found a large plastic bowl.

The kettle whistled, so he poured Kamali a cup of Irish breakfast tea.

"Here you are, Mazy." He settled the water bowl by Maize and ruffled the dog's head.

Quiet for a few moments, Kamali finished her breakfast. "Thank you. The eggs were quite filling."

He leaned across the table and wiped a stray crumb from her lips.

"Oh, thank you." She cleared her throat, glancing to the side. "Um…is the tea ready?"

"Absolutely." He blinked then grabbed Kamali's steeping tea off the butcher block "I'm sorry. I got lost in the deep mauve of your lips. I'm afraid the temptation of you will serve as quite the distraction in the coming days."

"I like the thought of that. Coming days. A future." She smiled then frowned. "I-I have something I feel I must say." She shifted in her chair and took a deep breath. "I have seen what I believe is a snippet of the future…a-and what I saw was terrifying."

"Did this vision feature Violet?" Nodin rubbed his hands up and down her chilled arms.

"Yes." Eyes wide, she jerked back. "How did you know?"

"I, too, have the seeing gift, and I've seen Violet struck down in a field." He closed his eyes, but he could not erase the picture in his mind. "Not all my predictions come true. We *will* change the course. Flint cannot...he won't...let's just say, if we lose Violet, we all suffer." Nodin raked his fingers through his hair. "This vision must not come to pass." With a white-knuckled grip, he clenched the side of the table. "She is the strongest of us all, and Flint's very soul."

The air stirred around him, ruffling Kamali's hair. His element surged in response to his emotions.

"The thing is, I also have another vision of Flint and Violet. One I find very hard to comprehend." He shook his head. "I see children."

Gasping, Kamali straightened in her chair. "Upstairs you said you couldn't have children, so how is this possible?"

"I don't know. Plus, I've never experienced conflicting visions before." He studied a spider web in the corner of the window. "Charles Darwin said, in *The Origin of Species*, 'Thus, from the war of nature, from famine and death, the most exalted object which we are capable of conceiving, namely, the production of the higher animals, directly follows. There is grandeur in this view of life, with its several powers, having been originally breathed into a few forms or into one; and that, whilst this planet has gone cycling on according to the fixed law of gravity, from so simple a beginning endless forms most beautiful and most wonderful have been, and are being, evolved'."

"So, you feel the Elementals could represent the higher animals?"

"In a way, perhaps."

"Or maybe it's as simple as nature finds a way. Haven't you ever watched *Jurassic Park*?"

Searching his memory, Nodin furrowed his brow. "The dinosaur movie?"

143

"Yes. The park starts out with all female dinosaurs, but they end up with eggs anyway."

"Eggs, Elementals, I suppose it's all tossed together in some evolutionary basket only people like Darwin can comprehend."

"Things change." Kamali shrugged. "We've changed. It's life. And now that we know more changes are coming, we will prepare." She tipped his chin with her finger and met his gaze.

As he gazed into Kamali's dark brown eyes, no longer opaque, he froze as another premonition tore like a tempest through his mind. *Kamali sat at that Oklahoma diner. Maize at her side. She turned to greet him with eyes full black.* "No." He shot out of his chair.

"Nodin?"

Her voice was a beat louder than usual, as if she'd been saying his name over and over. "I'm sorry." He turned, but avoided meeting her gaze, afraid of what he'd see. He needed a moment, so he grabbed her plate off the table and headed for the sink. What did that vision mean? Why were her eyes black?

"Nodin."

He almost shrieked when Kamali touched his arm. "What is it?"

"Nothing." He held her close, unwilling to consider losing her to Quint's dark essence now that she'd become his. "I'm just concerned about blocking our vision from Flint." Refraining from mentioning he'd have to keep his thoughts from her, too, he smoothed her hair over her shoulder. "Flint's concerned about Violet becoming mortal again once we defeat Quint. I almost believe he doesn't wish to destroy him at all. I understand that feeling, now. I think I would do anything to keep you safe." Nodin held her tighter, fighting against the vision of those dark eyes.

With all the uncertainty surrounding him, all the possible future changes and dangers, Nodin blocked all that out and let thoughts of her writhing in his arms erase his concerns.

Violet would survive.

Kamali would not be overtaken.

He must have hope.

And love.

With his hips, he nudged Kamali against the cabinets. "I want you again." He kissed a path from her jaw to her ear then down her neck. "What do you want?"

"You." Thick, dark lashes hid her eyes. "But, I'm frightened of what will come."

"For too long, I've taken life for granted." He held her face between his hands. "I must blow past all regret and sorrow. You've given me the strength to do that, Kamali." He kissed her forehead. "After all my breezy days, lost in the sky, floating along in my own self-importance, you've helped me see...I still have much to learn."

Kamali nodded and bit her bottom lip before gripping his wrists where his hands were locked on her cheeks. "Ah, but right now how about you become the teacher?"

He blew a soft breeze through her hair then caressed her breast through the thin T-shirt. "Let's start our lesson on the various uses of a wooden spoon and a spatula."

CHAPTER 21

Slumped and sated in Nodin's arms, Kamali tried to summon a modicum of embarrassment over her current predicament, breathless and half-naked on the castle's kitchen table. Yet, all she could think was—Nodin sure did serve up a fine breakfast.

"I'm sorry," he murmured against her ear. "I should have more respect for you than this."

"I'm fine...you respected me quite well." She giggled then together they burst out laughing.

"Nodin." Terran called from the direction of the kitchen entryway. "We've got a game plan. Come out when you're ready."

Still laughing, Kamali buried her face in the fall of Nodin's hair.

He pinched her side. "Come on, temptress, let's see what the chief has planned." Smiling, he met her gaze and kissed her once more.

A soft, seeking kiss. One of gratitude and quiet promises. Then he scooted her off the table and helped tug up her pants. While adjusting his own pants, more kissing followed, but she pulled away before she forgot her duties and begged Nodin to take her to bed. "I feel I should apologize, because I'm insatiable."

Nodin drew her closer and winked. "I don't mind."

"I think after twenty-three years of little to no affection, I'm gorging myself." She slipped her hands around his waist. "But I refuse to feel guilt or shame. I'm doing this."

"All right, then." Nodin kissed her once more as if he had all the time in the world to slide his tongue across hers, to tilt his head and get the angle of their lips just right.

Damn, this man knows how to melt a woman.

When she tried to wrap her leg around his hip, she watched him ease back. "Ah...you're no fun." She laughed. "I think we should see what we could do with that honey on the counter." She licked her lips. "Shall we?"

He glanced at the honey, then the door, and then the honey again. "I must be insane, but we do have to go, or Terran will drag us out by our ears."

"I know you're right, but that honey does look really good." She swatted his butt then whistled for Maize.

Nodin grabbed her from behind. "We'll find out how good later."

"Oh no." She wagged a finger. "Offer is only good within the next minute."

He bumped her bottom with his sizable erection. "Believe me, you'll need longer than a minute." This time, *he* spanked her ass and, while chuckling, led her to the door.

With each step, she sensed a change in his energy. Twisting his hair up into a ponytail at the top of his head, he shifted from a lover to a warrior. Due to her blindness, she hated admitting when she needed someone, but with Nodin, she freely conceded her life was richer and more complete. Yet, so many things stood in the way of their happiness. But, no matter. She'd grasp the now and not for one moment dwell on a future she could not escape.

She grabbed his arm. "Nodin, before we join the others, I want you to understand something. These moments with you may have been drawn by destiny's hand, but I willingly follow her path. No matter what comes, I chose you."

"I chose you, too." Nodin kissed her forehead then sighed

while glancing at the library. "We better go hear Terran's plan, even though he and Violet have been discussing it for five years." He took her elbow and led her down the hall.

"What's their plan?"

"Massive fire balls, an electromagnetic field, black holes, gravity, other dimensions."

"Say what?" Kamali halted. Those words required an after-school special to understand.

"Exactly. Mind blown." With his fingers, Nodin mocked an explosion coming out of his brain. "I'm not much on physics, but those mega-brains think their plan will work."

"Then we will believe, too." Kamali nodded. "All energy is connected. We must stand with them and project our hope and positive belief in their mission."

"I believe." Nodin brought her hand to his lips for a quick kiss. "I hope."

She nudged Maize forward. Her guide dog was still necessary, since she could not easily detect objects like tables or chairs. All sure ways to trip her up and knock her down. She kept a tight grip on Nodin's arm and knew he would never lead her astray.

Except on kitchen tables.

She was unable to stifle her laugh.

"What's funny?"

"Nothing."

Nodin hummed, but he didn't press her further.

CHAPTER 22

Sitting in the library with a fresh cup of tea in her hands, Kamali breathed deep of the musty smell of old books. She wished to escape in a complex story, perhaps a mystery with a hint of romance, but none of these were printed in Braille and she could read no other way.

"Violet and Flint are...um...resting," Terran informed them. "She and I have been over this plan a million times. But since you are new to this, Kamali, we felt we should educate you on our plan to defeat Quint."

Nodin led her to sit beside Maya.

The water-girl's aura glowed with pride.

"I imagine you are quite beautiful, Maya, but I don't really know. I can see your blonde hair and make out the blue of your eyes, but does that make you pretty?"

"Oh," Maya cried. "I'm not sure how to answer that. I think we each are beautiful in our own way."

"She's absolutely gorgeous," Terran interjected. "She has thick, blonde hair that waves around her shoulders. Her eyes are the color of the ocean, a clear unending blue. You dive in and never want to surface. Her smile is open and kind. She is taller than most women, but fits perfectly at my side. I won't describe her body, as that might distract me from my purpose." He chuckled. "Just know, she has curves in all the right places."

Kamali smiled.

"May I describe Terran, since he so kindly described me?" Maya bounced in her seat.

"Yes, please," Kamali answered, happy she had brought up the topic.

"First, thank you, my love. I am flattered at your version of my appearance." Maya made a kissing sound then hummed. "Let's see. How can I describe Terran?" She wiggled in her chair. "As he said, he is taller than I, although I'm not sure I know his proper height. He has thick brown hair and these brown eyes that remind you of a sad hound dog. His shoulders are broad. His muscles well-toned. He is my home, my everything. All wrapped up in a single package." Maya laughed. "A very nice package."

"Maya," Terran's voice took on a chiding tone.

"Let's move on from talk of packages." Nodin shook his head.

"Well, she asked." Maya flashed a cheeky grin. "I was just making clear that Terran has—"

"Enough, Maya. I've seen Terran's package a thousand times. And I really don't want Kamali envisioning such things, so let's go back to our original reason for being here, shall we?" Nodin waved a hand as he leaned against something, perhaps a table, which looked like a brown blur to Kamali.

"Yes." Terran sniffed. "Let's move on."

Maya giggled and took Kamali's hand.

"Our plan is to lure Quint to an open area, like our land in Colorado."

"With the amount of energy he and Violet will be generating, we can't have any humans around," Maya jumped in. "The heat will be too intense. The light too bright."

Terran paced next to Nodin. "I lost focus when our cabin was destroyed. Then, dealing with Raven and rescuing you from the hospital, I needed to take a breath and remember our plan.

Take each day steadily and not allow my emotions to rule my actions."

"Terran and Violet have spent hours working on equations and they came up with the idea to compress Quint's matter, like a dying star," Maya added.

"Our science is sound." Terran continued in his circuit back and forth through the library. "We plan to create a black hole within Violet's electromagnetic field. We'll superheat atoms and they'll vibrate, creating heat and energy, stripping off electrons and jamming neutrons and protons together. Then we'll draw Quint inside with the intense gravitational pull until he's trapped inside another dimension."

Kamali had done well in biology, but chemistry, physics, and all those other mind-boggling how-the-universe-works concepts remained a mystery. If Terran and Violet believed the plan would work, then she would trust that as fact. No sense getting a headache pondering neutrons and electrons, let alone the composition of dark matter. Or how Quint evolved. Or continued to exist. Or anything else about this crazy world. "What'd ya think, Maize?" Kamali rubbed her dog's head. "Seems hard to comprehend."

"Tell me about it," Maya huffed under her breath. "I've had to listen to this mumbo jumbo for five years."

"This mumbo jumbo will save lives," Terran scolded. "We will end Quint, essentially forever."

"I know," Maya cooed at her earth-man then whispered into Kamali's ear. "He's a tad sensitive about his brain matter."

"Maya." Terran filled that one word with exasperation and love. "Be serious."

"I try. I really do, but the thought of you facing off against Quint again…it…it tears at my very soul. What if I were to lose you? I cannot bear it." Cringing, Maya released a pained whisper, "I will not survive without you, so I must be lighthearted for a time. I must smile and affect an air of nonchalance, or I shall dissolve and never be whole again."

A slight mist filled the air before a wash of heat warmed Kamali's side.

Terran knelt at Maya's side. "I will not leave you."

"You cannot know this as fact." Maya's voice shook.

"I do."

"No, you don't."

Kamali squirmed in her seat, her heart aching for this couple. Their love stirred through the air. Clear even to one who could not see.

She had always believed she could survive anything life tossed in her path, but now she realized there were moments that could rip apart everything and leave her broken and incomplete.

Because her own heart couldn't take the unease circulating throughout the room, Kamali cleared her throat. "As I understand, you feel you should return to Colorado. Well, I am worried about my remaining family, so I—" She swayed in her seat as a wash of hatred ripped through her mind, and her head pounded with a searing bolt of pain that shot back and forth between her temples. Upon closing her eyes, she saw a gravel road nestled between two thick hedgerows.

"Raven's outside." Kamali gasped as she clearly saw her aunt's raging orange-black aura beside...beside..."Oh, no, she's got Sawni." Shooting upright, she gazed into Nodin's blue eyes, searching for something, anything, answers, prayers, hope this wouldn't turn out like a bloody horror film. Kamali gripped her guide dog's handle. "Maize, door."

"Where do you think you're going?" Nodin caught her arm.

"Do *not* ask me to stay here while that woman has my friend."

"What's wrong?" Heat filled the room as Flint arrived.

"Raven is outside the grounds with Sawni, Kamali's friend," Terran answered.

The Elementals were quiet for a moment.

"I know what you're doing. Don't shut me out," Kamali huffed. "I'm the only one who is safe from Raven's power. She can control your gifts, remember?"

Her aunt's vibe raged stronger than before. Harder. More intent and sharp like a blade. What would Raven do to Sawni? Why bring her here? "I have to go. Raven's changed somehow. She was malicious before, but now I sense a blank slate, one she wishes to coat with blood." Kamali bent at the waist as that foul thought shot through her mind from nowhere and everywhere. Blood. The scent, the stickiness, the deep red all seemed to cloak her senses.

"Kamali, listen to me." Nodin held her in place. "Wards are all around this castle and this land."

"Yes, for those of us inside. Sawni is outside of that protection." She yanked her hand away. "You think those wards are strong, but even now I sense Raven's inky claws trying to seep into you, control you. The dark aura has waded past whatever you've devised and seeks only to destroy."

Dark fingers reached for each Elemental's form, but bounced off, shriveling back. Repelled somehow.

Nodin clasped her shoulders. "We possess wards within our bodies."

"How?" She met his gaze, digging deep within the walls he'd erected. She broke through and something muddy yellow, indicating regret, drifted past. "What have you done? I don't want to, but I'll dig out the truth. Please, explain why Raven can no longer control you."

"Kamali, we only did it because we had to." He lifted up his hands then let them fall.

"Did what? You're wasting time, Nodin. Time Sawni doesn't have." With a glare, she opened the library door and stepped into the foyer then glanced over her shoulder. "Explain on the way down."

"It's not that simple."

Furious at his equivocating, she shrieked, "Nodin, just spit it out already!"

"We drank your blood."

CHAPTER 23

"You did what?" Kamali shoved both hands against his chest.

"Buddha says—"

"No." Kamali shoved again. "Don't you dare Buddha me."

He swallowed and tried not to remember the wash of her blood over his tongue. "Listen, Violet found a spell and when you were in the hospital, she obtained a sample."

"A sample." She glared, hands braced on her hips.

"Yes."

Kamali turned and shouted, "Did you all get a piece of me, then?"

"Kamali." Terran came to her side. "I understand why this may be distressing, but let's deal with your aunt and then discuss this…ah…issue another time."

"How do you know this isn't another one of your theories? Plus, I didn't think any of you had a lick of blood flowing through your veins."

Nodin rubbed his temple. "The composition of our bodies is—"

"Pfffttttt…I don't want to know." She stuck up a hand, palm out. "While the whole concept of you drinking my blood is quite disgusting, I agree Raven poses a much larger problem. She's pushing against my-my…blood barrier."

"I thought you wanted to help?" Maya drew Kamali outside.

"I do," Kamali huffed. "I'm sorry. I was shocked."

"And rightly so," Maya continued. "Now, let's go show Raven we have a few tricks of our own."

"Kamali…I don't think you should face off against your aunt." Nodin kept pace beside Maya and Kamali. "We don't have any clue what she could do to you."

"I will go. Sawni will need me."

He hesitated. Having his woman, a mortal woman at that, join in their fight wasn't something he'd foreseen. While fine with her detecting ill will, he wasn't comfortable with her actually facing their foes.

And yet, a much stronger danger lurked in the shadows, one they would all have to stand against. So, maybe, he should take Mother's words to heart, and let Kamali experience life through his eyes, be her guide. "All right, but stay by my side."

Already far down the path, Terran and Flint led the way across a bright green meadow before stopping at the edge where grass met the road.

Nodin considered that barrier. How in this moment Kamali had made her choice, whether she realized it or not. He'd been fighting Quint for centuries and would never wish that upon another, but his woman stood strong.

This moment would define her, would change her in subtle ways. She would come to see that those aligned with Quint had no mercy, no soul. She'd see true darkness.

He stayed right beside her, bare feet planted firmly in the grass as they faced off against their new foe. He hoped with all his heart that Kamali's friend would not become one more victim in this endless battle.

In a black dress more fit for a cocktail party than an old Irish road, Raven clutched Sawni at her side.

A cab idled a ways down, waiting off to the side.

Nodin drifted into Sawni's mind but found nothing but a gray wall, as if she'd been drugged.

"What did you do to her?" Kamali stepped forward. "Her aura is all wrong, gray and sick."

Nodin took her hand and drew her beside him. "Stay back."

"I see you've resorted to primal magic to deter my gifts." Raven's voice slithered across the gravel. "I've simply come to deliver a message. These trivial walls you've erected wouldn't stop me if I really wanted to play."

Kamali shivered at his side and then she rubbed her temples. "Nice try, but I can keep you out."

Raven merely arched a brow. "Kamali, your family is very displeased at your abandonment. You've left them open to Quint's devices. He'll leave your family be, if you return home *and* deliver his pretty Violet."

Flint's hands burst into flames. "Leave. Now."

"Calm down. Personally, I couldn't give a shit about your electromagnetic witch." Raven smirked then glanced at Kamali. "Aren't you the least bit curious about the power thrumming through your body? Curious as to why it was hidden for so long? I have the answers, and I can teach you to become so much more." Raven's smile turned acid as she glanced from Nodin back to Kamali. "Do not become your mother. Fawning over a man for whom you will always be second best. For your father, his primary focus was drugs and alcohol, and for this Elemental, he'll always hold his duties over you. Not only that, you *will* die."

A skull flashed in Nodin's vision, but whose? He glanced at Sawni, but she just swayed in place beside Raven. Were the drugs hiding something else? Something more sinister? He tuned back in to Raven's speech.

"I'll give a demonstration of one of your gifts. We can enter minds." Raven ran a red-tipped nail across Sawni's forehead. "We can make them see anything we wish. Make them believe...they are drowning."

Sawni tumbled to the ground and grabbed her throat, choking and gasping as her face flushed red before paling to almost light blue.

"No." Kamali gasped and lunged forward.

Nodin gripped her arm. "Kamali, don't pass the barrier. Stay within the wards."

"See? He's already controlling you. Doesn't care that your dear friend will die."

"Terran, Maya, Flint, glean with me. Together, we can block Raven." After sending that mental message, Nodin fought past Raven's influence and entered Sawni's mind.

With his Elemental partners using all their skill, they released her from the fake block in her throat.

So focused was he on Sawni, he hadn't realized Kamali had left his side.

She now stood toe-to-toe with Raven. "I don't need you to teach me anything. I know exactly who I am." Kamali clutched her aunt by the throat. "You want to experience choking? A sensation of helplessness? I'll be happy to teach you."

Maya shook Nodin's arm. "Stop her. You can't let her hurt her aunt."

Nodin drew a deep breath then released a strong wind against Kamali. "Let Raven go."

"She has to pay." Kamali's clothes billowed around her body, but she kept her focus on Raven.

"Don't let her death be on your conscience." Nodin blew a softer breeze, a light, calming caress through her hair.

"She's a blight." Kamali shook her head. "She'll never stop."

This time Kamali did turn and meet his gaze, and the little trickster tried using her gifts against him. He had no wards against Kamali, never thought he'd need them. A slight sting whispered through his heart, but then he considered this was her first battle. Her first chance to use those powers now coursing through her body. Yet, he was not the enemy here, and he wouldn't let her do something he knew she'd regret once the battle high was gone.

Still, he had to admit Kamali's gleaning power did have him considering walking back to the castle, just as she wished. "Don't do this to me, Kamali. You may be desperate for revenge, but don't use your mind tricks to push me away." He caught her eye and whispered through her mind. *This is not who you are. You are a builder, not a destroyer. Get out of my head. I will not leave you.*

"She is evil."

"Many in this world are evil." He stayed focused on Kamali, blocking her attempts to alter his will. *"We are not their judge and jury. You are no better than her if you use your gifts to control others."*

"I'm sorry." Kamali slumped and loosened her hold on Raven. "I lost control."

Nodin broke eye contact and rubbed his temples. "We'll discuss this later." He might have to break out the wooden kitchen spoon and pink her bottom after this latest infraction.

"The apple doesn't fall far from the tree," Raven choked out, rubbing her throat. "You have about as much control as your mother did, and an equally bad record at making your man happy. Although, I do applaud your attempt at restraining him. Good going, dear." She laughed, which came out more of a wheezing rasp. "Perhaps, if your mother had fought with equal abandon, she'd still be alive."

"I'll not let you bait me again." Kamali called Maize to her side. "Nodin, will you help Sawni inside, please?"

Unable to speak, he nodded. Still slightly disappointed in her, yet fighting the fact that same fiery nature turned him on.

Terran and Flint led Raven toward the castle.

Maya followed behind, mumbling under her breath about fires, and cabins, and stupid black birds who thought they were so clever.

Kamali wrapped her arm around Sawni's shoulders. "Nodin, will you help me?" She jerked back, eyes wide as she studied her friend. "Something isn't right."

Suddenly, Sawni convulsed and lurched forward, black ooze pouring from her mouth.

"Sawni?" Kamali knelt beside her friend. "What's wrong?"

Nodin whipped to her side. Quint had claimed yet another innocent victim. How would he explain this to Kamali? She was already on edge and ready to strike out against Raven.

"Nodin, what is happening to Sawni?" Eyes full of fear, Kamali clutched Sawni's deflating form in her arms.

"You stupid Elementals." Raven's words tore across the castle's front grounds. "You defy Quint, knowing there will be consequences. Sawni just paid the price for your defiance. Give him Violet and this all ends."

"Is this true?" Kamali asked, her voice barely above a whisper. "Nodin, please, her aura is gone. Where did it go?"

"Nodin, take her inside." Maya had returned and he hadn't even heard her approach. "I will care for your friend, Kamali. Please, you shouldn't witness this." Maya scanned the castle grounds then glared at the car waiting down the path. "I'll check on the driver, but I'm gleaning he's just a local cabbie."

"No." Kamali surged to her feet. "I-I don't understand. What happened to her? Nothing is left."

Maya shot Nodin a glance before answering, "Sawni was infected by Quint's seed and has passed. The human body cannot contain even a portion of what he is. Unfortunately, this is the result when he overcomes a human. They simply dissipate." She patted Kamali's shoulder, tentative, as if afraid she'd lash out at her touch. "I'm very sorry."

Kamali visibly swallowed before a low, keening wail poured from her throat, and she fell to her knees.

Nodin pulled her into his arms, breezed across the field, entered the library, and sat with her in the rocking chair before the fire.

Flickering yellow and orange, the flames stretched high in the massive two-sided stone fireplace.

Raven's shouts echoed through the stone walls as Terran and Flint led her deeper into the castle to what he hoped was a cold, dark dungeon.

"I couldn't really see." Sobbing, Kamali pounded a fist against his chest. "I don't even have a clear face to mourn. All-all I-I could see was a black, blurry blob, but her aura was pure and kind. Why her?" Her voice staccato as she poured out her grief. "Why didn't I see him inside her? I'm supposed to see."

Though unsure of that answer himself, he tossed out his only theory. "I think the drugs masked Quint's presence. And he wasn't fully inside her. He planted a small seed. After we chased him off last time, we spent the next few years fighting off all those small remnants he'd left in humans." He rocked them back and forth in the chair until she stilled.

Kamali breathed with short surges, as if trying to catch her breath after running a long race.

"Quint is a parasite. He has a form but with no defining features. He uses humans to mesh with the world and its inhabitants. But, as Maya said, the human body is not equipped to contain dark matter. Even the smallest drop of Quint's being will destroy its host." He swallowed hard while recalling the flash of Kamali's pure black eyes in his vision. Kissing the top of her head, he held her tighter and rested his cheek against her soft hair. "I'm sorry...there was nothing we could do."

For a long moment, the only sounds in the room were the crackling fire and the creaks from the old wooden rocking chair.

Kamali sighed, and then sang an old tribal song about lifting the dead to the Great Spirit.

Nodin closed his eyes and joined her, finding comfort in the tradition of their people.

After the song ended, she rested her head against his chest while he continued to sing songs he hadn't voiced in hundreds of years. This woman drew parts of his native self to the surface. Not native as the pale faces had labeled them, but native as in the man he'd been born to become. His father's son. A Chickasaw chief.

For too long, he'd let the other Elementals bear the brunt of the fight against Quint, but now was his time. An inner strength surfaced while holding this brave woman in his arms. A return to those days when he was a warrior, preparing to fight for his land and his people. Kamali, the Elementals—they were his people now. He would no longer turn to philosophy for reason in this unreasonable world.

Time and the forces of nature had turned against him.

But he was Nodin, Air Elemental.

He'd reverse the winds of change and sway the flow back in their direction.

He would not lose her…would not let her eyes turn black.

CHAPTER 24

Two days after the death of her friend, Kamali mentally prepared for the moment she'd again face Raven. Rocking in the castle's library chair, her favorite spot, she contemplated her next step. A face-to-face confrontation was inevitable now that Kamali had a stronger grip on her emotions.

Guilt still assailed her over their deception of Sawni's family. She'd lied and stated her friend was visiting. Once their fight with Quint was over, they'd agreed that all four Elementals would visit Sawni's family and explain everything that had happened, except…they wouldn't have a body.

Explaining that and the circumstances of Sawni's death were not par for the course for beings who were meant to live in secret. But in this instance, the Elementals felt that, due to the tribe's understanding of Mother Earth's spirituality and purpose, they would comprehend the struggle that had occurred the day of their daughter's death.

Still, understanding or not, Sawni's death was senseless and absolutely pointless in the larger scheme. That fueled her anger, but Kamali would not be controlled by that emotion again. Not after using her gifts to manipulate Nodin. Never again would she succumb to the dark thoughts that lived inside her mind. Controlling her gifts was the order of the day, and to do so she needed a deeper understanding of herself.

One woman held the answers. And she *would* answer.

The Elementals had kept her aunt confined in the west wing of the castle, which, according to Violet, hadn't been refurbished in decades and was likely cold and damp.

Such a pity.

Nodin had explained how Violet and Eamon frequently joined hands and stood outside Raven's door, murmuring stronger and stronger enchantments, which kept her aunt's energies suppressed.

No further discussion took place of using Kamali's blood as a ward.

Would they need a fresh batch? Not a pleasant thought.

Grimacing, she bit her bottom lip and studied Nodin sitting in the chair at her side. He'd been her strength these past few days, holding her as she cried. Last night he'd made love to her so gently and with such utter devotion, he'd soothed her grieving heart. He had only sought to hold her, but she'd wanted to feel alive. Even now, though he had a book spread before him, she knew his attention was on her. While she hated to disturb their cozy environment, she realized they needed to move forward. "I need to speak to Raven. I have questions."

Nodin placed his finger on a point in his book then met her gaze. "She'll lie."

"I agree, so I've spoken to Violet about a compulsion spell. She believes I can make it work."

Nodin sighed and closed his book.

"Violet believes I am stronger than Raven, because my mother was the oldest and I inherited her energies. I'm quite certain Raven somehow stole my mother's extra gifts, and I wonder if I could steal them back." Over the past couple of days, she'd noted everyone tiptoed around her, pampering her, likely feeling they shouldn't upset her during her time of grief. But whimpering in corners was not in her nature. Finding solutions to any and all roadblocks was how she'd lived her life and how she planned to continue.

So she would make clear to Nodin she wanted the rough edges, wanted to free her savage side. If she were to stand strong against a vicious woman like Raven, she needed someone to bring out the same in her mind, heart…and body.

From under her lashes, she peeked at Nodin, her body heated and more than ready. Prepping for battle made her mad with lust. "Nodin, before we visit my aunt, I would ask something of you."

"What is it?"

"Come closer, please." She refrained from flashing a wicked grin.

"Yes?" He stood before her in low-slung jeans and a blue T-shirt that highlighted the color of his eyes.

And, since his placement perfectly aligned with her plan, she leaned forward and bit his cock through his jeans.

"Kamali." He jerked back and glanced around. "What are you doing?"

"Biting you." She drew him back to her then undid the zipper before pulling out his thick shaft and drawing her tongue across the tip.

A breath whistled through his teeth. "Anyone could walk in."

"I don't care." She widened her mouth and swallowed him deeper.

He clenched his hands in her hair. "I don't, either."

She slid her mouth and tongue up and down, all while working her hand in tandem with her lips.

"Kamali." Nodin drew her hair away from her face. "That's good, love. Take all of me."

His hips joined in the sliding motion, so she let her hand fall away to massage his sac. She rolled them in her grip, eliciting a sharp gasp.

"Pull back. I-I…I'm gonna come."

She cupped his balls and nipped the tip of his cock before once more taking him deep.

After releasing a groan, his body jerked as he came.

Dropping to her knees before her chair, she laid back and spread open her arms. "I don't want you to make love to me, Nodin. I want hard and carnal. Take me to the edge and push me over."

Nodin raised a brow before glancing at the library door. "You may want to revel in your wild nature, but I think we'll do so with a blanket beneath your body. Stand up a minute." He helped her up, pulled a couple blankets from a large basket beside the chairs, and then placed them on the floor. "There. Your bed awaits, but first…" He bent and kissed her, not tame, not hesitant.

Lost in the dueling of their tongues, she released a soft cry when he pulled away and disappeared into air.

His clothes fell to the ground before he returned to his human form and tugged her to their make-shift bed. "I wish that trick would work for you, as well." Grinning, he lifted her shirt over her head then shimmied off her pants and socks. "Now we can begin." After bracing his body above her, he leaned down and kissed her again.

Kamali reveled in the heat and in the soft brush of their bodies rustling together, his skin warm against hers. She skated her hands up and over his shoulders then arched against him. "Take me. I'm ready."

"Are you?" He tested her assertion with two fingers, plunging deep before he spread her knees wide and entered her. "This what you wanted, Kamali? Deeper, without mercy?" He thrust hard over and over, gliding within her core before stopping and slanting down to kiss her mouth, her neck, her breasts.

"Please, Nodin. I need you to move."

"I'm not moving within you, Pakali." He breathed against her neck. "I'm taking, fucking you, until you scream my name."

She locked her ankles around his lower back and nudged him

deeper. "Yes, that's…exactly…what I need."

He reared up and rocked against her relentlessly, endlessly, until the waves of oblivion came, crashing, thundering through her body. As predicted, she shouted his name while raging across each undulating swell.

He, too, broke with a roar then shuddered against her.

She shivered as he surged forward with a single final plunge and her very blood melted, dissolving into another round of seemingly never-ending bliss.

He lifted from his sprawl over her body but did not pull from her core. Again he kissed her, feral and raw then pressed two fingers against her clit, slowly nudging his half-hard cock into her body.

His warrior nature now released, he pleasured her with his mouth and fingers until she cried out again, rocketing into pulsing pleasure.

Though sure she could endure no more, she shifted with him as he settled her onto her side, her back to his chest. Then he bent her leg over his hip, spread her, and then entered her from behind, whispering endearments in her ear and caressing the tips of her breasts.

"I can't," she panted as another orgasm teased and waited just out of reach.

"Oh, but you will. I'll not stop until you beg." With his fingers, he once more stroked her wet lower lips with one hand, then squeezed and pulled on her sensitive nipples with the other. He kissed her neck and plunged within her, holding her body tight against his.

No escape.

She begged for the impending explosion, for the stars that erupted behind her lids. In an attempt to stay grounded, she grabbed his teasing finger, brought it to her mouth, and sucked the tip until she clenched and came once more, squeezing his driving cock.

"Oh, that's hot." He pushed her forward onto her stomach and drove into her from behind, pulling her hips at an angle as he murmured in their native tongue.

Overstimulated, she bit her lip as the combination of his touch and deep plunge did exactly as she asked, pushed her over an edge until she fell and fell with nothing to break her fall. Lost to sensation, she let herself fly.

Shouting her name, Nodin stilled before delivering one final plunge. He gripped her hair in his hand and shuddered against her. Breathing with heavy pants, he collapsed against her back then rolled until they rested side by side.

"I'm begging now." Kamali huffed out a breath. "No more."

Nodin kissed her shoulder. "We'll see. If I want to go again, I will have you."

"And where has this side of your sexuality been all this time?" She arched a brow.

"You were a virgin." He shrugged. "There were considerations."

Closing her eyes for a moment, Kamali simply enjoyed the tingles still surging through her body.

The ancient grandfather clock nestled in the library's corner chimed twelve times, reminding her of her purpose in this whole sex fest. She heaved a sigh before pulling the arm Nodin had slung over her waist up to her chest and kissing his knuckles. "I must return to Oklahoma. I cannot leave my uncle and two remaining cousins defenseless. Quint is knocking off my family like dominos set up on a death board."

"I'd rather the outside world not interfere with this moment."

"I'd rather my friend wasn't dead. Two friends, counting Waya." She cursed and glared at the clock, ticking away moments from her life. "I long for release from this pain, but my mind won't stop spinning." Kamali turned to meet his gaze. "Are the Elementals planning to retrieve my uncle and cousins?"

"Yes, since you must discuss this now." He flicked the tip of her nose with a finger. "Terran and I are going."

"I want to come with you." She shifted to face him, sliding her leg between his thighs.

"No. You'll stay here." Nodin held her chin between his forefinger and thumb. "Terran and I can fly in and out, literally. Plus, we'll divide the weight."

Kamali laughed and shook her head.

"What's so funny?" Nodin tickled her side.

"I just pictured my uncle's face when he realizes he's not the one in charge."

"Hmm…how about you picture your face, when you realize I'm in charge?" Licking his lips, Nodin flashed a wicked grin before nudging her with his hard cock.

"And how would I do that?" She wrapped one hand around his shoulder, eager for what he had in mind.

"How about I show you?"

By the time the embers in the fireplace died out, Kamali had a very clear picture of what it meant when Nodin took the reins and led her soaring through the sky.

CHAPTER 25

Though Kamali had searched through Violet's closet and found a fleece jacket and sweatpants, she still felt a chill as Nodin led her down the castle's drafty corridor.

"I don't trust her." Nodin squeezed her elbow.

While appreciating the sentiment, she didn't need negative energies or doubt drifting into her consciousness. Her mind needed to be clear on one thing—she was stronger than her aunt. "I am not afraid of her. She will not overcome me, or you, again."

The click of Maize's nails against the stone floor and the jangle of her collar were the only sounds echoing down the hall.

"This section of the castle really is remote." Kamali gripped Maize's handle tighter.

Nodin huffed out a laugh. "Only the finest accommodations for your aunt."

"Are we close?" Kamali ignored the butterflies stirring in her belly. No fear. Only pure determination in discovering the whys of Sawni's death.

Nodin slowed then halted. "Raven is on the other side of this door." He gripped Kamali's upper arms. "If at any time I feel she is a threat, I will remove you, whether you like it or not." He kissed her forehead. "I won't have you harmed, and that means emotionally, too, not just physically."

Nodding her acceptance, Kamali gazed into his clear blue eyes. "I trust you to do what is right."

He brushed her hair over her ear then turned to her guide dog. "Maize, lie down. We'll be right back." He ruffled the dog's head before he opened the door and followed Kamali into the room.

Upon entering, she searched for her aunt's muddy orange aura and her form, but she only detected an absence, as if all Raven's powers were shielded and in their place was nothing but an empty hollow. "Clever, but I can still detect where you are." And Kamali did.

Raven was to the right, sitting in a chair with red-chipped paint.

Her aunt's aura had turned a deep orange-brown with black specks. These specks were clear evidence of a sick mind.

"Well now," Raven sneered. "You *are* coming into your own." She sniffed. "And isn't that cute, she's fallen in love."

Not daring to glance at Nodin, as neither had uttered those words, Kamali clenched her jaw. "I'm here to find answers. What did Malachi do to me, and why? Why mask my gifts? What purpose did that serve?"

Raven's aura shifted as she stood and began to pace. "Adler didn't like the power your mother held over his brother. When you were born he didn't want a repeat so, after a series of events, including the part where I took your mother's gifts, Adler got you...though a...tamed version."

Nodin took her hand and squeezed.

"You say you 'took her gifts'." Kamali arched her brow. "I doubt the taking was anything but harmless."

"Your mother was a waste. An alcoholic and an addict. She was lost to everything but love for your father. She'd do anything for him." Raven paused before delivering her blow. "Which did have me wondering sometimes, just how did they get all that money for drugs, when they had so little...hmm?"

Kamali narrowed her eyes. This woman's barbs missed their mark. Who her parents were twenty-plus years ago, didn't matter. She'd loved them. End of story.

"Raven, that's enough." Nodin tugged Kamali to his side.

"And what will you do, Air-boy? Blow me over?" Raven huffed out a laugh then released a long put-upon sigh. "Her parents didn't appreciate her abilities." She yawned, patting her hand over her mouth. "So, when I discovered your mother on the edge of death, I took them. I have no regrets." Raven's aura turned a lighter orange. "Dying after drinking and leaving you home all alone."

Kamali held back tears. The night of their death, her parents *had* left a tiny three-year old, abandoned for an addiction. Still, something didn't ring quite true. "Raven, you are not worthy of these gifts, either. You've done nothing to support the earth and its people. The moment you stole those gifts from your sister, you lost your soul."

"That would only matter if I believed in such things." Raven sniffed and flicked her long, red-tipped nails through the air as if waving away all guilt.

Kamali delved farther into her aunt's aura. Hidden deep was a seed of regret. "You believe."

Raven's heels clicked across the floor. "You can't see as much as you'd like, dear niece. You may be aware of your gifts now that Malachi has succumbed to Quint, but I've been at this game a lot longer, and I'm not afraid to pull the trigger. You, Kamali, will never fully embrace what you are, because you do not see both sides of the coin. I flip back and forth, at will. Dark and light, I choose whichever serves my purpose."

"No." Kamali jabbed a finger at her aunt. "Your days of freedom without consequence are over."

"Is that so?"

"I'd show you, but you're right, I'm not like you. I'll save my energy for a worthier foe, like Quint."

"Oh, you naïve idiot." Raven roared out a laugh. "You'll never defeat him. No matter what secret devices, science tricks, or ancient spells your Elemental friends use. Understand this, you'll never completely contain him."

"What makes you believe we wish to contain him? Are you looking for a partner in this cell? Shall we fetch him for you?" Though she went on the attack, Kamali's stomach churned. Had her aunt somehow discovered their plan to stop Quint? Had she warned him? Was that part of their plan, to get her mind-reading aunt within these walls to snoop?

Kamali did her best to keep her thoughts masked, blocking the woman from entering her mind. Though, she wasn't sure how much Raven could or couldn't detect in Nodin and the other Elementals' minds. Plus, other humans lived in the castle, those who cooked and cleaned for Eamon.

Just then, her aunt nudged around the outskirts of her mind, like a sharp tack stabbing a balloon. "Stay out of my head, Raven." After breathing deeply, Kamali expelled her aunt's continued plunges against her mental matter. "Shall we get back to the point of this conversation? Why you and Malachi felt masking my gifts necessary?"

"Pay attention. I already answered that question. I said, ask your uncle. Now it's my turn to ask questions. How much longer will I be forced to suffer in this brick hovel?"

"Until you repent, which will be never." Nodin crossed both arms over his chest. "You'll be here until you die. No manicures. No dye jobs. No pool boys. No fashionable clothes. Just this cell where you can consider all your past misdeeds."

"How sweet." She turned her dark gaze to Kamali. "Your boyfriend thinks he can contain me. Surely, you know better, dear."

Kamal refrained from rolling her eyes. "This picture you've painted of my parents is not anything I did not know. Life with my uncle was satisfactory. I was educated and never treated as if I were handicapped due to my blindness. If I learn Adler is somehow responsible for my parents' deaths, I may never forgive him, but I will remember all he did for me."

"In the overall scheme of things, your uncle's past choices are irrelevant. As you say, you've prospered as his ward." Raven picked at a jagged nail. "Let that be a lesson for you, Kamali. Men who have money make wonderful investments."

"Really, just don't." Kamali raised her hand, palm out. "I don't want or need any advice from you." She stepped closer to her aunt until she had her backed against the wall. "Your days of tormenting the Elementals are over. If I find you've hurt them, or anyone else, I will take back what you stole from my mother." She peered deep into Raven's eyes, seeing darkness swirling behind the deep brown, but searching for those short bursts of white she'd detected before.

There.

They sparkled, just out of reach, like a beacon guiding her home. "I see my mother's energy within you, fighting to be free. She calls to me, and someday I'll answer."

"You have no idea how to control anything, let alone think you could handle me."

"I will learn."

Nodin braced a hand on Kamali's shoulder. "Time to go."

Kamali gazed up at Nodin, focusing on his clear blue eyes, the color of air, of freedom. "Thank you for bringing me here."

Nodin smiled then lightly kissed her lips.

"Oh dear God, I just vomited a little in my mouth," Raven jeered.

Ignoring her ridiculous words, Kamali once more met Raven's gaze. "Remember my warning."

"After you leave, I'll continue not giving two shits about you and your stupid Elementals."

"Then you'll be making a grave mistake." Kamali clenched her hands into fists at her sides. "I see glimpses of what is to come, so when I ask you to heed my warning, I don't issue that message lightly."

"What do you mean?"

"That you will stay here until you are no longer a threat, because if you escape or leave before you have changed your path, you will die."

CHAPTER 26

Drifting across the Atlantic on his rescue mission, Nodin recalled he hadn't yet mentioned his vision of Violet's death to the Elementals. Not that he would reveal his concerns now, with Terran beside him as nothing but air—an insubstantial nothing composed of nitrogen and oxygen.

"Quint will be lying in wait." Terran's mental message interrupted his thoughts.

"I agree."

"I will hold him off."

"I don't need you to fight my battles." While Nodin appreciated Terran's assurances, he sometimes believed his Elemental partners didn't fully comprehend the power of Air. Now, traveling across the eastern portion of America, the Midwest, and then into Oklahoma, Nodin exulted in the freedom that came with becoming his element.

Terran sailed along at his side, not only as air, but also as his brother in arms. *"I do not believe you cannot fight, Nodin. I am merely reviewing our game plan. Your task is to carry Adler and his sons back to the castle."*

They hovered just outside the Oklahoma border.

"And, if you'll recall, my game plan involved not leaving your side, Terran."

"All right. If Quint is in the area, we will engage him together and attempt to retrieve Kamali's relatives. If we find he poses too much of a threat, we'll move on."

Nodin studied the much-too-open landscape, searching for a place to land. The era of hanging clothes out to dry used to make finding them much easier as he could sneak them off line after returning to his human form. As it was, they made sure they arrived just after midnight, so their nude bodies would only be visible by moonlight.

Adler's massive home sat on the outskirts of Thackerville, Oklahoma.

As air, they quietly bypassed all security, easily breezing up the front stairs and under the front door before returning to their human forms in the foyer.

"I'm only detecting two minds." Nodin glanced at Terran. *"The older brother, Caddo, isn't here."*

"Maybe at the casino?"

"Most likely."

"I'll grab Adler." Nodin flicked a hand toward the spiral staircase. *"You grab the younger brother, Isi."*

After passing four bedrooms along the right wing, Nodin followed Adler's brain waves. Without a sound, he entered the bedroom and whipped into a funnel.

All the items in the room knocked about. A lamp, blankets, and pillows circled Adler, who now stood by his bed, dressed only in underwear. "What is going on?" He opened the drawer on his side table and pulled out a gun.

"Remaining here is unsafe." With a gust of wind, Nodin knocked the weapon from his hand. "You are leaving."

"Who are you?" Adler braced a hand against the headboard.

"I'm here to make sure you don't miss your flight to safety." Suddenly, a rush of unstable air coursed through his lungs. "We need to leave. Now." Nodin swirled and swirled, lifting Kamali's uncle into the funnel and blowing down the stairs.

"Did you really believe I wouldn't be waiting?" Quint's voice snarled across his mind.

"We'll do this dance as long as we need to, Quint." Nodin shot back.

Pressure increased against Nodin's skull, and he fought to keep spinning fast enough to contain Adler. Nodin repelled shards of dark matter bombarding his mind.

Terran landed at his side. "He's out front, standing in the circular drive."

"Just two. This will be easier than I thought." Quint snaked through his head. *"Why do you continue this struggle? These humans do nothing for you. They spit upon your land, water, and air. Why do you fight for them? Let me rule them. Let me make them understand there are forces in this universe out of their control. They are nothing but mere specks of stardust."*

"I don't have time to philosophize today, Quint."

"I care not for philosophy. I'm a man of action, not words."

"Really? After that bit of pontificating on the value of humans, I disagree." Nodin whirled with Adler. They'd have to leave Caddo behind. Facing off against Quint with humans caught in the crossfire was unacceptable protocol. *"Terran, when we get outside, follow my lead."*

"You sure?" Terran had a grip on Isi.

"Everyone underestimates me, and at times that serves my purpose, but not today." Nodin blew the front door off its hinges then whipped outside. After locating Malachi, Quint's current form, he released a torrent of wind, pushing and forcing the dark matter creature deep within the earth. *"Let's bury him, Terran."*

Dark matter entered Nodin's spiral, but he blew the pieces away before they struck Adler.

Terran joined their whirlwinds together, passing over Isi. *"Take them and go."*

"No. I won't leave you." Nodin fought to maintain his grip on Adler and Isi as both struggled to break free. He couldn't keep up

his barrage against Quint and fight them at the same time. He entered Kamali's relatives' minds and put them in a calm state. *"Terran, help me send Quint deep into the earth."*

Together, Nodin and Terran combined their powers, shoving at Quint, driving him past each layer of the earth.

Laughing, Quint dug in his heels before clawing a hand in the earth and pulling himself free. As he rose from the hole, he caused a great rumble that shook the house behind them.

Nodin clutched his throat. A sludgy blockage obstructed his breathing. He coughed and fought to maintain his hold on Kamali's uncle and cousin. *"Terran, let's go."*

While the Earth Elemental may have held off Quint once before, Nodin understood there were no guarantees Terran could do so again. Especially, when Quint now controlled Malachi's magic.

Once more, Nodin and Terran combined forces and drove Quint a little deeper into the ground.

Terran coughed.

"Let me in, Earth-man." Quint's words tore through their minds.

"Go!" Terran's will surged across Nodin's mind in a burst of energy,

Black muck coated Nodin's form like quicksand where he couldn't move for fear he'd sink deeper. *"We must spin free together."*

"I want Violet, and I will have her." Quint sneered. *"You have three days to deliver her. Once the third day is over, I'll begin a killing rampage the likes of which you've never seen. I've got the medicine man's deadly poisons, which I'll use to destroy these humans on a mass scale. You decide. Death, or Violet?"*

A final wave of malice bogged down Nodin. *"Terran, together. Now."*

With a burst of power, Terran and Nodin blew Quint farther into the earth's core.

Then Nodin wrapped Adler and Isi tighter and travelled

across the country in a reverse pattern.

"Not much farther. We can do this." Terran joined his spiral.

With each breath, Nodin noted a rattle in his chest, as if the darkest venom had struck. He fought the compulsion to drift away and heal himself, because these men and his Elemental partner needed his help. *"I can make it."*

As Nodin crossed the ocean, rotating over one hundred miles per hour, he inhaled deeply as clean ocean air drifted across his form, cooling and cleansing him.

The green shores of Ireland came into view.

Hold on. Not much longer, and he could fly free.

Just inside the castle grounds, they placed the humans in the tall, swaying grass.

Once his burden was released, Nodin breathed deep, but dark matter still clogged his passages. *"I must go, Terran."*

Kamali appeared on the back porch, Maize at her side.

The dog barked in recognition, wagging her tail.

Nodin glanced at Terran, naked at his side. *"Care for Kamali until I return."*

Even while fighting against Quint's nefarious obstruction, he worried his woman's relatives would blame and harass her for hauling them from their casino empire. Kamali had explained Adler blamed her for his middle son, Waya's death. *"Don't let them hurt her. I'll be close by on Dursey Island. Please tell Kamali not to worry."*

Terran nodded then hefted Adler to his feet before lifting him across his shoulders and carrying him to the back patio. The Earth Elemental stopped at Kamali's side and glanced over his shoulder. *"Go. We will discuss Quint's words when you return."*

"Kamali?" Nodin gleaned into her mind.

"Nodin, are you all right?"

"I must rejuvenate my life force. Stay inside until I return. Once your relatives regain consciousness, do not let them bully you."

"I have lived with them long enough to disregard their harsh words. Go, and return to me quickly."

"I shall return and share my crystal-clear breath with you."

"Mountain freshness?" She chuckled.

"At its finest."

"Go. You sound like a cheesy detergent commercial."

Nodin escaped with the wind but carried the sound of Kamali's laughter with him until he landed on the tip of Bull Rock, relishing the blustering wind blowing across Ireland's Dursey Sound.

CHAPTER 27

"Do you understand the power and wealth under my command?" Adler stood above Kamali.

His muddy red aura an indicator of his rage, but she didn't need that bright beacon. His tone alone cut like ice.

"I can't disappear from the casino without alerting someone. I have enemies hovering in the wings, just waiting to takeover. This will give them the perfect excuse." He huffed out a breath. "I will not stay here."

While Kamali wished to placate her uncle, she remained disturbed over his likely involvement with her parents' deaths. Not that she truly understood Adler's level of participation. But she would—soon.

After a day of listening to her uncle bluster and whine while they sat in the castle's library, she wished she had Nodin's ability to escape with the wind. Now that her uncle's thoughts were racing through her mind, she didn't need a verbal repeat of each stern and censorious word.

She'd settled her cousin, Isi, in the kitchen with Violet and Maya. He'd seemed quite spellbound by the two beautiful women.

Her thoughts drifted to Nodin. When would he return? What would happen to her other cousin, Caddo? Would Quint follow through on his threat?

Kamali rubbed her temple. How did the Elementals shut off their gleaning ability? She needed a lesson in control and fast. Unwilling to endure another of his lectures, she interrupted. "Uncle, would you prefer Quint destroy you, Caddo, and Isi? We've lost Waya." Biting her bottom lip, she gripped the arms of the rocking chair. "He's overcome Malachi, and you have no wards, not that your medicine man's spells offered much protection, anyway." Sensing Nodin, she stood and turned toward the window. A warm breeze stirred around her legs before swirling around her body and up through her hair.

"You will not keep me here." Following her, Adler barreled on, his harsh breath puffing each word across the side of her face. "Do not test me."

"Get away from her." Nodin appeared just inside the library door, tugging on sweatpants.

Adler spun on his heel and jabbed a finger at Nodin. "You have no authority over me."

Nodin shook his head. "I refuse to engage in any ridiculous chest beating, Adler. You will remain, and you will treat your niece with respect. Your money may buy many things in your world, but it means nothing in mine. Now, moving on." He dropped a quick kiss on Kamali's lips. "Are you all right?"

She cupped his face between her hands. "I am now."

"What is going on here?" Adler exclaimed. "What are you doing with this man?"

"I am following my destiny."

"Never follow your heart, girl. Always your head. No future exists with this...this being...this insubstantial Air-man, or whatever he calls himself." Adler flicked his wrist. "Your place is with your family."

"My place is right here." Kamali clasped Nodin's hand before turning to meet her uncle's gaze. "I've had enough of your shouts and recriminations. You obviously have a lot to say, so how about you answer some questions about my past?" Her stomach roiled but, with Nodin at her side, she could withstand the coming unveiling of what Adler had done to her and her family.

"I want and deserve an explanation of what happened to my parents." Her voice wobbled a little as she made her request. This man had been her father, her mentor. She'd always followed his lead out of a sense of loyalty and gratitude, but now she believed those feelings were unfounded. Still, after living as his child, she had a hard time separating the little girl who needed love from the adult who needed the truth.

"Kamali." Adler used his familiar, placating tone, one that never failed to raise her hackles. "Your parents died because they were alcoholics."

"That's not entirely true." Kamali patted Maize's head as her trusty guide dog came to her side. "I see now, Uncle. You cannot hide behind the half-truths any longer." She took a deep breath and squeezed Nodin's hand.

"You are so beautiful in this moment." Nodin smiled. "Stay strong."

At Nodin's words, she turned and met his gaze. Within the sky-blue, she saw and felt...love. Though her heart skipped a beat, forcing her to catch her breath, she focused once more on her uncle. "I know my parents died because of you, Adler. You used Raven and Malachi to conspire against them."

"How dare you say such a thing?" Adler scoffed.

"I've seen within Raven's soul, and I see within yours." For the first time, Kamali raised her voice against her uncle. "I will have the truth."

Nodin tucked her closer to his side. "She knows, Adler. And she deserves the truth. I can delve and glean everything from your mind, and so, I believe, can she. But she's giving you this chance to come clean."

Adler huffed out a nervous laugh and scuffled his shoe against the stone floors. "I will not dwell on the past when my son's life is on the line."

Muddy, defensive pink entered his aura. Kamali sensed him blocking images of a lonely stretch of road with a car's single headlight glaring at the end.

"No need to dredge up the past during this time of uncertainty. We will stand strong together." Adler paced before the fireplace, where the fire had begun to wane. "Were you not treated well? Did you not receive the best of everything?"

"You stole my parents from me."

"And your mother stole my brother from me!" Adler shouted. "Her wiles and charms drove him to madness. We were a team until she took him away. Afterward, I did everything on my own." He paused for a moment, as if realizing how much he'd revealed. "She took him, so I-I...I took you." His voice wavered before strengthening again. "And I'd do it all again. Understand this, Kamali, *I* did not force them to drink. *I* did not put your father behind the wheel, but once I heard from Raven they had crashed, I did what I had to do."

Grimacing over the pain of those words, Kamali inhaled a ragged breath. "You speak of your brother falling prey to a woman's wiles. Did you not do the same? You fell prey to Raven's demands and her demented wishes."

"They were dying." Adler sank into the vacated rocking chair. Elbow braced against the armrest, he dropped his head into his palm. "That is all now, Kamali. I do not wish to speak of this."

"Dying does not mean dead." Nodin spoke in a low tone, as if careful not to disrupt the brittle reality of this moment.

"You let them die," Kamali whispered. Her aching heart took one last gasp before the truth splintered the vessel in two.

Nodin wrapped her in his arms. "I can show you the truth, you only have to ask."

Kamali buried her face against Nodin's bare shoulder. "I want to know."

"Don't do this to her." Her uncle glared at Nodin. "You

think to judge me, but you weren't there…you weren't there." Shoulders slumped, he shook his head.

Fighting the urge to comfort her uncle, Kamali closed her eyes so she wouldn't see his pain. "Tell me, Nodin. Please."

"Come sit with me." He led her to a loveseat set off to the other side of the huge stone fireplace. After resting her head in his lap, he squeezed her shoulder. "Are you sure?"

"Yes." She nodded. "I need the truth, and I won't dig into his mind. I don't know why, except I see him as my father. I've been warned too many times about breaching his privacy."

"I'll begin." Nodin combed his fingers through her hair for a moment before actually speaking. "When Adler arrived, he saw your father's car wrapped around a tree. He searched for your parents' bodies, as they'd been shot through the windshield due to the force of the impact."

Kamali focused on the hypnotic tone of Nodin's voice. She followed him back, back to the past, and could see the picture he painted with his words.

A wash of blood poured from your mother's mouth, nose, and ears.

Raven paced back and forth beside her body. "She's not worth saving, Adler." She clutched his shirtfront. "Give her to me."

"Raven, she is my brother's wife." He slapped away her hands.

"Your brother is dead," Malachi said, coming to stand at his side.

"No," Adler gasped, eyes wide. "Take me to him."

Malachi led him to his brother's body.

Adler pressed his fingers against his brother's neck, finding a slight pulse. "I feel faint life. We need an ambulance." He tugged his phone from his back pocket.

"Think of the girl, Adler." Malachi urged, placing a hand over the bulky phone's buttons. "Kamali is better off with you. Her skills, though not yet clear, will benefit you far more than they would this wasted shell of a man. Let them go. Let Raven take what she needs, and you will see the benefits will far outweigh the loss."

Adler's index finger hovered over the 9-button. He gazed at his brother's still body and then he turned to Malachi. "He is my brother."

"No, he was your brother. He is gone."

Adler once more checked his brother's pulse. Nothing.

Anger, pain, and blame all mixed together in Adler's mind.

The one person in his life who mattered was dead, and so he would do the same to the one responsible—his brother's wife. "Do what you want with her." He flicked a hand toward Kamali's mother. "That bitch deserves to die." Adler walked away, leaving Raven and Malachi to execute whatever ritual was necessary to gain their prize.

"He walked away and let her die." Kamali breathed deep, her voice barely above a whisper.

"She was already dead." Adler heaved a sigh and crossed both arms over his chest.

"I don't understand something." Wishing she had a tissue to wipe the tears from her face, Kamali bit her bottom lip to stave off true sobs. "How did you know where my parents were?"

"The bartender and I had an arrangement." Adler crossed his legs and leaned back in the chair. "Your father frequented that bar, so I asked the bartender to alert me when they'd had too much to drink and needed assistance." Adler drummed his fingers against the wooden armrest. "That night, he called before they even left."

"If you'd just called an ambulance, you could have saved them." Kamali shot upright, glaring at her uncle.

"No, Kamali." He shook his head. "I saved you."

"Don't feed me those self-righteous lies." Kamali jabbed a finger at her uncle. "Perhaps you've stuffed your conscience with those platitudes over the years, but they mean nothing to me. They were dying." She choked back a sob. "You did nothing. You are to blame."

"Life is about choices, Kamali." His tone turned paternal once more. "Have I not also lost people? My parents? My wife? My brother?" He paused then, in a soft tone, said, "My son."

Though she had sympathy for his losses, she could not

forgive his dismissal of two people's lives, no matter his pain.

"Life *is* about choices, Uncle. Quint has returned, and in the coming days, we will all have to make them. What will you do? You have no control over Quint. No one does." Kamali considered her uncle for a moment. She read no regret in his aura. "If you return to the casino, you will be used as a pawn in Quint's game. I do not trust you to make choices for the greater good." She turned to Nodin. "We must send him away, because he cannot be trusted to think of anyone but himself."

Adler blasted out of the chair. "I made the choices I had to make and you, young lady, benefitted, so I'll hear no more of your accusations."

"We cannot change what has come before, only make the best choices for the future." Nodin leaned forward with his hands folded between his knees. "Kamali knows the truth now. She will decide whether or not to forgive you." He stood and took Kamali's hand, pulling her to her feet. "Mother Nature will be here shortly to take you someplace safe until we finish our battle with Quint."

"I will go back to where I belong." Adler stormed around the room, knocking books off a side table. "You will return me to my casino. I do not care if I die there. It'd be a fitting end."

"Adler, you have no say. No choice." Nodin bent and dusted off the book Adler disturbed in his childish display of defiance. "Just like Kamali's parents, and just like Kamali when you chose to take their lives into your own hands." He dropped the book back on the table. The loud boom reverberated throughout the room, emphasizing the finality of his words. "While away, I suggest you ask Mother to teach you a thing or two about humility, and I'd pray to the Great Spirit for forgiveness."

CHAPTER 28

"Let's go upstairs." Leading Kamali out of the library, Nodin decided she needed some quiet time. The poor girl had gone from her ordered life to one with witches, Elementals, evil beings composed of dark matter, and hearing truths no one should have to bear.

Holding an entire Kleenex box in her hand, Kamali wiped her eyes and then her nose with a wadded tissue. "I don't know...I should...maybe I should take Maize outside first."

"Maya can take her." Nodin drew her into his arms, ignoring the pointy edges of the tissue box digging into his chest. "I'm sorry for everything. I hate to see you so sad. Let me help you sleep." He sent a mental message to Maya. "*Maya, come get Maize, please.*"

"I don't like being sent to my room, Nodin, but I agree. I'm overwhelmed, and I didn't sleep last night worrying about you. Plus, I'm terrified of what Quint could do to Caddo...and just...well, everything." She sniffed. "I'm fighting to be strong, but a ball of fury and sorrow is building just here." She tapped her breastbone. "And I'd rather you didn't witness my fall when it breaks."

He lightly kissed her lips. "Then I won't. Come on, I'll put you to bed."

Maya rounded the corner, approaching from the kitchen. "Need me to watch Maize for a bit?"

"If you wouldn't mind." Kamali nodded.

"Of course not." Maya glanced at Kamali. "Are you all right? I know your uncle has been quite verbal in his displeasure."

Kamali bit her lip, keeping her gaze on the tissue box. "I don't know if I'm all right, but I will be."

Maya wrapped her in a hug. "We're friends now. If you need to talk, find me."

Kamali's eyes widened at Maya's words.

Perhaps she hadn't had many friends. This was true of Maya, as well. The water-girl had spent decades with only him and Flint as confidants. Poor thing needed more females in her life. "I'm taking Kamali upstairs to rest. She needs a bit of consoling."

"Is that what they're calling it now?" Maya smirked, arching a brow.

Nodin rolled his eyes. "Take Maize outside to play and keep your dirty mind to yourself."

"Yes, sir." Maya kissed his cheek before taking Maize's leash.

"You two are funny together," Kamali noted as he led her up the stairs.

"Living the life of an Elemental is quite lonely. Your whole world is a secret. For so long we only had each other, but then Terran came along and filled a gap in Maya's life. I'm happy for her."

"Then I am, too. She's a lovely person, both inside and out." She squeezed his arm.

Arriving at her bedroom, he led her to the bed. "I'll stay for a while."

"I thought Elementals didn't sleep."

"No, but at times I close my eyes and pretend. It sort of reboots my system." He sat on the edge of the bed. "I'll sit very still on the summit of a mountain and let the wind batter against me until I feel as if I've been tumbled and dry cleaned. Then I begin again with a fresh perspective."

"I'd like a reboot." She sighed. "I feel as if my whole life has been lived in a shadow and, though the veil has lifted, I am still in the dark. Are there any more secrets? Lies? How much longer will my new gifts remain? Where will I live? Where will I work? I have no grasp on my future, because I feel as if I don't know who I am."

"I know who you are. You are the woman I love." Nodin drew her into his arms and kissed her, capturing her gasp. "Kamali, we will find answers to your questions. I have no doubt about one aspect of your future—you and I are together." He trailed a finger down her cheek. "We shall steal this moment and just be, Nodin and Kamali."

She shivered as he trailed kisses along her neck.

"Are you cold?"

"Yes." She gripped his hips and drew him against her lower body. "But I don't believe I'll be so for long."

Smiling, he tapped her nose with his index finger. "I may not be a Fire Elemental, but I can still bring the heat."

She chuckled. "Goodness, I think I liked your philosophy quotes better."

"No, you'll like this better." He lifted her shirt over her head then tugged her pants down along with her pink panties. After situating her on the bed, he nudged her legs apart and kissed his way from her ankle to her inner thigh. He stopped at her apex before going down her other leg.

She leaned down, bunched his hair in her hands, and tugged.

He hummed out a laugh and kissed her just below her bellybutton. "You trying to direct me, my little Pakali?"

"I am on edge emotionally, don't keep me there physically." Licking her bottom lip, she bent her knees. "I need this."

"Then I'll do as you wish." With his tongue and fingers, he used his years of well-honed sexual skills to bring her to orgasm quickly, just as requested.

At her release, she tightened her fingers in his hair and her entire body flushed as she murmured his name while writhing against the sheets.

From his kneeling position, he smiled down at her. "Ready to rest now?"

"No." She cocked a brow and pushed against his chest. "Your turn. Stand at the edge of the bed."

"What?" He furrowed his brow and shook his head. "Kamali, I don't need anything. You should rest." He shifted to stand while watching her trail her fingertips between her breasts. A natural tease. He'd enjoy teaching her everything—and after four-hundred plus years...there was a lot of everything.

She sat up and wiggled to the bed's edge before caressing his throbbing cock. "I'll rest after I take care of this."

More than happy to follow her direction, he let her draw him closer and then groaned as she wrapped her lips around the head of his shaft. Her positioning on the bed had him sliding directly into her mouth.

She hummed around him, and the sound vibrated through every inch of his body.

"Kamali, that's perfect, love." He placed his hand at the back of her head and watched as she engulfed his cock in one deep glide, then eased back and teased the tip with her tongue. "Yes...just like that."

After nipping his tip, she drew back. "I want you to thrust inside my mouth."

"You sure?"

"Yes."

He couldn't say no to those deep brown eyes. "All right. I'll take it slow." He started a slow rhythm, rocking into her wet mouth. "Touch yourself, Pakali."

His rod hardened to pure steel as he watched her pinch both nipples, hardening each pink tip. He momentarily lost his rhythm and stuttered out, "I'm close...so close."

She wrapped both hands around his bottom and helped guide him deeper.

"Enough. I want us to finish together." He pulled free of her gloriously capable mouth, lifted her ankles to his shoulders, and then slammed into her wet core. "Oh...yes. This is what we need."

Arching against him, she lifted her hands and squeezed her breasts.

"That's my girl, now pinch both nipples."

At the sight of her following his commands, he increased the pace, his balls tightening and his cock screaming for release. Yet, he had more he could give.

Tonight she would soar high enough to touch the stars, and he would fly right beside her. To reach that peak, he took her right hand and placed two fingers into her mouth all while continuing his deep plunge. He directed her wet fingers to her mound, and together, they brushed against her clit.

He directed her other hand back to her breasts. "Keep touching yourself. I want you to come hard."

Gasping, she bit her bottom lip. "It's too...too much."

"No...it'll never be enough." Arcs of pleasure whipped down his spine, and wanting to ramp up the visual pleasure, he placed a finger in her mouth. "Suck me."

As he watched her suck hard then bite, he lost all control. His rocking orgasm heightened when she tightened around his cock. His entire body shuddered but kept driving, delivering her ultimate pleasure.

Cries tore from her lips as her body shook. Her skin blushed a bright rose and her hair fell in disarray around her face.

He had no seed to take root, and for a moment regret breezed across his airy heart. He shook his head, unwilling to dwell on such things now. Instead, he studied the well-loved woman and exulted in their combined heat and satisfaction.

After one last prod with his semi-hard cock, he remained

buried in her wet heat. Feeling wicked, he lifted her fingers to his mouth, licking them clean.

"I should find that dirty, and I suppose I do." Kamali flashed a cat-in-the-cream smile. "But, I like dirty."

He felt her clench around his again-interested shaft. "Nothing we do is dirty, except maybe this..." He bent and kissed her, sharing the taste of her pleasure.

"Mmm..." She moaned against his mouth while simultaneously scooting up the bed and drawing his body down to rest on hers. "I want you again."

"You need to sleep." He shook his head but, seemingly out of his control, his hips rocked against her body.

"So, put me to sleep. Love me until I can no longer open my eyes." She drew him down and kissed him, lifting her legs to wrap around his waist. After a moment, her kisses turned carnal, licking and biting at his mouth while her tongue dueled with his.

"Are you challenging me, Kamali?"

She stretched her arms above her head, her hair a puffy cloud of thoroughly ruffled dark strands. "You've breezed across my body and my heart. Do you understand what that means to a girl who has only dreamed of this moment? Can you possibly comprehend what fires through my heart when you make love to me? I had no hopes for moments like these, because I had no basis of understanding love and affection...until you. You have lifted me from the darkness and shown me what love means." She drew a circle with her index finger around her heart. "You are here, and because of that, I do not challenge you...I surrender."

"Then, so shall I."

Though unsure of their future, as he remained a peri-mortal and she was all too human, he shut out those worries and lost himself in her arms. No matter their course, he would remain at her side until her last breath.

And though he lived as air, he knew deep within his heart that her final breath would be his, as well.

CHAPTER 29

As Kamali slept, Nodin breezed into the library and spent the rest of the day planning with his Elemental team. Though he understood Quint wasn't bluffing about the tactics he'd employ to obtain Violet, Nodin remained unsure of their strategies.

They planned to release Raven, as she might lead them to Quint.

Kamali would aid them in their final battle, detecting Quint when he came within a certain radius. And, as a precaution, they decided to drink her blood again. Nodin refused to take part, which resulted in a verbal, and then physical altercation with Flint.

Terran pulled them apart.

As the sun set in streams of purples and reds, Nodin knew he could not stand against Quint without offering Flint an apology.

After checking on Kamali, Nodin slipped back downstairs and out the patio doors before calling to his Elemental brother. *"Flint, meet me by the stones."*

Nodin breathed deep of the fresh Irish air, unsure of what tomorrow would bring but unwilling to face the next day without mending their relationship.

A hint of heat stirred in the breeze.

Nodin glanced toward the castle.

Each step Flint took across the damp grass created heavy steam which folded around him like a cloak.

His friend's anger remained palpable, but Nodin believed he was actually more frightened over his lack of control of Violet's life. Understandable, as her immortality would end if, and when, Quint was destroyed. Not to mention, Nodin's vision of her death. A picture he buried deep in his mind as Flint approached.

"What?" Flint braced both hands on his hips.

"You already know." Nodin shook his head.

Flint huffed out a sigh. "Why would I ask if I knew?"

"I tried, my friend. I've circumvented this moment for five years. I waited to bring Kamali into the fold so you and Violet could have those years together. I understand that it's never enough. I want more, too. I want you to know, if we survive the coming days, I too, will become human. I will not let Kamali walk alone in this world."

"There's a difference." Frowning, Flint paced away.

"Explain, please."

"Violet will remain a witch. *She'll* still have powers." Flint met his gaze, his expression one of utter desolation. "I'll be nothing. But what choice do I have, because when she dies…I die."

"Perhaps Mother knows of another way."

"No." Flint raked his fingers through his coal-black hair. "Mother granted Violet and I this time. Once Quint is gone, I do not believe she has the power to prolong Violet's life."

"Then perhaps a spell."

"Spells cost." Shaking his head, Flint glanced back at the castle. "With magic something is always lost or given. I would not have her become something else just to serve my selfish needs. I have walked this earth so long, my brother." He clasped Nodin's shoulder. "I think I am ready for a simpler life. Perhaps, I'll father children. Maybe, I won't remember much of this life. I don't know how the transformation works, but I do know I will not live without her."

Dear Great Spirit, may my vision be false.

He'd hate to see his friend destroyed by the loss of a love he'd waited centuries to find.

Yet, a moment ago, Nodin had a repeat of another vision. One that made no sense. He'd brushed it off, thinking his own wishes were interfering with his seer gift. "You need to speak to Violet." Nodin studied his friend, contemplating how much the man had changed since meeting her.

Flint heaved a sigh. "I do try to talk to Violet, but I...I've lived so long that an end or a change in my life seems impossible. I keep thinking something will happen to alter this choice, but the closer we come to fighting Quint, the more I feel the end. How will I go from living six hundred years to perhaps only sixty more?" Flint cursed and paced closer to the stones. "Violet has broached the subject of her mortality, and I-I...I try—"

"No." Nodin clasped his friend's shoulder. "You stomp and storm until all she feels is guilt. How do you imagine she feels about ending a life that has lasted, as you say, hundreds of years? When you do not speak, she will fill that gap with words that may not represent how you truly feel. This is why you should drop the cocky demeanor and let her see the times you are unsure and weak."

"I'm not weak," Flint growled.

"No. You are not." Nodin pulled his hand from his friend's shoulder as all of a sudden Flint flared hot. "Listen, Violet needs you strong, not torn apart by a future *you* cannot see. I, however, can see, and I think you'll be interested in my most recent vision."

Flint furrowed his brow. "Enlighten me."

"While I was waiting for a half hour for you to join me"—Nodin cleared his throat—"I leaned against these stones and had a vision of three children playing in this field—two boys, both with dark hair and one girl with red hair." He waved a hand at the land between the castle and the stone ruins. "I felt their joy and heard their laughter."

"Don't say this to me. Not if it isn't true." He placed a hand over his heart. "I can't...don't give me false hope..."

Nodin studied his friend. Though he knew his visions could change, this one was very clear, almost as if he'd transported into the future and joined the jolly children as they played. However, this clashed with the picture of Violet's death he and Kamali had seen before. Nothing made sense, and perhaps he shouldn't have spoken of this to Flint, but he needed his friend strong in the coming days. And maybe, just this once, life could surpass death. "All we have is hope." He glanced at a high castle window, knowing his own hope was waking from her slumber.

Flint clutched Nodin's shoulder. "The children were happy. And you said there were three?"

Nodin nodded. "However, there was something I didn't quite understand."

"What?"

"It was winter, and they were all dancing around a fire."

Flint shrugged. "So?"

Nodin met his gaze. "There wasn't any wood."

Face pale, Flint whispered, "Holy shit."

CHAPTER 30

On the third day following Quint's threat and after updating Kamali on their plans, Nodin spun to a stop within the cover of Colorado's Rio Grande National Forest right outside the area that used to surround Terran and Maya's cabin.

"You really think Raven is working for Quint?" Kamali reached for his hand.

"Yes, I believe she'll deliver the message to meet us here, if she hasn't already." Nodin guided her over fallen branches, leading her closer to where the Elementals would face off against Quint.

"I can't believe you let her go." Kamali shook her head. "That'll teach me to sleep."

"You needed the rest." Nodin halted and brushed her hair from her face before kissing her cheek. "And *we* needed to get Quint to an open location so Terran and Violet can create their black hole." He sighed, not even wanting to delve into that physics theory. "Not only that, we were limited on time. We must distract him before he follows through on his threat to destroy more people." Tilting his head, Nodin studied her, noting the faint purple circles under her eyes. "Once we're through with Quint, we'll go someplace tropical and rest for days on a warm beach."

"I'd rather not *rest* with you." She flashed a cheeky smile.

"Oh, but you will rest…after." He kissed her. Unsure of what would come today and who would still be standing at the end, he released the reins and simply reveled in her sweet lips. They would never have enough time, so he would take these small moments as they came. With this kiss, he let her know she was cherished and loved before drawing away. "I love you, Kamali. I know it seems as if I've fallen for you in a very short time, but I believe we were destined. This feeling between us was waiting dormant for hundreds of years and now soars free."

She placed her hand on his breastbone. "I love you, too. I know our future may end today, and I accept that. I've seen love and that's enough."

He gripped her hand and kissed her knuckles. "I hate that you must be here, but we need you. I'm worried about our vision of Violet's death. We can't lose her." Though he would rather disperse into air and carry Kamali away, Nodin led her out of the forest. "Let me know right away if you feel Quint, even if it's a flicker."

Kamali nodded. "I can do this." She winced and pulled his hand off her arm, brushing two fingers over the bandage at her left elbow where the needle had drawn her blood.

"I'm sorry. Did I hurt you?" Regardless of his threats and arguments, Violet had performed a protection spell on them all again, using Kamali's blood, but he hadn't swallowed a drop.

"No, I'm fine. I wish you could see that once I understood the purpose, I was happy to help." Kamali pinched her lips together, holding back a smile. "Although, I did notice you turned a little green as each person drank from their vial."

"Elemental vamps." He shook his head. "I never thought I'd see the day."

Walking across what was once Maya's backyard, they skidded to a stop when they heard her scream.

Already on alert, Nodin lifted Kamali in his arms and rushed toward the sound. Upon arrival, he noted Maya crying and locked in Terran's arms, but he detected no danger.

Water formed in puddles at her feet.

Once he glanced around, he understood the reason for her tears—their cabin was rebuilt, and was slightly bigger than before.

Terran rocked Maya back and forth in his arms.

"What a nice surprise." Nodin chuckled and dropped Kamali to her feet. "How Terran kept her from gleaning this, I'll never know."

"What is it?" Kamali tugged on his arm.

"Right, sorry." Sometimes he forgot she couldn't see everything clearly. "Terran rebuilt their cabin."

"Maya's aura is bright pink, full of love." Kamali beamed, a dazzling smiling spreading across her face. "Can we get closer?"

Inspired by the joyous moment, Nodin stooped down and kissed Kamali again.

"Geez, Pigpen. How'd you pull this off?" After exiting their rental car, Flint tugged Violet around. They'd left last night, taking a long flight into Denver then to Monte Vista Municipal Airport.

"Honestly, I don't know." Terran kissed the top of Maya's head. "Maya, we'll look at the house later, all right? I'm sorry, but we need to start the fire."

She nodded, the tip of her nose still slightly pink from her happy tears.

"Wait a minute." Nodin pulled Kamali over and wrapped his arms around Terran and Maya. Violet and Flint joined in until they were a mass of warm, huddled bodies.

"This moment is why everything matters," Kamali spoke from within his arms. "The love you all have for each other is so strong, and nothing, absolutely nothing, defeats love. Remember that today as you battle against Quint. I see you all so much more clearly now, but I don't need to see to feel."

Flint pounded against Nodin's back and pulled away. "Let's light it up."

Maya hugged Kamali. "Flint's not one for public displays of

affection, but your words touched him." She tapped her temple. "I know."

Violet simply nodded, her purple hair waving in the slight breeze. Her fingers pulsed white. "Thank you, Kamali. I-I cannot allow such soft emotions. I must become what my ancestor spelled me to be. Vengeance and fury, and nothing else." She turned away to join Flint, who stood beside a massive wood pile composed of all the builder's scraps.

A sense of unease rippled down Nodin's spine. He did not sense victory on the wind, only something he could not quite grasp, as if hidden by shadows. He glanced at Kamali, wondering if she, too, felt the negative energy.

Kamali stiffened and bent over at the waist. Eyes wide, she shouted, "Tell them to get ready. Now!"

Staving off panic, he sent a mental message to Terran and Violet. *"Quint is coming. Start the fire."*

Terran volleyed back, *"We'll begin."*

"How far out?" Flint fired to Nodin's side.

Kamali's whole body shook. "H-he's close."

Nodin knelt so he could see her face and held her shoulders. "Breathe. You're doing great."

Her pain became his own as he watched her spear her hands into her hair and wince. "He's in Trinidad, which is a bit east of here. He's moving fast in this direction."

"That's only one hundred and twenty some miles." Nodin glanced at the now-blazing fire. Fuel for the weapon they planned to use against Quint.

The Earth Elemental stood beside the raging fire. Violet remained at his side, her entire body now glowing with white light. Using her control over the electromagnetic field, she worked at compressing the flaming raw material into a miniature black hole.

"I've got Kamali." Nodin glanced at Maya and Flint. "Hold back Quint while Terran and Violet work together."

Kamali moaned and collapsed onto her side. "So dark, so

evil. Nothing is there. His aura's like a vacuum, sucking you in until he buries you alive." Blinking, she met Nodin's gaze. "He wants Violet, and he won't stop until he has her."

Nodin drew her into his arms. "Stay with me."

Flint nudged his shoulder. "Where is he now?"

Kamali murmured, "Moving...quickly." She paused a moment, taking a deep breath. "He's using Malachi's magic to travel. Raven is with him. She's attempting to redirect your thoughts by creating an alternate reality. Nodin, you are not safe." She straightened and gripped his biceps. "You should have taken my blood."

"Do not worry." Nodin shook his head. "With you by my side, you're all I see."

"She's digging, poking. In your head, in mine." Wincing, Kamali met his gaze.

Pacing beside them, Maya growled, "That crazy cuckoo bird isn't destroying my house again. And yeah, I feel her trying to dig her tacky red claws into my head. No go, psycho."

"Terran." Nodin sent a mental message. *"Quint is almost here.*

A wash of immense heat blasted across the yard.

Now that Kamali had alerted them to Quint's presence, Nodin needed to remove her from the area in case Violet lost control and the fire blazed too hot.

Even now, she coughed and blinked against the smoke pouring from the burning wood.

Too late.

Quint sauntered around the back of the cabin, dressed in a fine, black business suit. He waved a hand toward them all. "Nope. No discussions. No pleas and no fight." The dark menace slithered forward on his overly shiny high-dollar shoes. "I'm taking my prize."

Flint circled their perimeter with a wall of fire, even encompassing Violet and Terran's blaze.

Worried about Kamali, Nodin blew the blaze outward, so the

fire stretched four feet from its source.

Quirking a brow, Quint snapped his fingers, and the flames went out. "I said...no games."

Flint glanced at Nodin and Maya. "Snappy little fingers you got there. But you're wrong, we *are* playing a game, and it's called Annihilation."

Together, they fired wave after wave of water, fire, and air, using the forest around them as fuel for their battle.

But Quint simply waved away their bombardment.

Kamali had dropped to her knees by Nodin's feet, keeping her gaze locked with Raven's.

Her efforts most likely stopping the woman from entering his mind.

The earth rumbled under their feet, forming cracks and knocking Quint and Raven to the ground.

After the dust settled, Terran and Violet stepped forward.

Swirling between her arms was what had to be a black hole. An undulating circle, held in place by Violet's power over the electromagnetic field. Due to his connection to the earth, Terran had this same ability. His entire body was a bright shade of red as he walked at Violet's side.

As Nodin watched this ensemble, he considered that perhaps Flint should have maintained the heat energy while Terran assisted Violet in holding the black hole in place.

Violet gritted her teeth. *"If you want me, come and get me. I won't take another step."*

"And what is that you have for me, dear?" Quint moved closer to his prize. "Just look at her, Raven, all that power and beauty wrapped up in such a small package. Ah...I've waited lifetimes for you."

Suddenly, the skies opened and poured down rain.

Mother landed between him and Violet. *"This must end."*

Nodin glanced around at his team, unsure, because Mother never interfered with their battles. She'd explained once, but the ridiculousness of the idea aggravated him to the point he'd disregarded her excuses.

Kamali gasped and shot to her feet. "Humans are coming. They will see your gifts." She tugged on his arm. "Raven is calling them to this place."

"Who?" Nodin gripped her upper arms. "What do you mean?"

"Newsmen, police, firemen. They think a disaster has occurred. She's compelled them."

Nodin glanced at Mother Nature.

She had buried her legs into the ground and they'd sprouted roots. She spread her arms and became a huge tree, wrapping her branches around Quint. *"You must hurry before the humans see."* Mother's urgent tone shot a spike of adrenaline down Nodin's spine.

Kamali gripped his hand. "The people are just outside of Monte Vista, heading down a two-lane highway, twenty miles out."

Nodin detected the whop-whop-whop of an incoming chopper. He glanced at Raven.

She smiled and blew him a kiss.

A sharp *ping* burst against his temple as she fought to overcome his mind. Shaking her off, he took Kamali's hand and squeezed. "Concentrate on Raven. We must break her hold on the humans' minds. Together, we'll send them away."

A piercing crack ripped through the yard, sharper than a rifle shot.

Mother's tree splintered and faded to gray, but her spindly arms still kept hold of Quint.

Violet and Terran joined hands and stood before the tree, chanting the binding spell to compel Quint into the black hole.

Skin melting off his body, Terran fell to his knees but remained at Violet's side.

Maya held Terran's other hand and kissed him, pouring her

healing waters down his throat.

Flint joined in their chant.

Violet had used this magic incantation to bind Quint once before, but, as before, he'd likely escape since the humans were drawing closer.

"We can't stop them. Too many are coming, and I-I don't know where to focus." Kamali peered up at Nodin. "I'm sorry."

A chopper passed overhead.

In a swirl of dust, news vans poured down the gravel driveway, followed by police vehicles and two fire trucks.

Mother's tree burst into dust.

Particles fanned through the air, blocking their vision.

Kamali coughed and waved a hand before her face.

Quint's dark form stirred within the dust, and then shot across the yard before firing into Raven's mouth and nose.

"Oh, no!" Kamali exclaimed. "Quint's inside her." She stepped toward her aunt.

Clutching her head, Raven screamed and fell to the ground.

Then Quint's voice speared through Nodin's mind, surely doing the same to Kamali as he saw her shake her head.

"I will not be bound. I am more than your spells. I am eternal. Do not say I did not warn you. Your three days are over."

Screaming, Raven clawed at the ground, groping for purchase. Her rail-thin body undulated and shook as Quint's dark essence overtook her completely.

For a moment, Raven quieted, before lifting her hand and releasing a dark wall between herself and the Elementals still chanting the binding spell. She stood and dusted off her pants.

Hypnotized by his desire to keep the humans from seeing these unexplainable events, Nodin didn't detect the true danger.

Until Raven met his gaze and winked.

And Kamali was ripped from his side.

CHAPTER 31

The woman on the floor of Adler's office roared up, gasping for air.

Quint, back in his semi-damaged Malachi suit, merely rolled his eyes at Raven's theatrics. "Welcome back. I'd thought for sure it was bye, bye, black bird."

She held a hand to her throat and glared.

"Don't worry, I left a little bit of me inside you, dear." He bent and cupped her chin in his hand. "If I hadn't, then you'd be dead, not to say you won't die, anyway. Though, seeing how long you can last with me inside you should prove entertaining." When he received no response, Quint shoved a palm against her forehead and stepped away. "While inside you in that field, I quite enjoyed your gifts. Delving into others' minds, but I could only read the humans' minds, not the Elementals. A pity your tricks don't work on them."

Raven avoided his gaze, wiping her mouth with the back of her hand.

"Nothing to be ashamed of, dear. We all have our weaknesses. Except for me, of course."

"Seems to me you left the scene quite quickly."

Her voice had taken on a raspy tone, evidence of his influence, most likely.

"Law enforcement. They bore me, and they were swarming the place." He shrugged. "Though, I suppose you are right, I do pull out of battle, because I always wonder if this will be the one time those Elementals succeed in destroying me. Yet, after centuries and centuries their struggle remains."

Pacing by the wall, he wondered why he'd revealed such a thing to this woman. Perhaps his emotional deluge stemmed from that foreign feeling he'd experienced earlier, and from that time in the hospital parking lot. Only this time, the pull was much stronger, and Mother had finally decided to join the fight.

Why now?

Well, the gloves were off. Time for bare-knuckled brawling.

He glanced over his shoulder at Raven still lolling about on the floor. "I felt this internal pull today. Did you feel anything?"

"What?" She shook her head. "No."

"You didn't feel as if the world was fading away? Did you see the black tunnel?" He cleared his throat and gazed back out the cracked window at all the gamblers below. "This sensation was all Violet's doing. Once she's mine, she'll explain these tricks, and together, we'll rule the world." Pensive and a bit concerned because he'd felt something Raven hadn't, he barreled across the office, knelt down, and punched her stomach.

Raven gasped for breath.

"That's exactly how I felt today. As if I couldn't breathe, and someone was leading me into a dark tunnel." He sniffed. "Not something I wish to experience again, and I won't have to, because of why, black bird?"

Raven shook her head, lying on her side at his feet with her arms wrapped around her waist.

"No answer." He yanked her up by her hair. "Don't you listen? I've explained this over and over." He shoved her back onto the floor. "The Elementals don't sacrifice. All they'll care about now is saving Kamali. But they'll fall right into our trap." He rubbed his hands together and stepped over Raven on his way back to the glass window. "I'll make sure they think she's dying, and then they'll turn to me for help. I'll say, well of course, as long as you deliver my perky little Violet. And they'll do it, believing they can rescue her after I turn over Kamali, but once I have Violet, all bets are off."

Quint tapped a finger against the casino's glass in Adler's old office, ignoring the raging erection that always flared to life when considering his Violet. "Still, I find I'm curious about what they were up to. The whole thing was out of character. They usually don't all face off against me at the same time." He ambled back over to Raven, hands tucked in his dress pants' front pockets. "Did you glean anything? That was your whole purpose, Raven. What did you discover?"

"Fuck you."

"Already done. Can't say I'd go again." Although this bloated shaft between his legs *could* use some release. He glanced down at Raven. She smelled of smoke, her eyes and nose were red, and her eyes were full black. Not to mention her hair and clothes were in complete disarray. Perhaps he'd coax some cocktail waitress downstairs into relieving this human ache. "Go speak to that niece of yours. Make yourself useful, and take a shower. You stink."

She stunk. This reanimated carcass he lived inside stunk, hence his need for a violet to freshen his days.

He kicked Raven with the tip of his shoe, wiping some dust on her shirt. "Discover what those Elementals have planned. I'm heading down to the casino to fulfill my promise." He strolled to the door then stopped and leaned against the panel. "What shall I poison? The rum? No, these wrinkled fucks inhale gallons upon gallons of free coffee. What shall I sprinkle in the grounds? Hmm... I'll have to pull something from Malachi's memories." Grinning over his plan, Quint turned to leave once more, firing his final volley over his shoulder. "When I return, I expect you to have answers. Get them, or I'll end you." He straightened his jacket's lapel. "Now, where do they keep the coffee?"

CHAPTER 32

"No." Slashing his hand through the air, Nodin paced the castle library's stone floor. "I must go to her. You don't understand, in a recent vision I watched her eyes turn black. Quint means to destroy her."

"I'm sorry, my brother." Frowning, Flint shook his head. "I believe you are right. There is no other explanation for how she so suddenly disappeared."

Nodin pounded a fist against the sturdy wooden bookcase, eliciting a round of dust from the books lining the shelves. "Perhaps her disappearing act was simply a result of Quint using Malachi's magic." He glanced at Flint. "Still, I believe they came for Kamali. Raven either wanted revenge for her perceived mistreatment here, or she plans to strip Kamali of her gifts." Halting before the library's patio doors, Nodin flung them open and fought to breathe. "I'll give Terran and Violet a few more hours to develop a plan, and then I'm leaving, with or without you."

"You're wise to wait." Flint ambled to his side. "Perhaps Quint only used a small seed inside Kamali. When we fought him here five years ago, he said he'd learned not to put all his eggs in one basket." He lightly squeezed Nodin's shoulder. "Don't speculate until we know for certain."

"Exactly, nothing is for certain." Nodin rubbed the back of his neck, trying to ease the day's strain. "I've seen enough visions to know this is true."

"Nodin." Terran knocked on the library doors. "It's Raven." He waved his cell phone. "She wishes to speak to you."

Though Nodin didn't own a phone, he understood how to use them. When the only people he spoke to were Elementals, and those calls were done through mind messages, he saw no reason to have a phone. Plus, during his transformations, he'd just lose it. He glanced over his shoulder at the Earth Elemental. "I will speak to her."

Terran weaved around the library furniture and handed Nodin the phone.

Flint braced both hands on his hips. "I won't turn Violet over to Quint. Don't ask that of me."

"We won't." Terran shook his head. "We'll find another way."

Nodin clutched the slim phone in his hand, missing the days when these communication devices had more substantial receivers. One you could slam down when finished. "What do you want?"

"You'll crush it." Terran pulled the cell phone from his grip and put it on speaker mode.

"What kind of greeting is that?" Raven asked, affront lacing her tone. "I'd watch how you speak to me, as you're in quite a bind, aren't you?" Raven paused. "Or, wait, maybe Kamali is in a bind. Yes, that's right, she's the one bound this time."

Nodin glared at the phone sitting on the table's edge and imagined pounding it to bits. A blast of air stirred papers off the library table, and they fluttered to the floor.

"What do you want?" Terran asked the question this time.

"I'm delivering a message," Raven responded. "Although, I tire of these high-handed men using me like some personal assistant."

"Get on with it." Nodin glanced at Terran, who prowled before him like an alpha wolf waiting to hear where to lead the pack.

"Has Maya been back to your cabin, Earth-man?" She hummed a laugh over the line.

Nodin's stomach sank, yet as he met Terran's gaze, he held no doubt his friend would simply rebuild. They had forever, after all. He tuned back in to Raven's speech.

"Speaking of the cabin, how did you explain to all those humans what you were doing?" she asked. "Aren't people fined for starting fires? I find it interesting Mother Nature would care more about shielding you from human view than protecting someone you cared about. And look where that got you. Kamali is with me...and Quint."

Nodin couldn't respond due to the choking fury building within his body. Mother *had* once again made a choice. He actually agreed with Raven's assessment. They did have to sacrifice, over and over again. When would it end?

"We easily gleaned their minds and sent them home." Terran again jumped into the conversation.

His friend's words were a bit of a lie, because changing so many minds had required a considerable amount of effort on their parts.

"Let's get back on point," Terran demanded. "As you say, you have Kamali. I imagine this is the part where we talk exchange?"

"Exactly, you really are the smart one in the bunch." She huffed out a laugh. "Kamali for Violet."

Flint's hands burst into flames. "He will never have her."

"Now, you see, therein lies the problem," Raven replied. "All the chaos and that bonfire, and the humans, plus whatever else you had up your sleeve last time, Quint wants none of it. A simple exchange with no tricks. And hear this, if Quint so much as detects the air temperature is one degree higher than Mr.

212

Weatherman says, he'll rip Kamali limb from limb. So, I'd keep Flint at home. You know Quint doesn't make idle threats."

Nodin clenched his jaw before meeting Flint's amber gaze and then Terran's deep brown eyes. Whatever happened, these two men had his back. They'd stand with him through the coming days, and whether they retrieved Kamali or if Violet was taken, they'd endure and fight together. He punched the phone off speaker and lifted the device to his ear. "I want reassurance Kamali is safe. We won't make the exchange if either she or Caddo are compromised."

"You're bluffing." Raven snorted. "You'll take the blind bitch any way you can get her. Please, I'm a master manipulator. Don't try to turn the tables on me."

"Tomorrow afternoon. Maya and Terran's land in Colorado." Nodin ignored Flint's low growl and the rush of heat firing through the room.

"Perfect," Raven answered. "Enjoy tonight, because tomorrow, everything in your fairy tale world ends. And how will my world be, you ask? I'll admit to a few road bumps but we are past that now, and I will reign as Quint's queen."

Nodin chuckled then bent over at the waist, laughing.

"What's so funny?" Raven asked.

"Ah, *you* are the fool," Nodin shot back. "Not so long ago, another woman spoke those same words. Her name was Pillar, and she followed your path." Nodin rolled his shoulders, shaking off those bitter memories. "In the end, Pillar met the same fate as all the others. She was overtaken by Quint's dark seed, and she died when Death obliterated her life force." He heaved a sigh, pitying this woman regardless of her treachery. No one remained at Quint's side. Ever. The dark creature only destroyed. "I'd do what you can to leave now, Raven. This path will not end well. We've heard such proclamations before, and yet, we're still here. Now answer my question, how is Kamali?"

"I already told you."

He narrowed his eyes. "She's bound?"

"Of course."

"Why would you do such a thing?"

"Oh, do you so easily forget how you treated me during my last visit?"

"You were not bound." Nodin pounded a fist against the library table.

"Wasn't I?"

Nodin fought for calm, and though he dreaded the answer, he still asked, "Is she or isn't she overtaken by Quint?"

As the phone went dead, he feared he'd received his answer.

CHAPTER 33

Sitting in a leather chair in a grouping of couches surrounding a coffee table in her uncle's office, Kamali studied the smoky black aura surrounding her cousin, Caddo. A hopeless grief exuded from his thoughts *and* his aura as he stood by the one-way glass overlooking his father's casino.

Releasing a jaw-cracking yawn, Kamali ran her fingers over the wooded armrests, elaborately carved with forest scenes. She'd spent many an hour in this very seat when working for her uncle. These familiar surroundings had her missing Maize. Her cousin, Isi, was hopefully drawing comfort from her guide dog's company in whatever location Mother Nature had hidden her family. Maize was safe, which was more than she could say for herself.

Luckily, Quint had left Caddo alone due to his ability to run the casino. She glanced at her cousin. He'd been quiet after asking if she needed anything.

Once again, she peeked into his mind. Concern for his family and the casino blared right at the forefront, along with a sense he wasn't as clever or ruthless as his father. All these worries intermeshed with contemplations of revenge for Waya's death.

"Caddo, you cannot defeat Quint." Kamali rubbed her wrists, which were practically scraped raw from Raven's rope bindings. "Do not even think such thoughts in Quint's presence, or Raven's. You are lucky he is letting you live."

After Raven had deposited her on a stinking cot, Kamali remained unaware of how much time had passed before one of her uncle's security men entered and released her from her aunt's makeshift dungeon.

The tinkling sounds and flashing lights from the casino's games didn't disturb this room. The innocent humans below had no idea of the cosmic struggles occurring above. If Kamali could, she'd pound on the glass until it splintered and warn each and every one of them to leave. They were in a viper's pit and had no idea when the hissing head would strike.

But she knew.

Quint's poison was lethal.

Caddo crossed the room to stand before her and gripped both her hands, twisting each upward to study her sore wrists. "The salve should help." He sighed, gazing at her with his deep brown eyes. "Are you sure Father and Isi are safe?"

"I am sure they are well hidden. I cannot say if any of us are truly safe as long as Quint continues to exist." Kamali blinked back tears, fighting to keep her mind in the present, not worrying about the Elementals…or Nodin. She'd sent a zillion mental messages into the universe, hoping Nodin would hear her silent pleas: *Do not come. Stay away.*

When she woke this morning, she'd felt weighted down, as if her lungs were filled with cement.

Or dark matter.

Throughout the day, she'd continually coughed as the small stream of Quint's darkness became a raging river through her body.

"Cousin, you seem quite pale." Caddo tilted his head as he brushed a hand over her cheek.

"I'm dying." Kamali squeezed her hands together in her lap. She'd yet to speak the words out loud, but that hadn't made the truth any less real. There was no escape. She only prayed her life would end quickly, without giving her time to dwell on all she would lose.

"Why would you say such a thing?" Caddo yanked back his hand then settled on the armrest. He gripped her chin between his forefinger and thumb, twisting her head from side-to-side. "Is it Quint?"

"Yes."

"Are you in pain?" Caddo shifted to sit at her feet. "What does his possession feel like?"

"I feel dirty." She swallowed then tried to clear her throat. Soon, she would be nothing but an empty vessel. Perhaps her entire body would disperse in a great burst of energy, or maybe she would wilt into nothingness. Either way, a yawning void awaited her. The seeping darkness grew with each beat of her heart. "My main concern is that the Elementals will fight for me when I am not worth saving."

"Don't say that." Her cousin rested his head on her lap.

"I will not last much longer." Kamali rested her head against the chair and combed her fingers through her cousin's silky hair.

"We will find a way. The Elementals will save you."

She had chosen to enter this fight. She would not regret a single moment, no matter the dark stain currently erasing her life. "The Elementals have the entire world to save. I have no hope of surviving, and I will not—" She straightened as a vision of coffee cups overflowing with black sludge ripped through her mind. "Oh, no." She shoved Caddo from her lap. "Get the people out of here. Quint's done something to the drinks. To the coffee." Kamali shot out of her chair and made for the door. "Caddo, hit the Evacuation button."

Caddo rushed to his father's desk and pressed the button. "What's Quint done to the coffee?"

Alarms sounded in the casino below.

"I don't know. I just saw something bubbling out of cups. Something's in the drinks."

Caddo's eyes went wide. "The employees. They gather in the lounge before and after their shifts. I need to get down there." He shoved past her and raced toward the stairwell.

Kamali heard him on his cell, directing the security chief to evacuate and keep everyone away from all beverages. She jogged down the hall at a much slower pace, already well aware of the effect Quint's poison could have on the body.

What did he use? One of Malachi's potions? Why would that thought occur? She prayed this seeming omniscience was false.

Were the employees already infected? And with what? What cures existed against dark magic and an even-darker creature?

Kamali pressed the button on the elevator.

Caddo's voice erupted across the hotel's speaker system. "Forgive the interruption. We've experienced a water line break and will be closed today. Please exit immediately. Do not drink any liquids, as the water is contaminated. Any employees who have drunk anything this morning, please remain in the break room for further information."

With a heavy heart, Kamali rode the elevator down to the ground level and then weaved around slot machines to the break room. Though her eyesight might be sketchy, her ears worked just fine.

Cries and shouts came from the employee area.

Security guards raced past.

Shaking so badly she could barely keep upright, Kamali halted in the hallway just outside the door, closed her eyes, and offered a prayer to the Great Spirit for the deliverance of each person in that room. Prayed that human doctors could discover the source. Prayed for families sure to be torn apart. Prayed for peace in a world suddenly gone mad.

Mad, or part of Quint's plan? He'd warned them, and now he'd fulfilled his promise, grimly and without mercy.

Suddenly, someone gripped her by the shoulders.

Kamali shrieked and opened her eyes. Caddo stood before

her, a look on his face that could only be described as pure terror.

"They're all dead."

CHAPTER 34

Late fall in the Rio Grande National Forest brought temps in the low sixties, though the cool breeze and slight autumn rain made the temperatures seem chilly.

Nodin shook the damp hair from his face. Nothing would faze him. Nothing would detract his focus from Kamali. This time, *this* fight would end it all and they would begin again.

His Elemental team had left Ireland last night, plan in place. Flint would join Terran in creating the intense fireball until Violet could compress it with her electromagnetic field.

This morning they had gathered as much firewood as possible. The spruce beetle infestation of more than 550,000 acres of spruce and fir trees meant there were plenty of dead trees to burn.

Violet had used a spell to cloak Terran and Flint's activities while they started a fire up in the mountains.

Their main concern was whether Violet had enough internal power to sustain the black hole, or if all her energies would be depleted before Quint was captured.

Maya stood beside him, clipping and unclipping her long blonde hair. She'd seemed rather Zen after finding her cabin destroyed once more. Perhaps, she understood they could build again. Or maybe, she was more worried about Terran.

While at the airport, Violet and Flint had seen the news reports out of Oklahoma this morning about the strange deaths at Kamali's uncle's casino. Luckily, Caddo had evacuated the premises right after opening. This gave Nodin hope that Kamali was well. He believed his brave girl had warned them.

Nodin gazed at the mountain, detecting a small trail of smoke. Terran was to use his Air gift to keep the smoke at a minimum to avoid detection by Quint.

He itched to join his brothers. Was Terran capable of controlling more than one of his Elemental gifts at a time? And if so, for how long?

Violet stood along the edge of the forest line, her fingers sparking with white and blue arcs.

Upon the wind, Nodin detected the smell of burnt wood. He blew a breeze in the direction of the scent, keeping the area clear of anything that might alert Quint to their plans.

A royal blue SUV lumbered down the drive.

He sent a mental message to Terran. *"They're here."*

After the vehicle rolled to a stop, Quint stepped out of the back seat, tugging Kamali along at his side.

She swayed then stumbled to her knees.

Nodin surged forward. "Something is very wrong."

About ten feet from Kamali, Maya blocked him, holding his arm.

"Where is Violet?" Quint glanced around the yard.

"I am here." Violet waved a hand, though she remained along the forest's edge.

His Elemental brothers were making their way down the mountain, bringing the fireball closer and still cloaked by Violet's spell.

Nodin glanced at Kamali and sent her a mental message. *"What's wrong?"*

She wouldn't meet his gaze. *"Do not make this exchange. I am not worth losing Violet."*

"We won't lose her."

"Quint knows no mercy."

"Then neither shall we."

"Where are the others?" Quint turned in a circle. "I don't believe they didn't come to see you off, dear."

Violet brushed her purple hair over her shoulder. "You got what you wanted, I'm here. Now hand over Kamali."

Kamali shook her head. "Please, don't do this."

Quint shoved her forward.

Nodin lunged and caught her before she fell.

She shivered and was struck by a racking cough.

"Kamali." He rubbed a hand along her back. "Are you all right?"

She didn't respond, only shook her head again.

Quint hadn't shifted his gaze from Violet. "You have her. Now, Violet, come with me. Everything will be perfect, you'll see." He snapped his fingers, then turned and glared at Kamali. "The girl seems to have caught a cold." He shrugged, shifting his gaze back to Violet. "Come now, dear. No more stalling."

Nodin braced for an attack, a stream of particles or a blast of energy, but nothing came.

Maya brushed against his shoulder. "Something isn't right."

Nodin tried gleaning Kamali's mind and found nothing but despair. Everything was off kilter. Why wasn't Quint attacking?

Brow arched high, Quint frowned at Violet. "What tricks are you planning? Why not just come peacefully? I've held to my end of the bargain, and I can assure you that if I leave here without you, the tragedy at the casino this morning will seem like child's play."

"There is no peace while you linger on this plane." Arcs of electricity leapt across Violet's body, as if her veins were filled with flashing lights. "I will follow you nowhere."

A low roar rumbled through the forest.

Nodin turned to see a fireball lighting up the entire forest.

Ashes drifted through the air, landing on his skin. "Maya, the heat will be too intense for Kamali. Let's lead her away."

Quint kicked the SUV's tires. "I knew it. But, I still don't understand why. We'll just be here again at some later date. Why threaten those humans you all hold so dear by continuing this fruitless fight? You're all mad." He stomped across the field toward Kamali. "I'll take back my bargaining chip."

Terran and Flint blazed out of the forest, walking beside a large ball of flame.

Quint halted, lifting a hand to shield his eyes. "The fireball again? What do you mean to do with it?"

Blue bolts shot from Violet's chest. She opened her arms, encompassing the fire within her electromagnetic field. Yellow, red, and gold flames were surrounded with what looked like blue and white fencing.

The fire's sphere began to narrow.

Now that the black hole began to form, Maya and Nodin spoke the compulsion chant, which drew Quint closer and closer to the shrinking ball of fire.

"What is this?" Quint fell to his knees and clawed at the ground, trying to halt his forward momentum.

Without warning, Kamali flew from Nodin's arms, her body somersaulting through the air, closer and closer to the developing void. She glanced over her shoulder.

Nodin glimpsed her empty black stare. "No." The reality of his vision hit like an uppercut to the chin. Only this nightmare was so much worse. Not only was Kamali infected, but because she held Quint's darkness inside, her body was also being drawn into the black hole. Disoriented by this assessment, Nodin lost precious time. He jolted to attention when Kamali surged even closer to the dark void.

Violet compressed the mass further and further until it flashed white then full black.

"Wait, you must stop." Nodin waved his hands and stepped

across the yard, gripping Kamali in his arms. "Kamali has been poisoned by Quint's dark matter."

"What are you doing?" Maya came to his side. "It's working."

"No." He struggled to keep Kamali in his arms. "Violet is pulling Kamali in with Quint. The spell doesn't know the difference. Kamali has a dark seed inside. We must stop."

"No." Maya glanced at Violet. "We stopped the spell once before, and Quint returned. We must finish this."

"We will find another way." Nodin had to believe their story wouldn't end this way. He'd just found Kamali.

Maya shook her head. "If Kamali is polluted by Quint then there is no hope for her survival. I'm sorry, but we must fulfill our duty to mankind." She placed a hand upon his cheek. "Kamali is already lost."

A bright light flashed across the yard, so bright it blinded him. He braced his feet apart, gripping Kamali in his arms. Her life may be forfeit, but she would not end in an alternate dimension with only Quint by her side.

Within his mind, Nodin heard Quint chuckle. *"I'll keep her alive on the other side, Nodin."* Then the dark menace tumbled closer to the pathway to another dimension.

Where would that lead? Were they damning another society by sending Quint through? Or would he remain within the black hole, spinning and spinning forever?

Nodin dropped to his knees and used his gift to knock Violet away from the spinning black hole, but the gravitational pull was too strong. *She* was too strong. *"Terran, Flint, please stop Violet...Kamali is infected and will go through the portal with Quint. I can't lose her this way."*

Flint tore his gaze from Violet and shook his head. *"Violet cannot do this again. We end this now."*

"You would condemn Kamali to the darkness, then?"

"You do not know what is on the other side."

"Neither do you, but on this side we have love. Please, let her die in peace."

"You ask too much of me."

"I ask as one brother to another. I've seen your future, let me keep a small piece of mine."

A moment later, the flames ebbed, and the tug against Kamali ceased.

"What did you do? What was that?" Eyes wide, Quint stumbled backward before disappearing with a sonic boom that sprinkled his dark dust across the grass.

Violet fell to her knees, bracing herself with her arms on the ground. "We had him." She punched the grass before glaring at Flint. "Why did you stop me?"

"He didn't stop you, I did...for Kamali." Nodin lifted Kamali in his arms. Second-degree burns blistered her skin, her hair dull and brittle, and her entire body emaciated. She wavered at the edge of death.

And no cure existed for her...or for him.

CHAPTER 35

"We had him." Terran landed in the castle's bedroom just behind Nodin. "This is the second time you've stopped us from completing the spell. How many times have you said, 'we cannot let our personal feelings interfere with our elemental duties'? And yet, here we are."

Nodin sidestepped Terran's jabbing finger and placed Kamali atop the bed's blue and green quilt. "Five years ago, I did step in, yes, because, just as today, I couldn't let the people I loved die." He fluffed the pillow behind Kamali's head, and then brushed a finger down her cold, hollow cheek. "The moment I do not fight for life is the day I do not wish to be an Elemental." For his part, Nodin would accept the scolding from his brethren, yet nothing penetrated his heart or mind except Kamali and the fact she was slipping away. "You've said your piece. Now leave me be."

Terran combed his fingers through his short hair before drawing closer to the bed. "I am not pleased, but I would not have Kamali's death on my conscience, either."

"Living this peri-mortal life, we forget how precious time can be." Nodin heaved a sigh. "I knew I would lose her, but I thought I had time...and now I'm too late."

"No." Terran rubbed his chin. "Perhaps there is a spell. Something that can remove Quint from her body. We'll look. I promise we'll do everything we can to find a way." He turned to leave the room, but he stopped in the doorway. "We'll discuss our plans for Quint later. I don't know what I would have done if Maya was the one dying, but...we must consider the greater good. I don't know the answers, but we'll move past your actions today." He tapped the door with his fist before saluting. "I'll head down and help Maya look through the spell books."

"Thank you." Nodin glanced at the clock ticking away on the side table. Each movement of the ornate second hand mocked him.

He leaned over the bed, took Kamali's hand, and whispered in her ear, expressing hope and love, telling stories he'd never shared with anyone. For over four hundred years he'd evaded death, but this tightness in his chest, this inability to take a full breath, this ache in every part of his body...this was, in a sense, his end.

When she breathed her last, she would find peace. But what was in store for him? More loneliness? More aimless wanderings? Turning to look out the window, he watched dawn streak across the sky in a wave of gold.

Kamali's breathing turned raspy, each breath a harsh puff.

After brushing her hair behind her ear, Nodin rubbed his eyes. "Stay with me just a little longer."

Mother Nature entered and slowly inched across the room. Her movements seemed measured, and her coloring lacked its vibrant shine. She still suffered from their last fight against Quint.

Nodin returned his gaze to Kamali. "Is there a way to save her?"

Mother took his hand. "If a solution is found, Kamali must fight, as well. As with any magic there is always a price. If we succeed in saving her life, then she must accept what she's become."

"Consequences and repercussions matter little in this moment." Nodin clenched his jaw. "Not when she's struggling to breathe, and her entire body is being sucked dry by Quint's dark matter." An idea occurred, and he shot out of his seat. "Transform her. Turn her into the Air Elemental. I'll change places with her. Just, please…do something. She doesn't have much longer."

"She is too close to the edge, and I am still weak." Mother shook her head, causing her red-gold locks to glimmer in the morning light.

"She never had a chance to live." Nodin clasped Mother's hand and held it to his forehead. "She is so young."

"I'm sorry, my child."

"I saw it, you know. The darkness in her eyes, but I thought I could keep her safe. And now, I've put everyone in danger. I made a selfish choice, but I don't wish it otherwise. I could not send her into that portal with Quint…I just couldn't."

"We all face hard choices." She sat on the bed beside Kamali, placing her hand just above her heart. "Go help them search for a spell. I will keep watch and offer what strength I am able."

Heart aching, Nodin gazed at Kamali before bending and kissing her dry lips. "I love you, Pakali. You will bloom again…you must."

The answers had to lay within the spell books…because he couldn't live without her.

# # #

Walls closed in around Nodin.

The grandfather clock kept ticking.

Stacks and stacks of books lay beside him with words and spells blurred together.

Nothing.

No answers.

Where was Eamon? Maya had left him a message two hours ago. Wasn't he a supposed supreme wizard? Where were all his tricks now?

Maya had called on Flint mentally to ask which books Violet thought would be of best use. She had her blonde head buried in the recommended tome now. Beside her, Terran read another.

"Nodin." Mother's lyrical voice spoke in his mind, portending an end.

"No. I need more time."

"I'm sorry."

"Maya, do you have anything? Terran?"

Terran met his gaze with a solemn one of his own.

Maya held up a finger. "Maybe."

"I have your answer." Eamon stood in the doorway, leaning heavily on a cane. Gray tufts surrounded his ears, and he had wise violet eyes.

"You should be resting." Maya frowned. "I could have come to you."

"Take this spell." Eamon handed over an old tome full of loose parchment papers. "But, know this, you'll each absorb Quint's matter and Kamali might not be the same. I cannot join you, as I am unable to purge Quint's darkness. This spell will work, but it will exact a price."

Mother's voice tore through Nodin's mind. *"I believe you should come upstairs, now."*

"I'll pay it." In a daze, Nodin pushed back in his chair.

Eamon rubbed his bearded chin. "Be careful what you freely give. The price isn't always yours to pay." After issuing his warning, he shuffled off.

"We have to go upstairs. Mother is calling me. We have to do this."

Maya and Terran joined hands and nodded.

Upon entering the bedroom, they found Mother standing by the bed. In her quiet tone, she conveyed the gravity of Kamali's condition. "It must be now."

"Everyone, gather in a circle around Kamali's bed," Maya

directed. "Join hands. Now, I'll speak the words and you repeat. Sound good?"

Nodin spared a final glance at Kamali's body before closing his eyes and linking hands with Maya and Terran.

Maya spoke the spell's words and they all repeated each line.

"Seeker, seeker pull her free.
For her death is not to be
Remove the darkness from her core
And into each Elemental pour
An equal drop of the black seed
Because within we do not bleed."

Nodin jerked as pain billowed through this body. The words now clear. He could remove Quint's blight, while Kamali could not. Why hadn't they thought of such a simple solution before? Would she survive, now that Quint's dark matter had transferred into their Elemental forms?

Maya continued the spell.

"Pour from this well all that is foreign
And before we finish this chant
All will be as it was meant
Magic thank you for time spent
As one we make this desperate plea
By combining earth, air, nature, and sea
We ask, dear Death set Kamali free
As we will so mote it be."

After Maya finished the spell, Nodin opened his eyes and studied Kamali. A slight blush had returned to her face.

"I feel Quint's dark matter, don't you?" Maya coughed and glanced at Terran. "We'll have to heal."

Nodin sank onto the bed. "Maya, before you go, would you mind giving Kamali some of your healing waters, in case the spell wasn't enough?"

Maya set her lips upon Kamali's dry ones and released trickle after trickle of her healing flow.

"Don't drown the poor woman." Terran tugged on Maya's hand. "We need to rejuvenate."

"Wait." She stayed by Kamali's side. "I want to see if my waters helped."

Kamali remained still, but her breathing began to clear.

"You have to fight, Kamali." Nodin kissed her forehead. "Please, come back to me."

Suddenly, she gasped then her entire body stiffened. A smoky gray wisp poured from her eyes.

"What the hell is that?" Nodin glanced at Maya. "What's happening?"

"I'm not sure."

The smoke separated into four streams and shot into each of their mouths.

"I-Is that the last of Quint's matter?" Nodin sputtered.

Kamali breathed deeply, and then she exhaled a puff of pure white smoke from her mouth and nose. The mass hovered over each of her eyes before disappearing.

Terran cleared his throat. "Maya, we should go. You, too, Nodin. You need to rejuvenate."

"But, what was that?" Nodin glanced at Terran, and then Mother.

Neither would meet his gaze.

"What aren't you telling me?"

Mother took a deep breath. "The spell removed all that was foreign. I worry that it took her back to her most natural state."

"What does that mean?" Nodin rubbed Kamali's cold hand between his.

"I can't be sure, but in taking away Quint's influence, we may have removed all her other special gifts, as well." Mother offered a sad smile. "Which means, she'll no longer see auras...or..."

"Or me. She won't see me." Clutching the bedpost, Nodin fought to catch his breath. "I never meant for that to happen." His body shook from Quint's inky presence, yet he refused to leave Kamali's side. "I don't understand. *We* sacrificed. *We* took Quint's stain from her body."

"Magic doesn't discriminate. We can't ask the spell to remove unnatural items, but expect it to differentiate between the good and bad." Mother clasped Kamali's free hand. "The spell only did as we asked."

Nodin shook his head. "What have we done?"

Terran placed a hand on his shoulder. "I'm sorry we did not see this possibility, but she lives. She is the first human to be pulled from Quint's grip. Will it matter if she has no gifts and she cannot see?"

"Absolutely not." Nodin glared at the Earth Elemental. "I need to leave. I can't breathe with Quint's matter rattling around in my chest." He took Mother's hand. "You will stay by her side?"

"Of course."

"Her blindness never mattered to me, but I can't imagine how heartbroken she will be."

"Within our lifetime, however long we each live, we make choices and those choices have consequences that we can't always see or understand. Yet, we go on, Nodin." Mother squeezed his hand. "Move forward. That is all we can do."

"I'll leave you to watch over her." He nodded at Mother, and then headed downstairs and pushed past the front door.

His love for Kamali would see them through. As Mother had said, he'd made so many choices throughout his vast lifetime, and all had led to this moment. They would move on, regardless of the spell's costs.

Floating over the Irish countryside, soaring higher and higher, he considered his future with Kamali. If she wished, he would transform into a human. If she chose to blame him for her loss of sight, he would accept that, as well.

But his woman was a fighter. This removal of her gifts would *not* keep her from living a fulfilling life. He had to believe she knew that. Hadn't she said so, many times before? When he returned, he'd clarify how much he loved her. All of her.

Perhaps, Mother was wrong. Maybe Kamali would fully heal. Maybe the spell hadn't taken her gifts. Something that was passed down family lines wasn't really foreign or unnatural, was it?

Shaking his head, he chastised himself for worrying about such things when he should be grateful Kamali still lived. Hadn't Osho said, 'Life should not only be lived, it should be celebrated'? This was never truer than in the moment they'd pulled her free of Quint's clutches, from the very cusp of death. Nodin sent a mental thanks to the Great Spirit for answering his prayers. He'd seen few miracles, but today surely counted as one.

But, would Kamali feel the same? Would she still see their love?

Or had that been erased from her vision, too?

CHAPTER 36

After Mother left her side, Kamali lay stunned. Each word the mystical woman had spoken still roared through her mind.

They had performed a spell to free her from death.

But now...

Now, she'd returned to darkness.

No auras. No shadowed forms.

Just darkness.

"I must learn to live another way." She fought to keep from hyperventilating as she looked around the room but saw nothing. "I'm of no use to Nodin...or anyone." She clutched the blankets in her hands.

Maize nudged Kamali's hand with her cold, wet nose.

"Not now, Maize." Mother had returned her guide dog, understanding she would need her now more than ever.

Lost to bitterness, Kamali threw her pillow across the room. Why give her a glimpse of the world then rip it all away? Why let her see the beauty of a man then offer nothing? Why offer a hint of love then rip out her heart? Not that she and Nodin ever truly had a future, anyway. She would die. Did Nodin believe he could keep her alive forever with spells and tricks? How much would the magic take from her each time? What sacrifices would it demand? "I will *not* be a walking corpse."

Maize brought the pillow back to the bed.

"No, girl. We aren't playing fetch." Kamali sighed and ruffled Maize's head. "I missed you. We'll leave once I'm stronger and forge our way forward. We'll go back to where we belong."

"You belong here." Nodin's voice breezed through the room.

Drawing on the remnants of her fading inner strength, Kamali straightened her shoulders, fighting to convince herself that she would not cry over no longer seeing his handsome face. His lean body. That red-brown skin and those beautiful blue eyes. And that sure smile with those deep red lips. Colors were only memories now, just as he would be.

"I'm sorry, Kamali." He took her hand.

For the first time since Mother left, she felt a faint sense of warmth flickering through her body.

"We didn't know the spell would take everything. I'm so very, very sorry." He kissed her hand.

Kamali breathed deep once then twice, fighting the overwhelming sense of loss, of knowing the chill would return once she let him go. "It doesn't matter."

"I think it does…very much."

"I'd like you to leave." She swallowed hard against the lump in her throat. "I need time to process what has happened, and to be honest…I don't…I'd rather you not watch me fall apart."

"Kamali…when you love someone, you stay through everything. I'm sorry I wasn't here when Mother explained the repercussions of the spell." He sank onto the bed beside her. "But know this, nothing has changed for me. You are still my future."

"I am no one's future." *Please*, she mentally pleaded, *just go*. Her entire world hung from a very thin thread, and with each word, he whittled away at her tenuous grip on sanity. If he didn't leave, he'd see her at her worst. As she crashed and tore and burned through all her raging emotions. No one should witness that. Ever. "We both know I no longer serve any purpose here;

therefore, once I am better, I think it's best if I return home."

Nodin was quiet for a moment, circling her palm with his thumb. "Our purpose is to love one another."

"Is it? Why?" she practically shrieked, slipping closer and closer to that thread snapping in two. "There was never any hope for us. I was here to help with Quint, and I can no longer do that. So, I'll go back home, live maybe another sixty years, and then die."

"Don't say that." Nodin's voice was barely above a whisper. "Don't speak of your death as if it means nothing when it means everything." He rested his head against her stomach and drew her hand to his lips again. "Don't you know that? What more must I prove? I gave up everything to keep you alive, and I'd do so again."

"My death is a certainty." She crossed her arms over her chest, denying the urge to run her fingers through his silky black hair. "You, on the other hand, will live forever. Therefore, we're non-compatible." For unfathomable reasons, she suddenly wanted to hurt him, wanted to hurt everyone. Maybe because he wouldn't leave? Maybe because he made her feel guilty when she wanted to bask in misery? Or was this sudden anger because she didn't feel worthy of his sacrifices?

Wallowing in self-pity wasn't who she was, so why couldn't she stop?

Him. His presence beside her ripped at her heart unlike anything she'd ever felt before, because she couldn't *see* him. "I don't want to say hurtful things." She clenched her jaw and choked back tears. "I can't see, Nodin, and right now that hurts...real bad. But you sitting here, with me not seeing you...the man I love but can't have, the man who showed me the colors of bliss. Can't you understand how that's tearing me apart? Can't I please, have a moment to adjust before you come in here and talk to me about a future I no longer envision?"

"Kamali Kiwidinok, you may not have the ability to see the

future but at least you have one."

"That's not fair." She turned away as the tears started to spill. "You're not fighting fair. I have no value to you, and I've lost something precious, something that defined who I am. What will become of me, Nodin? I just need time to figure everything out." Done. So done with this conversation and the conflicting thoughts racing through her mind, she turned on her side and curled into a ball. "Please, go."

"All right, Kamali. I will go, but first I need to say something." Mercifully, he stalled only a moment, running a hand up and down her quilt-covered hip before he stood. "You are being very unfair to those who live fantastic lives without sight. You know this. I shouldn't have to remind you."

After hearing that reprimand, she detected the sound of padding feet, which signaled his departure. He was right, of course, which only made her feel worse, as did his next words.

"And you're wrong, your life is all I value. I have spent hours thanking the Great Spirit for your life. I loved all of you before, and I love all of you now. Don't lessen what we have together."

She heard Nodin sigh, and then the jingle of Maize's collar.

Just when she thought she was alone, she practically jumped out of her skin when Nodin spoke once more. "I ask that you consider what I've said, and for now, I'll do as you wish and leave you be."

And for the next two days, he did just that.

CHAPTER 37

Itchy, so itchy and so sick of this bed. Kamali grumbled out a curse and scratched at the side of her seriously-in-need-of-a-shampoo head. After wallowing for far too long, she needed a shower in a bad way. While her body recovered, she'd steered clear of self-pity, especially after Nodin's stern talk. This morning, she'd finally eaten more than just a few bites from the tray Violet and Maya delivered. After speaking to her new friends, she realized how close to death she'd been. Nodin had gone against his Elemental team and put the world on hold—for her.

But, the scope of his choice was hard to process when her head pounded, her body ached, and her heart drooped.

Still, a single thought kept racing through her mind. Nodin had saved her, but for what? How could she make that sacrifice worthwhile?

He loved her.

And she did love him, but she'd needed these past few days to recuperate both mentally and physically. Sitting alone for hours, she'd devised a plan. A way she could again help the Elementals. A way to bring the fight back into her spirit.

Nodin would throw up roadblocks but she needed to do this, for the Elementals and for her mother. And maybe even a little for herself. Actually, a lot for herself.

She would face off against Raven and retrieve the gifts stolen from her mother. Gifts that belonged to her. Hadn't they called to her from within Raven? Wasn't restoring her rightful claim on her mother's powers her due?

Raven used them for evil.

Kamali would not, could not.

Maize ambled back in. Maya had taken her for a walk this morning. The dog smelled wet, which proved true when she plopped her paws on the bed.

"Oh, girl, no. You'll get this quilt dirty." Kamali ruffled her ears. "Why didn't they dry you off?"

Maize made a groaning sound then flopped onto the floor.

"Are you tired from your rambles, girl? I'm tired, too." Kamali sighed. "Is it fair to rip away Raven's powers when she is suffering under Quint's thumb?" She shifted to the side of the bed and sat up, blinking away a wave of dizziness. "Maize, come."

Maize bumped Kamali's hand with her nose.

"You are my lifeline. My eyes." Kamali gripped her guide dog's handle. "I only sent you with Isi and Uncle Adler to keep you safe."

Maize wiggled between her legs and licked her hand.

"Nodin loves me. And he'll help me...after I apologize." Mentally crossing her fingers, Kamali placed her big toe on the cold wood floor. "I just needed a purpose, and now I have one, and even if this doesn't work...well then...we'll do what we can, won't we?" She placed her foot full on the floor and followed with the other. Stretching, she closed her eyes against the lightheadedness and realized perhaps she should have eaten a lot more breakfast and surely a gallon of tea.

"Oh, you're up." Maya's voice came from the doorway.

"Yes." Kamali clasped her hands together at her waist before clearing her throat. "I'd like to thank you, Maya. I haven't been a good patient these past few days, and I'm sorry for that. I'm leaving that bed and with it my despair, my anger, and my complete lack of courage."

"Kamali." The water-girl responded with a soft, understanding tone. "You've been through change after change for weeks now."

"I need your help, but first I'd like to shower. Will you show me the way, please?"

She heard Maya's sniffle then the pad of feet across the floor was followed by a warm touch on her elbow.

"Any time water's involved, of course, I'm your girl. Let me tell ya, it's a good thing you offered, because this afternoon, I was planning on hosing you off myself." Maya chuckled and led her into the bathroom.

Moments later, Kamali stood under the spray and let the woman she was wash away and accepted the woman she'd become.

#

In the chair by the library's crackling fire, Nodin rocked back and forth, listening but not engaging in the plans developing around the table.

Though grateful Kamali had finally rejoined the living, he remained...well no other word...or philosophical quote could say it any better, he hurt. She hadn't believed in their love. True, she had escaped death and needed to heal, but didn't she understand they were stronger together?

His Elemental partners had suggested he give her time to come to terms with her changes. Easier said than done, especially when, with each day, he'd felt Kamali slipping farther and farther from his grasp.

She wanted to leave him. Return to Oklahoma without him at her side. How could she walk away from everything they had become to one another? Unsure of his place in Kamali's life, he sat quietly and listened to her and his team develop a plan to retrieve her gifts.

Her voice was animated. Not dripping with misery. *This* was the fighter he loved. This woman would not accept life as it was, she would ask for more. Was taking back Raven's stolen gifts a harsh form of revenge? Possibly. He turned that thought over in his mind. Were they no better than this female villain? He didn't believe so, because Raven had stolen them from Kamali's dying mother. She had, in fact, caused the woman's death.

Still, in the end, the retrieval of these gifts mattered little. He loved Kamali as she was. The gifts had only counted in the beginning. But, as he rested against the wooden rocking chair, he conceded that detecting auras *was* a part of her. A part she could regain. And since her happiness mattered, perhaps instead of remaining wounded by her words, he should help make plans.

If their retrieval was successful, Kamali could continue in their fight against Quint. He halted his rocking. Quint and Kamali together again? No. Just no.

Frowning, he tuned back in as Violet discussed the challenges of their course and what magic they could employ.

Magic. He no longer trusted it. What would the price be this time? What if they somehow transferred a part of Raven's evil soul? Hadn't they dallied with forces they didn't understand long enough? Not to mention, how would they hold Raven long enough to pull those energies free when she had a menacing cloud of dark matter hovering nearby?

The stakes were too high.

He'd already paid with each drip of his heart, falling like worthless coins at Kamali's feet.

Damn it! Who is lost to self-pity now, Air-man?

"Nodin." Kamali spoke from her seat at the table. "You are so quiet. What do you think of this plan?"

"I wish you the best with it." He shrugged then stood and stretched, unwilling to be brought into the conversation.

"You do not think it sound?"

"I lost too much after that last spell. I hate to think what I'll lose this time." He headed for the door.

"Nodin, I—"

"Forgive me," he interrupted, refusing to further display his damaged heart by delving into deep discussion before all his friends. Let them soothe her worries. He no longer had the strength. "I need air."

CHAPTER 38

"Nodin, wait." Kamali reached for Maize's leader bar. "May I speak to you?" He'd been so quiet and still in the corner as they talked and planned. But she believed he wasn't quiet on the inside. He surely had a lot to say and he deserved his moment.

"I'm going outside."

"I'll follow. Maya, would you watch Maize, please?"

"Sure." Maya took her elbow and led her across the room. "Nodin, wait for Kamali."

He huffed out a half-sigh, half-growl then replaced Maya's hand at her elbow. "Fine."

They walked along in silence for a few steps. She sported a pair of Maya's flip-flops. All her clothes were borrowed: Violet's T-shirt, Maya's pants. She missed her apartment back in Oklahoma. Things were organized there, not foreign or confusing.

A cool breeze lifted her hair off her shoulders and reminded her of her purpose. "Nodin, allow me to apologize. I-I needed a few days to come to terms with so many things. But that does not mean I don't appreciate my life and what you did for me. Thank you for keeping me here. I'm not finished yet. I want more, and I'll get it, thanks to you."

She halted along their path. "I'm happy to let you lead me, I just need to know where we are going. Today we walk along this path, and tomorrow we'll take another." After clearing her throat, she tugged on the neck of her T-shirt. "Still, I need to know that you'll continue to walk by my side. Unless I've ruined our chances? Please tell me I haven't."

He released her arm. "You say you want me at your side, yet you never spoke to me of your idea. You just floated down the stairs, and the lot of you went into planning mode. Sending you back to Oklahoma, facing off against Raven and Quint." He growled. "He's likely to drop you where you stand, and this time you won't get back up." He practically shouted the words. "Kamali, how can you do this to yourself...to me? I don't know that I could save you this time. Are you so eager to take another step toward death?"

"I will not die."

"And you are so sure of this why?"

"Because you will keep me safe." She had to believe this truth. There was a reason she had lived when all others had died from Quint's infestation, and she would discover that reason with Nodin. "My journey is not yet finished."

"I've done a horrible job of protecting you so far. If you leave, if you follow through with this plan, I won't even be with you."

"Yes, you will. Take my hand, please." She brought his hand to her heart. "You'll be here."

"Am I?"

She ran her hand up his arm to his shoulder. "Always. You sacrificed so much for me. I must do this for you and the Elementals. I've seen the lengths Quint will go to in order to prove his point. After that morning in the employee lounge...he must be stopped."

"And if it doesn't work? If he simply uses you to strike against us again?"

"Then at least I was brave enough to try." She threw up her hands. "After all I've received from you, I will not continue without fighting back. Stand with me. Let me choose my own way, and if I end, then I do so at your side."

"I almost lost you, and now you ask me to follow you to your death. I was already there." He cupped her face in his hands. "I don't know if I can do as you ask. I just…" He halted, and a quiet moment passed.

The breeze, along with her fear she'd have to walk her path alone, shot shivers through her body.

"Damn it, Kamali." Nodin grabbed her arm and practically lifted her off her feet in his haste to get her back inside. "It's too fucking cold out here. You've been unwell, and you're making all these plans and walking around in summer clothes, and you haven't even recuperated from death. You're not talking sense."

Good. Emotion laced his tone again, even if it was anger. And since that seemed to be working, she pushed her luck. "I can walk on my own, you know, and I don't know where all this foul language is coming from."

"You think to face off against Quint again, and you're worried about my language?" He jerked to a halt. "I'm the one who has to live with visions of your decimated body. I'm the one who has to go on if your plan backfires."

"It won't."

He grumbled out another curse. "It might, Kamali. Wake up. He almost killed you." He heaved a sigh then, after a moment, gripped her elbow again. "We'll discuss this again after you've rested. Maybe then you'll have a clearer head."

"If I rest, will you stay with me?"

He didn't respond, only continued to lead her inside and carted her up the stairs.

"Wait." She placed a hand against his chest. "Is there another room we can use? My bedroom…it…it's messy, and I don't want to be in there anymore. I want a fresh room." And a fresh start. Though she'd been a complete disaster for days, she now had faith. He had said he loved her, and that emotion didn't disappear.

Even the deepest of loves may fade at times, but echoes always remained, waiting to once more shout from the rooftops. Perhaps she should show him how very sorry she was, and that she loved him, too.

"This bedroom door is unlocked." Nodin opened the door and whisked her across the threshold. "There is a bed, but no sheets. I'll set you over here in this chair while I go get some." He suited actions to words as she heard him plod back toward the door.

"Nodin." She rose from her seat. "I don't care about sheets. What I care about is mending what is broken between you and me." No sound came from the room, but then she heard a rustle. "Will you sit beside me so I don't have to guess where you are?"

He sighed again. Then the sound of a chair being drug across the room filled the emptiness.

"Is the chair heavy?"

"Not especially."

"Then why drag it?"

"What does it matter?"

She held back a grin at his grouchy tone. "May I touch your face?"

He cleared his throat. "I suppose so." He led her hands to his face.

She traced the contours, keeping her eyes closed as she recalled each and every feature. "I am very sorry for my behavior and for asking you to accept my plans, but I must do something. I must repay everything—"

His head shook back and forth between her palms.

"Please, let me finish." She tipped up his chin, and though she couldn't see him, she needed to feel as if he maintained eye contact as she spoke. "I was buried beneath a deep gloom. I no longer saw any color, and I didn't know how I was supposed to feel. Please, forgive me." She moved her hands down his face to rest on his shoulders. "I took out my frustration on you, the one person whose shoulder I should've leaned on. I was so angry with you, and myself, at everyone, because I lost something precious. Can you at least try to understand, a little?"

"I do understand. And you weren't fair. You shut me out. How am I supposed to trust you, if you don't trust me?"

"I didn't trust *me*. I had to figure out who I was meant to become." She huffed out a half-laugh. "Most people take years to find themselves, I only took a few days."

"This isn't funny, Kamali."

"I know. I'm sorry." She bit her lip to keep from smiling. At least he was here. He hadn't left and he was still listening. How much farther would he let her go? She caressed his face again with one hand while massaging the back of his neck with the other. To touch him again when she could have died brought her to life in every way. "I would ask for your support again. Help me regain what Raven stole from my mother. If my plan doesn't work, I promise I will not wallow again." After tracing his lips with her fingers, she leaned forward and kissed him. "The future will be what we make of it." She squeezed his shoulder. "Please, know you own my heart, forever."

Nodin placed her hand on his heart and covered it with his own. "Though only air flows through my veins, please know this is yours. Never doubt it again."

"Will you hold me?"

His answer came as he lifted her into his arms and she landed on his lap. She nestled against his shoulder and fiddled with a long strand of his hair. "Do you think me cruel?"

"For what?"

His deep, warm tone rumbled through her body, lighting up all the spots that needed confirmation of his love. And right then, she decided, sheets or no sheets, she was using that bed. "What?" Distracted, she'd forgotten her question. "Oh, right, do you feel I'm justified in removing my mother's gifts from Raven?"

"They *are* rightfully yours." He kissed the side of her head.

"I'm just not sure I trust the magic involved."

"Do you feel I should just accept who I am now?"

"I believe you have." He ran his hand up and down her arm. "However, I also believe you will use Raven's skills to help those in need. Your reasoning is no different than removing a knife from someone who would wield it for pain."

"I'm being selfish." She snuggled against his chest. "I want more, and I do wish to be of value to you and the Elementals."

"As long as you understand you can live just fine without these powers."

She kissed his cheek. "I know." Her words came out half inaudible as she released a long groaning yawn. "I'll live just fine with you."

He hummed out an agreement then kissed her fingers. "You need to lie down, but first...come with me." After bumping her off his lap, he led her into another room. "Stand right here for a second."

The door clicked shut and then a faucet turned on, likely for a bath.

"While the water heats up, I'll rustle up some soap and towels. Sit here." Nodin nudged her onto a cold toilet seat.

Smiling so wide her face would likely hurt after too long, she sat quietly and awaited his return. Though her feelings had been buried deep last week, she had missed him. She may no longer see him, but she could still touch him.

The door opened once more.

"Steamy." Nodin's voice joined the thick, moist air in warming her body. "I brought a space heater, too. I don't know that there's heat in this part of the castle unless you light a fire. Let's hope there is enough hot water to enjoy a bath."

"Will you be joining me?"

"After almost losing you, yes, I'll be joining you. Likely joining with you over"—he kissed her shoulder—"and over"—another kiss upon her lips—"and over again."

Practically quivering with need, she stood and raised her arms. "Undress me."

Each tug of her clothing was followed by a hot kiss upon her skin. Once he'd removed all her clothes, he wrapped his arms around her from behind and angled her head to the side to meet his hungry lips.

His skin was a warm and smooth sensation against her back.

Each punishing kiss warned her of one thing—he planned to take his aggression and worries out on her body. She didn't mind—at all.

Nodin slid his lips down her neck all while shaping her breasts in his hands.

His hard shaft nudged against her back.

She arched against him.

"No. You'll wait. I'm more of a mind for slow torture."

Kamali locked her arm around his neck, undulating against him. "I'll take torture as long as it ends in pleasure."

"Maybe I'll withhold what you want." With the tip of his tongue, he licked the rim of her ear then bit down on her lobe before sliding a finger deep within her wet heat.

More than ready to revel in their love, Kamali captured the side of his face and brought his lips to hers, devouring his mouth and matching each thrust of her tongue to his invasion of her body.

Quickly, so quickly, she arrived at the precipice.

His finger left her pulsing core. "I don't think so, my sweet flower. I'm not ready for you to bloom. Besides, the water's ready." He clasped her hand to help her settle into the tub before landing behind her, splashing warm water over her legs.

The silky glide of wet soap travelled over her breasts while Nodin kissed the side of her neck and nipped her ear. He slicked his sudsy fingers through her sensitive folds. "What shall we do with this?" He plucked at her pubic hair. "Shall we trim or leave as is?"

"You're crazy." She laughed. "Leave my landing strip alone."

"Hmm…and do we have this waxed?"

"We do."

"What?" He tensed. "By who?"

"Nodin, a woman's beauty routine includes things no man should know."

"As long as that remains true. No *man* need know, right?"

"In case you've forgotten, I am blind. Therefore, I require others to at times…well they…you know…keep me trim, for lack of a better term."

"I can do that."

"Oh my gosh. You're killing the mood." She buried her face in her hands.

"Listen, every part of you is mine and every part of me is yours." He gently drew away her hands. "I will take care of you, Kamali."

"I can take care of myself."

"You just said you need help with…things."

That was it. The final straw. He'd driven her to a sexual edge, and now he wanted to discuss her personal hygiene. She turned, bracing her knees on each side of his thighs and splashed him over and over.

Laughing, he secured both her hands behind her back.

The temptation of her heaving chest must have proved too great, for he buried his wet face between her breasts and thoroughly, and oh so meticulously, speared his tongue over each peaked tip. His skill so perfect she almost came from that sensation alone. "Release me," she begged, feeling as if steam were literally pouring off her body.

"No. You cause too much trouble."

"You like my trouble."

He groaned and brushed his lips over her breast before once again lightly licking the tip.

"I'm going to kill you."

"I told you…torture."

She wiggled on his lap, almost enough to shift his cock right where she wanted it. Buried deep.

Freeing one hand from its vice-like grip at her back, he swatted her bottom. "Not yet."

Since begging wasn't working, she changed tactics and revealed her fears. "I've missed you. I was so frightened while Raven kept me prisoner. I knew Quint had infected me, knew my life was over, and all I could think about was you."

That seemed to work, as he hissed in a breath then held her close before kissing her. A driving, thorough kiss. One that said life was not lost and their love remained strong. One that proved their passion for each other with each flick of the tongue and crossing of their lips.

"Show me fireworks in the darkness, Nodin," Kamali panted against his damp lips. "Show me that I can still see the stars."

With his hands on her hips, he lifted her above him and then lowered her onto his thick cock. Once he'd settled deep, he stopped for a moment, brushing her wet hair over her shoulders. "You're my air. I cannot breathe without you."

After she found a rhythm, she took over and clasped his upper arms to keep steady. Over and over, she rocked against him while water splashed over the tub's edge.

Gasping for breath, she momentarily halted as he cupped her breasts and ran his thumbs over her sensitive nipples. Overcome by pleasure, she locked her legs around his waist and lifted once more before rolling her hips. Every sensation heightened by the steamy water and the hot, hard man, thick and heavy inside her.

"Oh, yes, this is what I've missed." Her entire body shivered. "Please, no more." She eased away from his teasing tongue and heated kisses. "I just want to feel you. Solid. Strong. So real inside me."

Nodin grunted out a, "yes" and a breathy, "faster, please" before gripping her hips.

"Oh, please…yes…help me get there." Kamali dug her fingers into his shoulders.

Nodin's hold tightened, and he met each of her downward plunges with a steady upward thrust.

Everything waved closer and closer to the ultimate peak, until her entire body tightened and she dove right over that edge—hard. Plunging deeper and deeper as she lost herself within the pulsing maelstrom of glory. "I-I'm still…I'm still…"

Utterly lost to bliss, her entire body went slack. Yet, her torture didn't end.

Nodin maintained the assault on her neck before he finished with one powerful thrust, shouting her name as he practically shot her off his lap. Again and again, he swayed against her before kissing her until they couldn't breathe.

"I thought you were…supposed…to be my air?" Kamali forced out the words around his lips.

Nodin blew out a deep breath. "Kind of difficult when you come so hard, you practically black out."

She kissed his forehead. "Same for me."

"Bath tub sex is a winner, then?" He drew her against his chest.

"Um…hmm…gold star, all the way." A sexual lethargy settled over her senses and she closed her eyes.

Though half-asleep against Nodin's wet chest, Kamali breathed him in, memorizing his essence. All man. A little sweat tinged with that crisp scent of awakening she'd inhaled each spring. Fresh air that was warm as it travelled through her nostrils, bringing with it a trace of vitality and hope.

She'd never seen the wind blowing through the trees or watched a cloud float by, but she'd experienced those moments with her other senses. Nodin's scent reflected those times.

Like a new beginning after a long cold spell.

Whether her final breath was today, tomorrow, or ten years from now, she realized it didn't matter. This man would carry her

out of any dark season and show her each bright bud, lighting the
path she could not see.

CHAPTER 39

Three days later and still not fully recuperated, Kamali swallowed every ounce of fear while sitting quietly before Adler's desk. Though exhausted from the international flight from Ireland to Oklahoma, she'd been dragged to this office for an interrogation. Seeking comfort, she ran her fingers through Maize's soft fur.

Her guide dog whined, fully aware of the tension in the air.

Raven jetted back and forth before her, just like the black bird she'd been named for. The swish of her skirt a clear indicator of this pacing movement.

After hours of planning with the Elementals, arguing with Nodin, and cloaking herself in magic, Kamali was fulfilling her plan. Heartache and loss were the only emotions Raven, and hopefully, Quint, would read from her mind.

Violet had needed her blood again to complete the spell, but sacrifice was the mantra of the day. Still, Kamali kept her mind clear of the softer moments between her and Nodin. These past few days, when they weren't arguing over what he'd deemed her 'foolish plan' they reignited their love and celebrated being alive in the most elemental way possible.

Kamali blinked, and then buried those thoughts in case they were readable. Stealth and care were needed, since she'd entered the lion's den.

A deeper part of her heart knew she didn't belong in this Oklahoma casino any longer, yet she was strangely calmed by the comforts of home. The familiar smells and sounds grounded her.

Whatever magic Violet had weaved and Nodin had altered through gleaning had certainly crisscrossed all her circuits, because she winced in pain anytime she tried remembering the Elementals and their plans. All she did know was she wouldn't be here for long...would she? She scratched her forehead.

After this was over, Nodin better remove whatever duct tape covered her thoughts. Regardless of what men thought, duct tape did *not* fix everything.

"You know what?" Raven's voice squawked from somewhere to Kamali's left.

The words brought her focus back where it belonged.

"I'm not wasting my time with a scared, weak little girl. I mean, really, the first sign of adversity, and you run back home." Raven huffed out a breath. "You thought you could save the world and look where that got you...nowhere with nothing. I warned you, but did you listen to dear Auntie Raven? No, you did not."

A swoosh of air struck Kamali's face, right in front of her nose. She remained still, unaware of her aunt's intent.

"Look at you. You can't even tell if I'm going to slap you. Not even the slightest twitch." Raven sighed. "What fun is that?"

"Raven, enough," Caddo commanded. "I'm tired of listening to you ask the same questions over and over. Kamali needs to rest. You've had your time with her, now leave her be."

"Do not speak to me in such a manner. Quint might need you at the casino's helm, but I'd have no trouble sending your puny, weak mind on a trip to an isolated island where it'd stay locked forever."

"I really don't know why you lay about my office all the time, Raven. Are you scared?" Caddo suggested. "Frightened to face

Quint alone? This building has other offices. Go visit one of those. We don't want you here."

"I've never cared what you want. Now, Kamali, I'll ask again, how did you break free of Quint's matter? What did the Elementals do?"

Her aunt spoke from directly in front of her now. Though Kamali couldn't see, she still envisioned Raven peering straight into her eyes, probing her mind, but finding nothing. They'd been at this for what had to be at least two hours.

Kamali certainly hoped the spell wouldn't wear off. "I already explained they used a magic spell, and because of that, I have nothing." She slumped her shoulders, adding to her defeated persona.

"You're a spy. I just know it."

Caddo heaved a sigh. "For the last time, Kamali is *not* a spy. This is her home. She's been through a trauma, and my duty is to help her assimilate to her new situation."

"*She* is right here, Caddo," Kamali piped up and waved a hand. "I'll get around fine with Maize. Things are familiar here. And speaking of familiar, I'd like to return to my apartment if someone could drive me."

Caddo took her hand as he settled onto her chair's armrest. "You're no bother. Did you eat on the plane? Can I get you something? Honestly, I'm shocked you've returned. I find I'm at a loss as to what to do for you, dear cousin. It's not safe here. For anyone."

"My life is here." She squeezed Caddo's hand. "I can no longer help the Elementals, let alone myself." She let her gaze drop to the floor and offered a sniffle. "Once I lost my gifts, well, Nodin…he didn't want me anymore."

"Can you even feed yourself?"

"Raven, that's enough," Caddo raged, shooting off the chair. "Get out of my office."

Kamali remained alert and tense as sounds of a scuffle

ensued. Raven cursed Caddo to the devil and back. Then Kamali heard what sounded like a slap.

Maize growled.

"I've never hit a woman, but with you, I'm tempted," Caddo spoke in a low, deep tone, through clenched teeth. "Get out of my office."

"I'm not leaving until Quint arrives," Raven responded in a too-sure tone. "I want to see what he'll do with her."

A chill slithered down Kamali's spine when *he* spoke—Quint.

"I won't do anything with her."

Kamali didn't need her aura-sensing abilities to know the air shifted and the room felt darker, menacing.

"The Elementals have sent us this pretty Trojan Horse. My sweet girl, don't think I don't know what the Elementals are planning. I know they'll come after you."

Maize whined and crowded against her legs.

All was still in the room, until Kamali felt Quint flick a finger through the back of her hair. Had to be him, no one else evoked this kind of terror that instantly froze her bones and stopped her heart.

"I don't know how you did it." Quint tugged on her hair. *Hard.* "No one has ever survived my invasion. Violet played a part, no doubt. You understand her power now, don't you? Actually, you may be the only one who truly understands why she's everything to me. And now that you're back, I'll see her again soon."

Kamali refrained from correcting his false belief Violet had saved her. His ravings were that of a madman, obsessed with something he would never have. Unfortunately, that made him more dangerous, and one hell of a lot scarier.

He released her hair, but kept a hand on her shoulder as he moved around the chair and sat before her on the coffee table. "You are quite a beauty, Kamali, but I fear you're not experienced enough for my taste. Too pure. Plus, I like my woman to *see* what's coming. Coming." He laughed. "Get it…coming?" He hummed out a chuckle.

Raven joined in.

Kiss ass.

"Anyway," Quint continued, "I enjoy seeing fear in a woman's eyes as she realizes what's about to fuck her isn't quite human." He ran a hand along the inside of her knee. "I'd never fuck a woman with a blank stare. Just the thought gives me the creeps."

Suppressing a chill, Kamali hoped he was through toying with her, but then his fingers pressed against her forehead, shoving her backward in her chair.

"Leave her be." Caddo's voice took on a tone she'd never heard before.

"You think to order me, boy?"

"What I think is that my cousin is no threat. I'll send her home. I never wanted her here, but apparently she has nowhere else to go."

"Oh, Caddo, do you really not understand my capabilities?" Raven purred. "I know you are aching for the poor girl. Your widdle heart is all blue. Still, get her out of my sight."

"Whatever," Caddo responded. "I'll call Creed to come get you, Kamali."

Though on shaky legs, and frightened Quint would still strike, she scooted off the chair and called for Maize.

One step at a time. She knew this room, she just had to move slowly and sure and she'd make it out. Nodin would be proud, though, furious she'd faced off against Quint again. Still…

Right before she stepped out into the hall, she swayed as a force shoved against her back. She yelped and, arms flailing, grabbed for the doorframe to steady herself.

Quint stood behind her. Had to be. Why else would the hair on the back of her neck be standing on end? She took one deep breath before taking another step forward. "Maize?"

Then *he* spoke again.

"How long do you believe their elemental magic tricks will work?" Quint whispered in her ear. "They saved you once, but can they do it again? Would they? I know that team. They'll never sacrifice. They aren't heartless enough. You're the perfect example of why they'll always lose." He shifted to stand before her, blocking her escape. "They saved you, a useless blind girl, instead of saving the entire world." He trailed a finger down her arm. "As Raven says, stay out of my sight. I don't wish to see you floundering about. Your weakness disturbs me."

Kamali took a deep breath. "*Everything* has a weakness."

"That's where you're wrong, girl. I have none."

"I thought pride was a weakness."

"Interesting. Pride, yes." He pinched her chin and shoved back her head. "One more thing. Don't bring that beast in here again. If you do, I'll barbeque the bitch and chew on her bones, understand?"

Bracing for an attack, Kamali nodded and tugged Maize closer to her side.

"Caddo," Quint barked. "Put her in one of the hotel rooms near Raven. They'll come soon enough, and I'll not miss my chance to obtain Violet."

Great Spirit, have mercy. He was making her plans too easy. *Wait, don't think about that. Don't. Just don't.* "I'd prefer to go home. I've been away and I need my things."

"Caddo, remove her."

Raven snickered.

Caddo took her elbow. "Don't argue."

Kamali nodded. "Fine, but can you at least ask Creed to bring me some clothes? I'll give you my key."

As Caddo led her and Maize farther away, she stumbled and fell.

"Kamali, what's wrong?" Caddo crouched at her side.

"Oh, nothing. Just thought I might get murdered back there,

and now that I'm still alive, my brave front is faltering a little." She took in one deep breath after another, to calm her racing, terrified heart.

"Let's not give Quint a chance to change his mind." Caddo tugged her to her feet. "I find the more you avoid his presence, the longer you live."

Kamali nodded. "So, I really have to sleep in a room next to Raven?" She pouted a little, continuing the façade.

"Yes, sorry."

She shrugged and followed him and Maize down the hall toward the elevators. "Well, at least tell me which side she's on, so I'll know where to place my hex."

"Your hex?" Caddo laughed. "You *have* been away too long."

She took Caddo's hand and offered a prayer to the Great Spirit. *Please, watch over him. Keep him safe.* Perhaps the Great Spirit heard her prayer, because a childhood memory popped into her mind. "Caddo."

"Yes." He drew her into the elevator.

She dug her nails into his arm, hoping he would understand her story had a purpose. "Remember when Waya would come into my room after he'd had a nightmare, because he believed I'd see any monsters floating around by detecting their auras?"

"Sort of." Caddo sighed. "Crazy kid. I miss him."

"Me, too." She bit her lip to keep from crying. She'd lost one cousin, she'd be damned if she'd lose another. "And remember Waya's nightmares got so bad, Adler took him to Malachi's sister and she performed a purifying ceremony that removed all his bad dreams."

As they exited the elevator, Kamali tugged on Caddo's arm, bringing him to a halt in the casino's foyer.

Voices, coins clanging against metal, and the musical jingles from the slot machines flowed through the room. Familiar sounds. She'd grown up racing through these very aisles with her cousins.

"How is she doing? Malachi's sister? Perhaps, it'd be best if you went to visit her." She turned to face Caddo and squeezed his forearms. "I think you should go tonight."

"You want me to leave?"

"Yes, you must go tonight, because Waya never told anyone…well, except me…you see, that ceremony…it worked."

CHAPTER 40

After Caddo left, Kamali sat against the headboard of the suite's queen-size bed and measured time by the passing of television shows. At the end of the sixth episode of *Big Bang Theory*, she figured enough time had passed. Plus, once she'd escaped Quint, she'd needed time to calm her mind and reiterate positive thoughts. She would succeed, because at this point, there was no turning back.

Kamali tiptoed to the hotel suite's adjoining wall and stuck her ear against the panel, trying to hear any sounds or movements within Raven's room. She'd heard obvious sex sounds earlier, but they'd stopped a short time ago.

Maize brushed against her side.

Ready to find a patch of grass, no doubt.

"I just need to breathe in and out, Maize. My heart is pounding so loud, Edgar Allen Poe is probably waiting on the other side of this wall, searching for his tell-tale heart. *I've* got a tale to tell, all right. Come on. We can do this." She reached for her guide dog's leader bar. "Door, Maize."

After being led to the door, Kamali once again pressed her ear to the panel. Not hearing anyone in the hall, she opened the door and stepped to the right. Caddo had finally answered her question regarding Raven's whereabouts as he'd settled her into her room. She couldn't worry about him now. She needed to concentrate on the wily woman next door.

Creeping along with a guiding hand against the wall, Kamali barely held back a scream when a brisk rush of air whipped across her loose short-sleeved shirt.

"Nodin?" she whispered when she really wanted to shout. Only one man could caress her skin in such a manner. "Nodin?" Glancing over her shoulder, Kamali waved him away.

Maize's collar jangled.

Her dog wiggled like crazy in her excitement over seeing Nodin again.

"Now look what you've done. Maize is making too much noise. Will you get out of here?"

"I couldn't let you do this alone." After whispering in her ear, Nodin clasped her grasping hand. "Not with Quint nearby."

Kamali fought back a sigh, because she really was grateful he'd arrived. She had no weapons except for the words of an ancient spell. Gratitude overcame her senses, and she wrapped Nodin in a tight hug before kissing him.

After a too-short kiss, he held her at arms length. "Are you truly all right?"

"I am now." She ran a hand down his arm then clasped his fingers. "Let's go."

"Now's a good time. Your ex-bodyguard wore her out, and then left about an hour ago."

"Gross, Creed and Raven? How do you know?" And she'd heard everything. Kamali refrained from gagging, because...*Eww!*

"I gleaned Creed's mind."

Kamali groaned. "Quint can detect your gleaning patterns. What were you thinking?"

"I doubt Quint pays attention to Creed, but you never know, so we should move things along. You've been here too long already." Nodin's voice seemed to carry with the air, drifting softly into her ear. "I'll direct a breeze under the door and open the lock."

"That isn't necessary. I have an all access key card. Uncle Adler gave it to me in case I needed to crash here. Caddo retrieved it from my apartment. So, here." She pulled the card from her back pocket.

"What?"

She didn't answer, just handed him the card. After a moment, she heard the door snick open.

Oh Great Spirit, what am I doing? She frowned when her heart thumped so loudly she could have executed a drum solo in a packed stadium.

Nodin took her by the elbow and led her and Maize into the room.

"Take my hand." His voice entered her mind. *"We'll speak the words of the spell together."*

Holding back a shriek, she placed a hand against her breastbone. Her chest had to look like some old-time cartoon character with a heart yo-yoing back and forth. She'd forgotten Nodin could glean her mind.

He tugged on her elbow. *"No fear, my brave Pakali. Let's move closer."*

As Violet had suggested, Kamali thought of her mother, letting her very last memory drift to the forefront of her mind. They were in the kitchen together: Kamali occupied with Braille books while her mom made peanut butter and apple sandwiches. Her mother sat beside her, drinking coffee and eating. Then she read Kamali page after page, acting out the characters with silly voices. Kamali still had those books buried within a cedar chest.

"Ready?" Nodin interrupted her recollection.

She nodded before pulling the bone-handled knife from her pocket and slicing open her left palm.

"She's been infected. I sure hope that doesn't transfer to you."

Nodin's concern came through even with his mental messages.

"I hope you can hear me, Nodin." Kamali turned toward him, and then brushed her good hand up his arm until she could cup his face. *"I know taking her powers may seem wrong, but perhaps our timing is good. If she is dying, she won't need her gifts. I know that's harsh, and I'm sorry for it, but she chose her own path. I choose to correct it."*

"Then we'll begin the spell."

Kamali jolted at the sound of his voice now speaking the spell out loud and hurried to join him.

"With the blood of one you've wronged, I hold you
With each drip, I seal your body
I, the seeker of vengeance, will have my due
Using the power of air within and beside me
As we will so mote it be."

"Hold my hand above her mouth, please." When her hand was held aloft, Kamali let the pooled blood in her palm drip past Raven's lips.

"What?" Her aunt sputtered awake. "What the hell?"

Kamali could just imagine the blood being spewed across the sheets and her aunt's struggle to rise. The spell was meant to hold her in place. "Did it work, Nodin?" Biting her lower lip, Kamali shook her head. Why had she ever thought she could do this mission alone?

"Yes, now the next one."

"This one is for you, Mother." Kamali closed her eyes and reached for Nodin. "Take my hand."

"From my mother you have torn
A gift that was not in you born
As her rightful heir I seek
That which is mine to keep
Only what is yours remains,
Remove each gift from her veins
All that was my mother's own
Stolen from her very bones
Fill my essence with this gift

I call upon the winds of change
Take what is mine and rearrange
With the blessing of air, fire, water, and earth
As we will so shall it be."

"No!" Raven screamed. "You little bitch. How dare you?"

"I'm taking back what is rightfully mine."

"Kamali." Nodin clutched her shoulder. "It's working."

"What is happening?" Sure her smile couldn't get any broader, Kamali stood still, wondering if she should repeat the spell. Wondering how Nodin could tell, because she didn't feel any different.

"I'll kill you for this," her aunt cried.

"A multi-colored light, so bright and beautiful, is pouring from her body into yours." Nodin's voice was laced with awe.

Kamali blinked and spread her arms wide as a sudden wash of warmth filtered through her entire body. "I can feel it. Oh, Nodin...I smell apples and peanut butter." Covering her eyes with her hands, she burst into tears. "Nodin, she's here. It's okay now. My mother's with me." Kamali opened her eyes and saw a blinding, soft pink aura. "Mom, I did it. I got them back to honor you, and I'll do you proud, I promise."

A soft brush, so much like a kiss pressed against her cheek.

Love, deep and forever, gathered around her heart. And for a brief shiny moment, Kamali felt a slight embrace from a mother too long gone.

"I am sorry, Kamali, for so many things. Use these gifts to color the world." Her mother's voice echoed through her mind.

The warmth faded, and when Kamali looked around the room she faltered, sinking to her knees. A visible aura surrounded her aunt, and Kamali could sense her vitriolic thoughts. She turned to Nodin. "Mother, because of you I can now see the man I love."

"You can? Oh, Kamali." Nodin wrapped his arms around her. "It worked. Pakali, you're back in full bloom." Keeping her in his arms, he twirled her around and around.

"I'm sad. I'm happy. I'm scared. I'm everything all at once." Shaking her head against his chest, she tried holding back tears, but they wouldn't stop. Her mother had been here. She'd been waiting for deliverance, and they'd given her wings. "I can see auras, but nothing else, except you. I can see you." Smiling, she eased back and then kissed his cheek. "I wonder if I have the ability to alter realities like Raven did? I can hear her thoughts in my head, so that's back, too."

Nodin cupped her face in his hands. "I would have loved you just the same."

"I would have loved me, too." She smiled and gazed into those clear-blue eyes. "Kiss me."

And he did. Very thoroughly.

Serenity settled over Kamali's soul. There was no cause for worry, because their futures were now on the correct path. Why she believed that when they faced such an evil foe, she couldn't say. But within her core a positive force pulsed to life and emitted a pleasing mix of peace, love, and hope.

"I'll just kill you and take it back." Raven's voice grated across the calm.

Nodin took Kamali's hand. "We must go. Quint is close."

A thick coating of malice bombarded her senses. "I feel him again. I could have done without repeating this horrid feeling. Raven, I'm sorry. You should be able to move soon. I wish you peace as you step into the next life, because your time is coming soon. Ask forgiveness for your foul deeds."

Her aunt's response was lost in the wind as Nodin swirled and swirled until Kamali no longer stood, but soared through the air in what seemed a horizontal position.

Was Nodin whisking them down the hotel corridor? Glass broke, and then cool air hit her skin.

Nodin abruptly halted, like a brick wall had been thrown up.

She tumbled to the ground.

Maize landed in a heap beside her.

"Nodin, what happened?" She patted the ground. Grass poked her fingers. "Where are we? Why did you—"

An orange aura, pulsing with sickly browns and greens, appeared in her vision, followed by insidious thoughts and a pure resolve for domination and containment of one thing—Violet.

"Now, Nodin. I don't believe you had a reservation." Quint's dark voice shot like poisonous arrows through her mind. "Kamali." The menacing form shifted closer. "Aren't you aware? This hotel has a strict no dog policy."

Maize yelped, and then started to whine.

CHAPTER 41

Fire alarms blared from inside the massive casino.

Luckily, Nodin had landed on a soft spot with Kamali and Maize and not on top of a car or the concrete pavement. Using the alarm as a temporary distraction, he whisked Maize and Kamali closer to his Elemental partners.

Patrons raced passed them, heading for their vehicles.

Funny thing was, there wasn't any smoke coming from the building.

"Fly Kamali to the Colorado clearing." Flint's voice fired through Nodin's mind. *"We are meeting Violet and Terran there. They've already started the process."*

Nothing and no one would stop them this time.

Nodin had made a pact with Kamali and his Elemental team, each agreeing to sacrifice for the greater good. Though Nodin still worried he'd falter when faced with losing one of his friends, he knew he had to let go this time.

Quint would end, one way or another.

"Kamali." He gazed into her eyes, their color now clear and as dark brown as melted chocolate. "Are you ready to see this through?"

"Yes."

He wrapped her in his arms. *"Let's fly."*

"Always, with you. Only you."

He twirled in a circle, spinning Kamali and Maize through the clouds, so bright and blue. What if they stayed right here and never touched the ground? What if they escaped all the dangers waiting below and just floated with the wind? Where would it lead them?

He'd contemplated his own future a lot over the last few days. Kamali's mortality was constantly on his mind. Could he be as brave as her? Could he start anew as a human man? Maybe there was a way to keep her alive longer. Hadn't Mother granted Violet life until Quint was destroyed? And what would become of Flint if Violet's immortality ended today? What if her years became as measured as Kamali's? That couldn't be, because he'd had a vision, a change in the Elemental pattern. Children. Would that still come to fruition?

These mind wanderings served him as he carried Kamali and Maize the short distance to Colorado. The remains of Maya and Terran's cabin appeared through the clouds. Intense heat from somewhere nearby fired across his bare skin. Slowing his spin, he landed, and then gently placed Kamali and Maize on the ground.

Maya rushed to his side and shoved sweatpants into his hand. "Is Kamali all right?"

While tugging up the pants, Nodin blew smoke and ash from Kamali and Maize.

Maize tried to stand, but kept toppling to her side.

Maya bent and petted Maize then formed a pool of water in her palm and held it to the dog's mouth.

Maize took five or six licks before scampering to her feet.

"Looks like your healing waters did the trick." Nodin patted Maize's head.

On her knees, Maya scrambled across the grass and peered into Kamali's face. "Are you dizzy?"

Kamali mumbled something.

"Open your mouth a little, and I'll give you some of my

water. We need you strong once Quint arrives."

While Maya tended Kamali, Nodin took a moment to appreciate the intense fireball Terran and Flint had created.

The fall air had chilled Nodin's skin as he'd raced across the sky, but that cool breeze quickly dissipated under the ferocity of the raging flames burning at the edge of the forest. He kept blowing the smoke away from Kamali and Maize.

Maize growled and barked, drawing attention to the dark menace walking up the drive.

Seemed the brave dog hadn't suffered any ill effects after Quint's earlier nudge.

"What kind of party are y'all throwing?" Quint kicked at a loose rock along Terran and Maya's driveway. "I didn't get an invitation." He glanced at Maya. "I'm done toying with you. I've amused myself with your pitiful games for far too long." He turned his black stare to Nodin. "You see, I know how to crumble your little wall. It's easy. You eliminate the weakest link."

Maya gasped then shot through the air, landing against a tree.

"No," Nodin barely breathed the word.

A loud roar erupted from the forest.

A sharp branch had punctured Maya's chest. Would they lose one before they even began? And what of Terran, could he remain strong?

Kamali took Nodin's hand. "She will not end."

Nodin barely registered her words as he watched Terran burst from the forest and fall at Maya's feet.

"Terran, you must fight. Turn the sorrow to anger. Become the fire." Nodin tried to break past the Earth Elemental's anguish.

Water poured from Maya's wound.

"That's two down." Quint stepped closer to Violet, who stood at Flint's side.

Her wild purple hair billowed around her face as she opened her arms and spread the electromagnetic field across the fire.

Quint shook his head. "You tried this trick before, and it

didn't work. I am not afraid of your little science experiment. A black hole. Really? I am a cosmic entity composed of dark matter and dark energy. Stepping through that portal would be like going home. So feel free to hocus pocus."

"If you believe that, then step right up." Violet lifted her arms above her head, creating a violet field which encompassed both the fire and Quint.

Nodin took the moment to rush to Terran's side. His friend remained in a daze, just staring at Maya as if not comprehending what he was seeing.

"Nodin. Terran." Kamali spoke from behind him. "I did receive my mother's gift of altering realities. I used it to remove Maya from pain and this place. Right now, she believes she's on a tropical beach. The sun in her face and the sand at her feet." Coming forward, she took Terran's hand. "She will not perish. Water *will* rejuvenate her. You must believe this, because right now, you are needed for a greater purpose."

"I cannot." Terran spoke barely above a whisper.

"Look." Kamali flicked a hand toward Quint and Violet. "I can only see their auras and feel the considerable heat, but they need you. Flint and Violet cannot maintain their energy without you. And believe me, the quicker we defeat Quint, the quicker Maya will heal."

Nodin clutched the Earth Elemental's shoulder. "My brother, I'll get Maya down and whip her to that stream that runs along the back of your property. Now go."

They both turned to glimpse Quint grabbing Violet by the hair.

Her field started to expand instead of compress.

"I will destroy him as he has tried to destroy me." After one final glance at Maya, Terran turned and rushed to Violet's side. "Hold him back." With Terran's ability to tap into the earth's electromagnetic field, he and Violet compressed the fireball even smaller.

"Kamali, stay back here." Nodin tugged her behind an evergreen. "The smoke might get to you for a few minutes, but I need to take Maya to water."

"Go." Kamali waved him off.

He spun off the ground, and then pulled Maya free. She slumped in his arms with a slight groan.

Grateful for that small indication, Nodin held her against his chest and breezed through the forest to lay her in the trickling stream. "Heal, water-girl. Terran needs you. We all need you." He kissed her cheek then, sure she'd renew in this clear water, quickly spun back to the clearing.

Once he returned, Nodin blinked then shook his head in complete awe of their combined power. "Kamali." He pulled her to his side. "It's beautiful. Like a small part of space has deigned to join us here on earth." He clenched his jaw as love for his team overwhelmed his heart. "I love you, Kamali. I love everyone. We're saving the world. Can you even imagine? I can't, not after all this time."

The gravitational pull drew Quint's form closer and closer.

"I feel their power." Kamali squeezed his hand. "Their positive energies. Quint's aura is narrowing and sliding into the breach. They've almost got him."

Flint's entire body, and the fireball he held in his hand, turned from orange to yellow.

Then an explosion of light and energy rocked the clearing, blowing Kamali across the ground.

# # #

They were winning.

Perhaps Quint *had* underestimated the Elementals this time.

Violet—his gorgeous, rare bloom—was the only reason they could spin this magic.

Was this to be his end? Not that he knew where he'd begun.

He'd formed over time, over space, into an entity with no form. Was it so terrible to want more? To seek out those who lived in order to breathe? To become something when he was nothing?

Were there more like him? He'd never felt the faintest of hints. So, why? What was his purpose, if not to rule and overcome those who were lesser?

He shook free of his human skin as it melted away. The heat and the gravity were too much for a mortal to endure. Fighting to break free from the unceasing tug proved fruitless as his natural form thinned to a narrow reed.

With Violet's control over the electromagnetic spectrum and witch's blood flowing from her maternal line, she, along with her Elemental partners, had devised the ultimate end game.

Smart bastards had finally found a way. He should've destroyed Terran a few years ago when the fool was human.

Unwilling to give up, he tried sending mental messages, warning them to stop. Tried blasting them all with his dark matter, but he no longer controlled his movements. He drew closer and closer to this science experiment gone mad. A perfect black circle surrounded and sustained by Elemental power.

Would he exist on the other side? Or would he simply knock about forever in an endless abyss?

Apparently, he'd been very wrong.

They were capable of sacrifice.

Too bad Violet was the one they would lose, because her power, stemming from her heart, was dying.

He may have lost her, but no one else would have her, either.

Grinning, Quint stopped fighting and accepted defeat.

CHAPTER 42

"Kamali." Nodin knelt at her side. "Oh, please, are you all right?"

She laid still, eyes closed.

Maize licked her face.

Due to the explosion of energy from whatever crazy science was occurring inside that Elemental powerhouse, Kamali had been tossed through the air before landing against a charred rectangular wooden flower planter. The sharp edge had injured the back of her left shoulder, leaving a large gash.

"Kamali, please wake up." He started to shake her before realizing that would likely prove even more painful. "I can't lose you now. I just got you back. We're winning. Quint's shed Malachi's skin. They've got him. I know you can't see it, but listen, please listen…I'll be your eyes. I'll show you." Careful of her injury, he pulled Kamali into his arms and brushed her hair away from her face before kissing her cheeks and forehead.

Maize whined and nudged Kamali's hand.

"They are doing it, Pakali. Quint's decreasing." He had no shirt to stem the blood dripping from Kamali's gash. Careful to avoid her shoulder, he tugged her shirt free, balled it up, and then placed it against the wound.

"Stay with me. Might be best that you're out, because I bet

this hurts like the dickens." Nodin kissed her temple then glanced at the action across the field. "Oh, this can't be good. Violet has dropped to her knees, but…she's keeping the lock around Quint. The fire's decreasing, and it's no longer any natural color, it's almost full white."

When Violet screamed, Nodin jolted.

A blast of white ripped from the center of the fireball.

Nodin rocked Kamali in his arms.

"Is Violet all right?" Kamali mumbled.

"Oh, thank the Great Spirit. Try not to move. Your shoulder is injured." The shirt Nodin held against her wound had turned a ruddy red and was almost soaked. "You'll need stitches."

"Don't remind me it's there. I'm already about to toss my cookies. What's happening? Is Quint gone?" She winced. "Please, move very, very slowly."

Nodin considered flying her out of there, away from the danger, but his team would need him to deliver them to their elements when they were done.

"The circle is now full black again. Quint's entity is being drawn inside as a narrow black streak."

"Good." Kamali hissed out a breath between her teeth. "Keep talking, please."

"Violet's hair has gone full white. She's very pale." Nodin studied Flint. The Fire Elemental was beating against the electromagnetic field, trying to get Violet out.

"I don't know if Violet can maintain the intensity."

"Why?"

"Oh, no, Terran has fallen to one knee, but Quint's form is just inside the black hole. He's halfway gone." Clutching his chest, Nodin silently offered a prayer of thanks to the Great Spirit. "As soon as this is over, we'll get some Maya-juice for your shoulder. She's likely almost back to full status."

"Nodin, something's coming." Kamali straightened, and tilted her head toward the sky. "Something even darker than

Quint."

Air leeched from Nodin's lungs and he wheezed then coughed.

The entire sky turned black. All went still. Not a peep or chirp came from the forest.

A sense of foreboding swirled down his spine.

Kamali gasped. "What aura is that? I've never seen anything like...there's grandeur and pride...and...and an overwhelming loneliness hiding deep within. Whatever this being is, its aura is pure gold, but I also detect silver specks. I don't understand."

An ancient scepter arced through the air and separated Quint's form from Violet. Terran and Flint maintained their control over the black hole, but it began blinking with white, waning without Violet's additional influence.

Death stood at least seven, maybe even eight feet tall, his black cloak billowing around his massive, muscled body. Under the hood was a face Nodin had glimpsed before. Eyes the color of well-aged burgundy. Pitch-black hair and a perpetual snarl twisting his lips.

"*I* will lead the dark matter creature into the other dimension." Death's voice thundered across the clearing. "You cannot sustain this power." He glanced at Flint. "This one sits on the verge of death. Heal her." After arching an imperious brow, he whipped open his cloak, encompassing Quint's writhing black mass. Then he jumped into the rippling black hole.

Nodin glanced at Flint standing at Violet's side. Yet, he had no vision of her death.

"I can see within," Kamali murmured at his side. "Death has kept one hand on the black hole's outer ring. And now, he's opened his cloak. Quint is spinning, meshing within the vortex of the black hole. It's over." She closed her eyes and then, after biting her lip, tears fell down her cheeks. "So, that is death. His aura has no violence or hate. He is but a means to pass into the next life." Kamali shivered. "Death, yet offering life, just in a different way."

Nodin studied the woman in his arms. "You do see within. And you say that Quint is gone?"

"He is." Kamali smiled and wiped the tears from her cheeks. "You are free to fly once more, Air Elemental."

He buried his face against her neck and, if he could form tears, he'd weep for all that had passed, the lives lost, the battles waged. Surely, they'd face others foes, but today, they'd conquered and survived.

Today, they would celebrate.

Kamali gasped. "Nodin. Violet, her aura…it's fading."

Nodin closed his eyes as his future came to him in a flash. All those questions…yet all along he'd known the answer.

And in this moment, he released…the air, the breeze, the freedom, and his connection to all he had been for over four hundred years. He lifted his face to the clear blue sky, knowing it would never look or feel the same, said a quick goodbye and offered a nod in gratitude. *"We will always be one, you and I, but I must pass this gift to another. She will serve you well. My thanks for each moment. I will continue to fight for the earth. For purity. Until I breathe my last."*

He kissed Kamali's hand, settled her against the planter, and shuffled to his feet slowly, but surely. "My love, it seems fate won't be denied. Know that what I'm about to do, I do freely and of my own will. I choose duty. I choose you. And above all, I choose love." He leaned down and kissed her lips, softly, reverently. "Forgive me, but I see no other way."

"Nodin, wait!" Kamali cried.

If he stayed, he might falter. He may not have chosen to enter this Elemental life, but he could choose when he left it. He spread his arms wide and, for the last time, transformed into his element and flew through the air, catching Violet just before she collapsed.

CHAPTER 43

Though Flint and Terran tried to break past Nodin's cyclone, they were weakened from the fight against Quint and unable to penetrate his barrier.

"*Nodin.*" Flint fired through his mind. "*Let me in. What are you doing? I-Is she…dead? Let me come to her, please.*"

"*She will not die, my friend. There is another way.*"

"*Are you suggesting…I can't ask you to do that.*"

"*And you didn't, I chose. Now, be still and call to Mother. We need her now. Violet is too close to death.*" Nodin closed his eyes and shut out all further contact with Flint and a few furious inquiries from Terran. He needed to focus. Now that he'd chosen, he wanted this done.

Violet didn't stir. Her hair was bright white, her skin pale, and her breath barely escaping her lips.

Keeping his spinning vortex moving around him and Violet, he called on Mother Nature. "*Mother, I ask that you transform Violet Levina into the Air Elemental. I freely offer my gifts and my peri-mortal life. Mother Nature, heed my call. My will. Only you have the power to transform her. Violet carries the Elementals' future. Save her from the brink of death.*"

Mother walked straight through his spinning gale. A hazy golden glow surrounded her. She stood over eight feet tall, both her red-gold hair and amber skin glimmering. Her eyes were the color of spring grass.

As she'd come in her full glory, Nodin bowed his head.

A song played from somewhere, a light melody, with a bevy of tiny voices singing words he couldn't understand.

"Be sure." Mother stood before him, her hands linked at her waist. "Once I begin the transformation, I cannot and will not reverse the effects."

Nodin stared down at the silent woman in his arms. Kamali was right, Violet *was* fading fast. "This is the right decision. She can be so much more. Her witchcraft, her power over the electromagnetic spectrum, along with the gift of air, she'll be a new type of Elemental. An evolution."

"I'm proud of you. This sacrifice is a beautiful kindness to those you love and to the earth. I thank you, Nodin Osi."

"Please, hurry." He jerked when the grass at his feet began to smoke. "I can't hold back Flint and Terran much longer."

Mother waved her spindly, branch-like arms above her head, and just that easily, they landed in a field full of spring flowers. The sky a perfect blue and the air so clean and crisp.

Would the air smell the same? He could actually feel it now, like a tangible thing, but he would not dwell on that now, he'd already said goodbye.

"We will begin." Mother knelt beside him. She took his hands and locked them together above Violet's heart, and then she placed Violet's hands on top of his and stacked her hands on top of Violet's. After Mother connected them, she sang a song.

The same tune he'd heard earlier. A beautiful, joyous song sung by Mother and what seemed a million fairy voices. The words were in no language he'd ever heard, but they touched his soul and he knew their meaning. They were asking for the Elements to come and bless this exchange. To guide and honor this choice and sacrifice. To bless the two Mother Nature had brought into their presence. The song full of reverence and hope. Purity and love. They cheered as they sang, clapping and laughing.

Yet, Nodin saw nothing but the flowers spread across the field. He closed his eyes and tried to comprehend the splendor of the moment, but he didn't belong on this plane where the oldest magic and fairy tales were born. This world was too close to the glory of creation.

Out of his control, his body breezed back and forth, hypnotized and swaying to the music. He fought to stop the flow of air rushing and pouring from his lungs. Quickly, too quickly. So much so, he couldn't catch his breath.

"Release, you must release." Mother's voice whispered through his mind. *"You are holding on when you promised to let go. The air is no longer under your command, Nodin Osi. You chose life and cannot turn back now. Calm your heart, remember your purpose, and close your eyes. Let go."*

Though losing a part of himself he'd controlled for hundreds of years tore against every survival instinct, he did as Mother asked and blew out a long breath. When nothing remained, he fell back against the soft grass carpet, and this time, as he closed his eyes, he caught a glimpse of fairy wings flitting by.

And the song…the song went on and on until it matched the beat of the heart now thumping in his chest.

# # #

Just when the pain in her shoulder and the irritating bombardment of Flint's and Terran's questions had her on the verge of passing out, Kamali heaved a sigh of relief as Maya's aura burst past the forest's edge.

Terran's aura met Maya's halfway. "We did it, Shoeless girl. Quint's gone."

Kamali heard what sounded like kissing.

Maya said, "Kamali is injured. I want to hear everything, Terran, but Kamali is in too much pain."

The grass crunched closeby before Maya settled next to her.

Kamali fought to stay conscious, but she'd likely lost too

much blood.

"Where's Nodin and Violet?" Maya asked from beside Kamali. When neither Flint nor Terran answered her, she halted in her investigation of Kamali's shoulder. "Here, Kamali, I'll pour my waters directly into your mouth. Open up and drink."

Maya's lips pressed against hers.

Water trickled into her mouth, and Kamali greedily drank each drop until the pain in her shoulder became only a twinge.

"Better?"

"Yes, thank you."

The ground rumbled, and they all gasped.

"What is it?" Kamali's heart pounded. Had Quint returned?

"Do not worry." Terran sank beside her. "Death's head, shoulders, and now his body are emerging from where the black hole had been."

Kamali gasped, lifting her hand to her mouth. "Is Quint coming back, too?"

"I left that nasty piece behind." A deep, baritone answered her question.

"You're not gold anymore." Kamali gazed at the aura representing Death. He was all silvers now, with a few shades of black.

"My penance is paid," Death answered. "I sacrificed for the greater good."

"Sacrificed what?"

"Well, I went into the bloody hole with that dark matter creature, didn't I?" he answered with a bit of an English accent.

"So, are you something else now?" Terran inquired. "I don't understand."

"Wait!" Flint hollered. "Where are you going?"

Kamali could only watch as Death's aura moved farther away.

"I go where I'm needed."

"Are you a human now?" Terran rephrased his question.

"Yes, of a sort."

"Thank you for helping my friends today." Kamali entered the fray. "I believe you are meant for great things. Don't let your dark moments as Death hold you back from finding what you deserve."

"And what is it I deserve?"

Kamali smiled. "What we all deserve…love."

"I've seen what love can do, it's not for me."

"I have a question. Will you answer truthfully before you go?" Terran tried, once more to engage Death.

"I will."

"Will Quint ever return?"

"No."

"How can you be sure?" Terran asked.

"His dark energy will remained compressed in that black hole for all time. Now, I'm off. There is someone I must find."

"We can help you," Kamali offered.

"No."

"But you have no powers now."

"Don't I?"

"He winked." Maya squeezed her hand. "And there he goes. Walking off like he wasn't Death five seconds ago. Cheeky bastard." A moment later, the water-girl gasped. "Oh, my God. Nodin? What has he done?"

Though slightly embarrassed to be in nothing but her bra and jeans, Kamali straightened and searched for Nodin. He lay on the ground on the other side of Terran's and Flint's auras. *Where did he come from? And why had he disappeared?*

Though frightened of what she'd find, she crawled to his side.

He looked the same, but the aura surrounding him was now human.

CHAPTER 44

Heavy.

Everything felt...heavy.

After being weightless for so long, the thickness of his legs, his arms, even his tongue were far from his known insubstantial form. An emptiness churned in his belly, and the air...the fall-scented air stopped within his lungs and came back out his mouth again. Odd. Eyes closed, he breathed in and out, in and out, slowly, surely again and again.

The sweet song had ended, but his mind remained in a daze. Where was he now? Would he need time to recuperate? Had Violet become the Air Elemental? And would she approve of his decision? Flint certainly would.

He wiggled his toes and even they felt...well, heavy. No other word described the sensation.

Though sure Mother's magic had transformed him into a human once more, he remained quiet and still. Unsettled, he took a long moment to grasp the momentous scope of his decision. Everything had happened so fast, but in the end, he'd known this conversion was coming.

Kamali was his life now. His future.

With no regrets, Nodin embraced his new reality and opened his eyes. There were repercussions to face, after all. He'd asked

Mother not to change his memories. He wanted to remember everything. She'd worried he'd be saddened, but he'd assured her he'd be more disturbed by losing his friends and his history. He hadn't chosen the blank slate as other Elementals had in the past.

He blinked and held his hand in front of his face, then squeezed it into a fist. The motion seemed odd and very, very slow, not fast like the wind. These new limitations would take some getting used to.

A blurry Kamali and then Maya came into focus behind his clenched hand.

"Nodin. How are you feeling?" Kamali touched his cheek. "Do you remember anything?"

"Only everything I'd forgotten."

"What?" Kamali furrowed her brow.

"Is Violet all right? Maya, are you all right?" He glanced at the water-girl.

"Do you remember what you've done?" Kamali persisted, hesitantly touching his shoulder. "You still feel the same to me."

Maya pulled at the hand he'd kept over his face, and then flipped over his wrist. "Blood now flows." She traced a blue vein. "Y-you really *are* human. Oh, Nodin, what have you done?" She burst into tears and placed her hand against his chest, sobs pouring from her slim frame.

"Maya, there was no other choice. I had to save Violet. Plus, my future is with Kamali now." He tugged on a strand of her blonde hair.

"It won't be the same."

He heaved a sigh, she was right. It wouldn't be. No more spontaneous meetings by the rivers and streams free flowing around the world. No more fighting at her side. No more late night discussion about the whys of their existence. He would miss those moments, but he'd made his choice.

Terran eased Maya into his arms.

Nodin glanced at Kamali then pulled her close and combed

his fingers through her long, black hair.

"I can't believe this. You didn't have to do this for me." She bit her bottom lip as tears trickled down her cheeks.

Maize whined at her side.

"Don't cry, Pakali. I knew this day would come." Lifting his hand, he wiped the tears from her face. "We are each other's forever now. I will stand by your side until the end of our days. I welcome our future together." He ignored the tears on his own cheeks, and what was that dripping down his nose? Human fluids, not such a pleasant thing, but a part that cemented his truth. He could bleed now, get sick now, eat food now—die now. When the wave of dizziness hit, he closed his eyes. "I think I might be hungry. Although, I'm not quite sure I can walk if I get up. My body feels...I really can't explain it."

Kamali quieted a moment before placing her hand over his heart. "Your heart beats, and your chest rises and falls with each breath."

Terran crouched at his side and brushed the hair from Nodin's forehead. "What you've done...my brother, this sacrifice, I've never seen anything so selfless."

"Where is Violet?"

"Mother has her. Since Violet was so drained from the fight and the transformation, she must stay with Mother for some time. Flint isn't pleased."

"I imagine."

"You understand what you've done?"

"I've done nothing but fulfill my purpose. Consider this my final duty as an Elemental. Were we not to protect the earth and its people? I believe I have done so in giving my gift to Violet." He grasped Kamali's hand, pausing as he considered the solidity of his own. "And I made the right choice for my own future. Plus, Violet will serve the Elementals in a much-greater capacity. She holds the future within her womb."

"Children?"

"Flint told you."

"Yes, after Maya gleaned it from his mind. So, you remember us. I thought perhaps you would forget."

"I didn't want to forget."

Kamali squeezed him tighter then leaned up and kissed his chin.

"I will help you adjust." Terran placed a hand upon Nodin's shoulder.

Flint dropped to his knees beside Terran and wrapped Nodin in his arms. "I've never said this to another man, but I love you. You selfish, heroic bastard. Violet's alive…and our children…how will I ever repay you?"

"You just did." Nodin smiled as he absorbed the heat coming from Flint. The Fire Elemental took up the whole right side of his body while Kamali took up the other side.

Maya joined in next, wrapping her arms around Kamali.

Kamali laughed. "You're a Nodin sandwich."

"I'm a blessed sandwich, and I have all the ingredients I need right here." He kissed the top of her head. "I'm okay with this, guys. I'm okay. I just need this, your support and love."

They were an unstoppable force. And together, after all their years, they'd defeated their greatest enemy. Maybe they'd finally found the right recipe: love and sacrifice.

Flint took Nodin's face in his hands and kissed his forehead. "You will always be my brother. Trust in me to keep you safe as you kept my family safe. You are still an Elemental and always will be."

Water poured from Maya's eyes. "I can't believe what you've done, you stupid self-sacrificing fool. I'll m-miss you so much, but I'm so proud of you."

"She's soaking me." With a chuckle, Kamali shifted to gaze into his eyes. "Clear blue. Your eyes are still as clear as the sky. I love you, Nodin Osi."

The five of them stayed locked together for a long moment,

arms wrapped around each other like a tight cocoon.

And though Nodin's human life would end before these three Elemental beings, he knew they'd stand beside him every step of the way. "Though the sacrifice be heavy, love makes it weightless."

Maya moaned. "All right, tell us, what great philosophical master came up with that quote?"

Nodin bit back a grin. "Why, the greatest mind of all time, a giant among men, the great and wise Nodin Osi."

Four groans followed his words.

"Good to know you haven't changed that much, Air-head." Flint shoved at his shoulder then rose. "Come on, Pigpen and Waterworks, let's leave them be for a moment."

The Elementals stepped away, and Nodin nudged Kamali's side. "Will you help me stand?"

She wiped her eyes and nodded. "Sure." She stood, brushed off her clothes, and then held out her hand.

As he gripped it, he wobbled a little.

Kamali wrapped her arm around his waist. "I will help you stand, and you will help me see. Since the first moment we met, we were stronger together. That hasn't changed."

Nodin wrapped his arms around her and kissed her. This felt the same, the meshing of tongues, the soft glide of lips, and the quick rise of passion. As he eased back, he met her gaze, lifting a brow. "Can you still read my mind?"

She bit her bottom lip. "Yes."

"So you understand."

"I do."

"And you know what I want?"

"In general, or after we kissed?"

He chuckled and swung her up in his arms. "By the Great Spirit, I love you, Kamali Kiwidinok."

She smiled and placed her hand upon his cheek. "And I still see only you."

EPILOGUE

Nine months later.

Sitting at his desk, Nodin hung up after talking to the plumber and braced his head in both hands. The man spoke of PVC pipe and valves. What did Nodin know of such things? He sighed and made a note to ask Caddo. Kamali's uncle and cousins were back at the helm of their Oklahoma casino and her family had given him a place in their organization.

He and Kamali were opening a Native American museum on the casino grounds. He had mementoes from his past stored away in northern Arizona. The museum was a true depiction of his people's history. Nothing was left out. Everything laid out in black and white and stained with red. He'd lived through the reality. History books tended to paint over unpleasantness. This museum would not.

A few weeks after his transformation, he'd married Kamali in Vegas. After a short honeymoon in Ireland, they'd returned to Oklahoma to begin work on their joint venture.

Maya, Terran, and Mother Nature were down in the Gulf, working on erasing an oil spill.

Flint and Violet remained in Ireland. She was adjusting to her Elemental life, though she hadn't yet transformed into air. She'd chosen not to risk it with three lives stirring in her belly.

During their visit, Flint had been at times grateful then suddenly switching to a ball of nervous energy. He'd cornered Nodin and expressed all his worries: *What did he know of fatherhood? Why three? How was this even possible?*

Nodin chuckled and leaned back in his leather chair. His fiery friend would adjust. Still, three demanding babies after hundreds of years living a solitary life? No wonder his friend was in a panic.

Violet had also pulled him aside and expressed her gratitude over his sacrifice. She'd given him an amulet blessed with good fortune.

And so far, whether through Violet's gift or due to his love for Kamali, he *was* very fortunate.

Some days he missed flying free. He wouldn't deny that ache in his heart. Yet, being human was a gift. Knowing he would come to an end made each and every day special. His musings were interrupted when Kamali wobbled into his office, led by Maize.

"Nodin, would you make me a cup of peppermint tea?"

"Sure." After leading her to the loveseat in his office, he thumbed through the pods until he found the right one then prepared her cup.

He'd slowly rediscovered food, and at the same time, he realized he needed to remain in shape. No longer frozen in the same body, he had to work to remain fit. Luckily, the casino had a work-out facility, and Caddo and Isi had showed him how to use weights. Though most days, Nodin would wake up early and run, reveling in the fresh morning air rushing against his face.

"How were the display cases?" Kamali ran a hand over Maize's head. "Are the security sensors in place?"

"Yes."

The coffee machine's light blinked, indicating the tea was ready.

Nodin carried the cup to Kamali, and then settled beside her, placing a hand over her rounded belly.

"Thank you." She held the cup between her slim fingers.

"Did you rest well?"

"Yes."

"Hungry?"

Freeing one hand, she linked their fingers together and rested them on her stomach. "I can't imagine how Violet will keep three fed when I think of feeding only one."

"Flint was quite attentive." Nodin put his arm around her shoulders and tugged her against his chest.

"Yes, much to her frustration."

"Can you even imagine what this means for him? For the Elementals? What an evolution." He rested his head back against the couch and considered again how much his friend's life would change. "I'm more worried about them ending up like Flint."

"Stop." Slapping his knee, Kamali shook her head. "You love him."

"I do, dearly, but after having no one depending on him for six hundred plus years, Flint should experience a rude awakening with three children seeking his attention." He chuckled. "Wish I could be there to see it."

"Understanding how Violet can be the Air Elemental, a witch, and a mother will keep him guessing long enough, but when those children come, he won't have time to think of anything."

Grinning, Nodin hummed out another chuckle.

"What is it?"

"Just an image of Flint changing a diaper. He'll probably incinerate them."

"Likely."

Nodin sighed, considering he'd be doing the same soon, but he had no extra gifts to help him through the process. "I've lived a blessed life. I hadn't realized how much I ached for children until we discovered you were pregnant. Just knowing a part of me and a part of you lives inside your belly fills me with a sense of wonder and amazement…and pride. I regret nothing. I was meant to be a father. I know this now. Thank you for giving me this opportunity, Kamali Osi. No words can describe the feeling within my heart except—I'm right where I'm supposed to be." He held her quietly for a few moments, reflecting on their time together. "The first time I saw you, I wondered, what does a blind girl see?"

"And what did you discover?" She leaned back and met his gaze.

"You tell me."

"Everything." Kamali cupped his cheek in her hand. "With love, she sees everything."

Thank you for reading *Air's Vision*. I hope you enjoyed Nodin and Kamali's story. If you did, please leave a review at your purchase site. Reviews are very appreciated by the author. I'm "moose"-assuredly grateful.

Visit **www.jillianjacobs.com**
for all available titles.

Please enjoy the following excerpt from *Water's Threshold,* **Book #1 in The Elementals Series.**

Since arriving in Wyoming only a few months ago, Maya had experienced a strange energy pattern that interrupted her sense of peace. A consciousness never felt before, as if something attempted to anchor her in place—a pull unlike anything she had experienced since starting this new life nearly one hundred and fifteen years ago.

This internal strife was because of him—Terran Forrester. Mother had warned this would come. He was part of her purpose in being in this place at this time. Her orders were to guide him, because their destinies were entwined. Having Mother Nature set her up on a "fate date" left her feeling like a contestant on a game show. During her human life, Maya strove to control her own destiny, never handing over power. As an Elemental, she remained determined to give her all to their cause, but it chafed when Mother asked for more—to open her heart. Why now? Why was this burden of love thrust upon her with a mate she had not chosen?

Mate. What a ridiculous word.

Maya blew out a breath, causing a bevy of bubbles to dance their way to the surface. She couldn't have children so Mother using that specific word made the whole idea more ludicrous. Yet, Mother's wishes had come to fruition and that fact rankled. When spying on Terran, Maya experienced emotions surfacing she'd thought buried in a deep well long ago.

Her duties included watching him as he went about his daily human life. She enjoyed observing his frequent visits to the banks of the Snake River where he filled little glass vials. A soft hum raced through her body each time she spied him doing ordinary things, like working up a sweat at the gym or grabbing a cup of coffee at the local café. Since her last sexual adventure occurred in the free-love laced 70's, she was more than overdue for male attention. Terran would, no doubt, approach sex with the same care he did his experiments—meticulously and thoroughly.

That trickle of lust thrummed especially strong tonight at the gas station, when he'd touched her shoulder, all concerned citizen, seeking to offer assistance to an unfamiliar woman. Her waterlogged heart had pumped like a steam engine traveling uphill.

About the Author

In the spring of 2013, Jillian Jacobs changed her career path and became a romance writer. After reading for years, she figured writing a romance would be quick and easy. Nope! With the guidance of the Indiana Romance Writers of America chapter, she's learned there are many "rules" to writing a proper romance. Being re-schooled has been an interesting journey, and she hopes the best trails are yet to be traveled.

Water's Threshold, the first in Jillian's Elementals series, was a finalist in Chicago-North's 2014 Fire and Ice contest in the Women's Fiction category.

Jillian is a: Tea Guzzler, Polish Pottery Hoarder, and lover of all things Moose.

The genres she writes under are: Paranormal and Contemporary romance with suspenseful elements.

Connect with Jillian Jacobs online

Website: www.jillianjacobs.com

www.ingramcontent.com/pod-product-compliance
Lightning Source LLC
Chambersburg PA
CBHW071447170626
46811CB00007B/2499